Michelle

Grade 6

Mrs. Cook-Brick

II

Basket *of* Beethoven

Susan Currie

Fitzhenry & Whiteside

Published in Canada by Fitzhenry & Whiteside,
195 Allstate Parkway, Markham, Ontario L3R 4T8

Published in the United States by Fitzhenry & Whiteside,
121 Harvard Avenue, Suite 2, Allston, Massachusetts 02134

10 9 8 7 6 5 4 3 2 1

National Library of Canada Cataloguing in Publication Data

Currie, Susan, 1967-
A basket of Beethoven

ISBN 1-55041-665-0 (bound). – ISBN 1-55041-666-9 (pbk.)

Title.

PS8555.U743B38 2001   jC813'.6   C2001-900776-0
PZ7.C9356Ba 2001

Fitzhenry & Whiteside acknowledges with thanks
the Canada Council for the Arts, the Government of Canada
through the Book Publishing Industry Development Program
(BPIDP), and the Ontario Arts Council for their support
of our publishing program.

Design by Wycliffe Smith.

This book is dedicated to three people—
to my husband, John, who is proof that miracles
occasionally happen; and to my parents,
Jean and Martin Terry, with thanks
for their love and support.

Chapter One

The supply room, of course, was the alien spaceship.

Sam Garretson began to pull crates into the center of the room. He would pile them up and then balance the lawnmower and some of the tools on top to create the control panel.

Weeeech, weeeeech, weeeeech!

Each scraping crate sounded like alien weapons shooting in the distance. Sam's own panting breath added an interesting rhythm that tumbled and surged in gray-red streaks. Sam always noticed the way sounds *looked*. Sometimes sounds almost drove him crazy.

At last the lawnmower teetered on top of the crates. Sam couldn't resist examining it. If he could figure out how it worked, maybe he'd be able to outwit the enemy before they returned.

Sam bellowed, "Beeeeep!" as he pushed the first button. The sound was startling in the silence of space: better to leave that button alone. It was sure to alert them, wherever they were.

The second control, when he grasped the lever and pulled sharply down, blurted out a "Blip-blip-blip!" so piercing and shrill that he ducked and waited for the slithering *sleeh-sleeh* of the aliens' return.

But nothing happened, so he tried the third control—the long string-like thing with a handle on the end of it.

It screamed, "Pheet-Pheet-Pheet! Pheet-pheetle-EEEEET, Pheeeeeeeeeeeeeeeeeet!"

Then, suddenly, the control board sprang to life, and one sound jumbled against the other: "Pheet! Blip-blip! Beep! Pheeeeet-Blip-PHEEEET!" It blasted a bizarre, otherworldly rhythm. Sam pounded an accompanying beat on the side of the lawnmower with a wrench.

Suddenly he stopped.

Had he heard something else?

Sam's heart began to pound so violently that he almost thought he could hear it. He tried to breathe naturally so it would relax, not give him away.

It was a real sound. Something was actually in the *hallway.*

The truth of the situation washed over him nastily. Here he was, new to the Lovett Co-op apartment building, playing by himself down in the supply room. You could never tell who might be lurking in basements of apartment buildings. This was the kind of thing adults always warned you about. And he was eleven, old enough by now to know better.

Hide, hide, hide, sang warning voices in Sam's head.

"HAH!"

A boy jumped around the pile of crates and shoved his face into Sam's. He was a blur of dark hair and peering eyes. He was much taller than Sam. A key dangled from his wrist. Sam recognized it as the key to the storage bin across the hall.

They stared at each other.

"I could hear you all the way up on the main floor," said the boy. "What do you think you're doing?"

"Nothing," said Sam. Then, to see if this boy could

understand, he added, "Well, I was thinking this was a good alien spaceship. I was giving it sounds."

He waited, hoping. Sam had never been able to find someone who could hear sounds the way he did.

"You're not supposed to be down here," said the strange boy after a moment. "Wait till Mr. Cockeral finds you."

"Nobody said I couldn't! He's not going to find out," said Sam, somewhat nervously.

"He's going to find out if I tell him." The strange boy lifted a wrench from the aliens' control panel and began tossing it up in the air and catching it again. Then he poked at the lawnmower. "What's this, the aliens' kitchen nook?"

Then Sam could see that there was a flat meanness in the boy's eyes, and something else. It was a tired, pinched anger, as if there was no room in his life for spacecraft sounds. There was only room for controlling things.

Sam knew that feeling—as if there was no point in trying to do anything, because it wasn't going to end up being important anyway. Whenever he and his mother were planning to move again, he felt it himself.

The boy said, "Hey, Astronaut Boy, you're doing what Pete Gower says from now on."

"No, I'm not," said Sam, nervously.

Pete Gower lifted his arm and threw the wrench down the hallway. It clattered across the floor. Sam tried to ignore the interesting clink-scrape of metal against concrete.

"You shouldn't leave Mr. Cockeral's tools all over the place," said Pete Gower. Then he picked up the grass shears and raised them over his head. Sam tensed, waiting for the blow. But instead Pete tossed them gently after the wrench.

"I saw you move in last week," Pete continued, conversationally. "You don't know the rules yet. But here they are: you do what I tell you."

There was no time to think. If Sam was going to escape, he needed to move quickly.

Instantly, Sam grabbed the only thing he could steal—the key on the elastic around Pete's wrist. The elastic snapped. Sam danced around Pete so that he was between the bigger boy and the door.

He dangled the key in Pete's face. "Want it back?"

Pete lunged at Sam, his face filled with dull surprise. Sam hurled the key toward the furnace room and launched himself in the other direction, along the hallway. Pete pelted behind. Sam reached the door, threw it open and pounded up the stairs two at a time.

He shot out through the Lovett Co-op's front doors. Some straggly bushes grew by the entrance; he dived into them.

Pete Gower burst through the doors and stopped. He stared around wildly.

At that moment, an orange-brown, tired voice shouted from a balcony, "What are you doing out there? Where's the diaper bag? Get back up here!"

Pete shouted, "It's COMING!"

"Well, go and get it, and stop hanging around!"

After glaring for another minute, Pete sighed explosively and slammed open the front door. He disappeared inside.

After five minutes had passed, Sam began to breathe normally. Finally he stepped out from the bushes. Peace gradually transformed into a thankful rhythm-pattern inside his head.

When he felt like himself again, Sam strolled along the walkway until he reached the road. He then jogged past a few kids sitting out on the curb, an elderly man shuffling along in the sunlight, and some older boys working on a car.

At last he veered onto a dirt path, followed it over the crest of the hill...and then stopped dead. He gasped.

It was like a miracle.

Below him yawned a ravine, green and wild and calling to him like a sweet, high flute. Suddenly the sound-patterns surged inside him. They mingled with bird calls and rustling wind, almost speaking with a human voice.

The weed-covered path plunged sharply, like a rip, down a nearly sheer cliff face. Sam joyfully hurled himself down, down, from the Lovett Co-op's peeling wallpaper and cramped apartments.

Then the sounds began to form into a movie sound-track. He was the hero, leading explorers into no-man's-land. The music soared, warning, *Captain! Enemy by the embankment!*

"Ha!" cried Sam, tackling. *Smash!* exclaimed the music. His men cheered enthusiastically.

The struggle ended quickly. The enemy wheezed, *I give in. You win. Let me up!*

With dignity, Sam helped him to his feet.

Then the soundtrack faded until all was silent, except for the rhythmic chirp-chirp of birds and the whine of cicadas. Sam's troop vanished around him, back into the blue sky. The smothering heat returned.

The ravine went on and on, miles of exciting waving

wildflowers and wild, ragged trees. Sam didn't notice the passage of time until shade bathed the weeds in light and dark. The sun had been inching across the sky all afternoon and now shadows gestured like fingers: *Sam, come home!*

Panicking, he checked his watch. Almost five o'clock! He had told Mrs. Hatch that he'd be home before now. Mrs. Hatch was their neighbor at the co-op—a stony, elderly lady who had just been hired by Sam's mother to keep an eye on him when she was at work. Whenever he went out or came back in, Sam was to knock on Mrs. Hatch's door and tell her. When his mother worked late, Mrs. Hatch would be coming in to cook his dinner. Sam was dreading that first dinner; Mrs. Hatch looked like the kind of person who'd think that gruel was a healthy meal for a growing boy.

His mother had promised to get off work early so they could buy school supplies for next week. She might even be home already, worried because he wasn't back when he had told Mrs. Hatch he would be.

Sam bounded back through the ravine. What was his excuse? He'd been at the library. The only way he'd get a good job was if he did well in school, his mother always said. And it wasn't really a lie, if you decided that "library" meant "ravine." It wasn't Sam's fault if nobody else knew the rule.

At the co-op, Pete was nowhere to be seen. Sam sneaked along the hallway toward Mrs. Hatch's apartment, trying not to make a sound.

He knocked softly on Mrs. Hatch's door, and waited. After a few minutes there was the sound of several locks being undone. Then the door crept open a few inches.

"Yes?" said Mrs. Hatch's face loudly, peering around the side of the door.

"I'm...I'm home," said Sam, somewhat embarrassed. He waited for her to ask him why he was late, and to say that his mother was angry about it.

"Good, good," said Mrs. Hatch. "Had a good day, did you?"

"Very good," said Sam. "I was at the library. That's...that's why I'm a little late."

"Always reading. That's a good boy. But you should get out in the fresh air, get some red in your cheeks."

"Tomorrow," said Sam. Inside, he was amazed that he had fooled her with the library story. Surely she could smell the ravine on him—the flowers, the waving grass!

Moments later, when he eased open the door to his own apartment, glorious silence greeted him. His mother wasn't home yet. He had outwitted them both. Relieved, he poured a glass of pop and slammed in the armchair in front of the TV.

Then her key squeaked in the lock. That noise was followed by the *thwump!* and *ting!* of her purse and keys landing in the hall table basket. Then she sighed quietly, a foggy, hopeless tune in his head. He knew she sighed because of him.

"Sam? Are you home?"

"In here."

His mother's face was drawn as if she had been up all night—which might have been the case, Sam thought. She often puttered around, trying not to wake him while he pretended to sleep.

"How was your day?" said Sam promptly, prepared for the usual.

"Oh, how was *my* day?" retorted his mother, her voice rising. "Unemployed fat cat businessmen, cocky new graduates, and the really *clever* types who think they've caught you in a spelling error. And being called 'girl' by clients younger than I am!" A gust of explosive air shot from her. "Some days I wish I had no responsibilities and didn't have to work for a living. There are actually people in the world who live like that!"

Sam felt his heart tumble crazily, the way it did whenever she mentioned her responsibilities. He was her biggest responsibility: he knew it in a flat, dark way.

"So how was *your* day?" his mother asked, after a moment.

"Fine," said Sam, briefly. "Mrs. Hatch told me I should get more red in my cheeks, so I went out." He thought about telling her how he'd met Pete Gower, but that would mean mentioning the basement of the co-op and maybe the ravine, where he was sure she would not allow him to go. There was a lot his mother didn't need to know.

"Remember about the school supplies?" he asked hopefully.

"Get your shoes on," she said, her voice like a stalled car. "And I don't want any arguments when we get there."

He began pulling his shoes on again. He imagined ice-blue erasers, glue that went on purple and dried clear.

The drive to the department store was eventful, as always. The car jerked and bucked as if it were as tired of being on the road as Sam's mother was. And there was a new sound—a kind of scraping creak, as if an important part of the car was dragging on the pavement.

"Shouldn't someone be looking at that?" Sam asked warily. She always barked at him when he mentioned anything about money.

"Someone should be doing a lot of things," she snapped. "Right now, food and clothing are a little more important."

The department store crackled with parents and children buying last-minute supplies. Signs screamed, *Save, Save, Save! The Bottom Line on Back-to-school!* Aisles burst with pencil cases, fluorescent pens and crayons, multicolored pencil sharpeners, glue-sticks, miniature staplers, and specialty binders of every description. There were notebooks with superheroes on the front and even mini-calculators you could wear like a watch.

Sam's heart started racing. But the harsh lights made his mother's face look even more tired and disappointed.

"Okay," she said, "five minutes. What do we *have* to get? Not, what do we *want* to get."

Minutes later, trotting back to the car, he reflected it was going to be another lousy year. Unless something unusual happened, which was highly unlikely.

Chapter Two

Sam prowled through the playground, focused on his mission. Where was Pete Gower hiding? This was the first day of school, and Pete had to be destroying things somewhere nearby. Whatever else happened, Sam needed to see Pete before Pete saw him—he needed to control things.

He sneaked past a group of kids leaping at basketball nets, another group pounding foursquare balls, and a gaggle of skippers twinkling in and out of ropes.

Then a familiar, scornful, ice-colored voice pierced everything.

"Gonna get it? Gonna get it?"

Sam muttered, "Enemy at three o'clock," and began gently repositioning himself behind a group of girls playing cards. Something must always be between himself and Pete—that was part of the mission.

From his vantagepoint, he could peek out and see what Pete was doing. Pete and another boy tossed a pencil case back and forth over a little kid's head. The boy scraped hopelessly at the air.

"Oooh, you gonna cry? Baby's gonna cry? Hey, Troy, baby's crying!"

They danced away down the pavement. Sam darted to the back of the foursquare line, so five players stood between himself and Pete. But he couldn't resist checking to see what Pete was doing.

Now, pencils soared gently through the air. The little boy was torn between grabbing at the pencil case and running to fetch the pencils.

Sam looked away guiltily. The obvious, brave thing to do would be to help. But he couldn't afford to draw attention to himself. Pete would be only too pleased to finish what he'd started in the furnace room.

As Sam looked everywhere but at Pete and Troy, an unexpected figure caught his eye.

It was a girl, standing coldly alone, hands clasped simply in front of her, as if she was hardly aware of everything tumbling around her. Only her eyes moved, flickering from group to group.

She seemed to be reading something dangerous in her head. She looked powerful and detached from the schoolyard.

An interesting little tune arose in Sam's thoughts, cold and stalking.

Just as he realized he was staring, the girl turned to look directly at him. She glared so blackly and scornfully that Sam glanced away, embarrassed. She seemed to be able to scan Sam's thoughts like a newspaper headline—*I am a coward, hiding in the foursquare line.*

When he looked out again, the girl was striding directly toward Pete Gower, his friend Troy and the little kid. She marched between them, easily ripped the pencil case out of Pete Gower's hand and gave it to the kid. Then she pushed the boy to show him that it was time to run.

Sam was dumbfounded. Just then, the school bell rang.

He lost sight of the strange girl as the teachers herded them into their new classrooms. But a moment later, inside his new room—5B—he noticed her standing alone, just inside the door, grimly waiting.

"Helen Alemeda, second desk," the teacher shrilled, pointing. Her voice squeaked with silver sparks. "Samuel Garretson, third desk."

Sam obediently sat where he was told. The strange girl slipped into the desk ahead of him, neatly, as if she didn't want to waste any movements.

Helen Alemeda. It sounded like she looked—coolly apart from her surroundings.

"Peter Gower, fourth desk."

Sam groaned aloud: "Oh, no!"

"I beg your pardon?" squeaked the teacher, turning to stare at him.

"Nothing," Sam muttered, flushing.

Pete settled into the desk behind Sam, then leaned forward to whisper heavily in his ear: "Found any aliens lately?"

Sam swallowed hard.

"Found any diapers lately?" he whispered back.

Pete flicked the back of Sam's head. Sam flinched.

The teacher wrote her name on the board. *Mrs. Jones.* Then she turned, beaming fiercely, to the class.

"Good morning, everyone."

A layered chorus of "Good morning" rose awkwardly from the class.

"Most of us know each other already, but we have one new person in our class this year. Helen Alemeda, will you please stand up?"

Helen Alemeda grew, like a dangerous vine, out of her desk. She stood, waiting.

"Helen's father is Frank Alemeda, a famous conductor, who has led symphony orchestras all over the world. We

16

are lucky that he has taken a permanent position with our city orchestra."

Mrs. Jones beamed at Helen, but Helen said nothing. Mrs. Jones continued, "Helen has lived in many different countries and has had exciting experiences. Helen, would you like to say a few words to the class?"

There was a long pause.

At last, in a clear voice, Helen replied, "No, I wouldn't, particularly."

"Well, can you tell us about your hobbies, what you like to do in your spare time?"

Helen sighed so softly Sam almost didn't hear. It was a menacing sigh, and it curled, grayish-black, inside Sam's mind.

Sam would have liked to sigh in just the same way.

"I don't have any *hobbies*," said Helen Alemeda. "I am studying to be a pianist. In the meantime, my tutor has been dismissed, so I apparently have to go to school. This was not my idea, however. I have no interest in anything or anyone in this ridiculous place."

Complete, stunned silence.

"Thank you, Helen," said Mrs. Jones, weakly. "You may sit down."

Whispers hissed and popped around the room, especially from the girls, who were offended. Helen Alemeda was supposed to wait humbly until they decided where she was going to be accepted.

"No interest in anyTHING or anyONE," Pete lisped severely from behind Sam, just loudly enough for the kids in his row to hear. The row erupted in giggles.

Sam tried to ignore Pete while Mrs. Jones reviewed math concepts they had learned last year. Nobody seemed to remember anything, and Mrs. Jones' face grew pinker.

"Helen Alemeda!" said Mrs. Jones, cheeks glowing. "Surely at least you can come up here and show us how to do this problem."

Gracefully, dangerously, Helen slid to the front and wrote the correct answer without hesitation. She bestowed the chalk upon Mrs. Jones before gliding to her seat again.

"Excellent!" said Mrs. Jones, holding the chalk lightly in her hand as if it was a strange species of butterfly.

"Thank you," said Helen in a chilly voice.

Then they read aloud. First, Amber McDonald stumbled through a paragraph. Then Helen's ringing voice pronounced sentences as if they were part of a clearly ordered melody. Next it was Sam's turn. He tried to be like Helen—to shape the sentences into a tune, making each word fit.

"Ow!" Suddenly he leapt to his feet, grabbing his back.

"Oh. Sorry," said Pete. "My mistake. My ruler slipped."

"Aggressive behavior is unacceptable in my classroom!" cried Mrs. Jones. "Turn around!"

"Which way?" said Pete. "To the front or back?"

Then grim silence fell, and everyone looked at Mrs. Jones to see what she would do.

"To the office," said Mrs. Jones with finality.

Pete flashed his golden smile at Mrs. Jones, and sauntered from the room.

After lunch Sam settled under a poplar tree, far from Pete. He closed his eyes and pretended he had run, tumbling, into the ravine again. He could almost hear the birdcalls—twittering green-yellow sounds.

After school, he would definitely return there. If his mom was working late.

When he opened his eyes, he saw Helen Alemeda. She slipped with precise, tiny steps to another poplar not far away, settled in a nook between the roots and opened the book she carried with her.

Glaring, she began to read.

He could almost hear the purple-black of concentration crackling around her. It felt impossible for him to stay quiet.

"What're you reading?" Sam called.

Helen ignored him, turning a page and scanning a new paragraph. Sam waited. Then he wondered if he had spoken loudly enough.

"WHAT ARE YOU READING?"

"I distinctly heard you before," snapped Helen Alemeda, "but I didn't think you'd have the gall to ask a second time. Especially after your performance on the playground this morning, cowering in the four-square line."

She raised the book in front of her face, dismissing him.

Sam stared at her, astonished.

Two things shot through his mind. The first was that he intensely disliked Helen. The second was that he wasn't going to allow her to win so easily. He would make her talk to him yet!

Desperately he peered at the front of Helen Alemeda's book, at the scowling man with wild hair. "Beethoven," he said, very loudly. "Bee-though-ven." He pronounced it exactly as it looked.

"Bay-toe-ven," Helen hissed, head popping up again. "Were you raised in a barn?"

"Who's Beethoven?" said Sam promptly, pleased that he had made her talk to him.

A sound twirled out of Helen's throat like steam rising from a kettle. "Beethoven," she said at last, glaring, "is the most famous composer who ever lived, as all but the most hopeless ignoramus knows."

"What's a composer?" said Sam. But suddenly he wished he hadn't asked. He sensed it was the kind of general knowledge you were supposed to have. It was like asking, *What's a painter?*

"A composer writes music, idiot," snarled Helen, so blackly that Sam flinched. "If you don't leave me alone, I'll get the teacher on duty to force you to do so. This is my private time, and you're intruding. Go. Away."

Sam blinked. He tried to ignore the sharp, embarrassing feeling inside him, as if Helen Alemeda had just told him that he'd never been important and would never amount to anything.

"Well," he said, determined to sound detached and mysterious like her, "it has certainly been nice talking to you. We must do this again someday."

While she continued to glare—a red flush creeping into her face—he got up and sauntered toward the baseball field. Now that he'd had the last word, he decided he would never talk to her again.

But by the end of the afternoon, he had forgotten everything but the glorious adventure that lay ahead. The ravine flashed in his mind like a promise. Even Helen Alemeda couldn't spoil it.

Mrs. Hatch was standing like a stump in the kitchen, when he arrived home. Pots were bubbling on the stove. They smelled brown.

"Your mother is working late," said Mrs. Hatch in her grumpy, muttery way. "I'm making dinner. It'll be ready in ten minutes. Wash up."

A triumphant chorus welled up in Sam. After dinner, the ravine. Mrs. Hatch was the one who had said he needed red in his cheeks.

He wolfed down the dinner, which tasted and looked as brown as it had smelled—great lumps of mystery meat, oozing in a muddy lake. Then he said to Mrs. Hatch, "I think I'll head outside to play for awhile. Some kids might organize a softball game."

"That's it," said Mrs. Hatch, gloomily. "But be home before dark."

"I will," Sam promised.

Minutes later he joyfully closed the door behind him.

First he needed supplies.

He remembered seeing a pile of old boards by the recycling bin, behind the co-op. It wasn't really stealing if Mr. Cockeral was planning to recycle it; in fact, Sam would be recycling it for him!

He sneaked out the back door of the Co-op, keeping an eye out for both Pete Gower and Mr. Cockeral. Neither was anywhere to be seen.

He dragged several medium-sized boards from the pile, carefully avoiding the rusty nails. Lifting the boards over his shoulder, he staggered down the road that led to the path that led to the glorious ravine.

The sun glittered as he climbed down the steep embankment, to the place where he would build his own world and have his own adventures—far from school, far from Pete Gower, far from everything.

Far from Helen Alemeda.

Unexpectedly, a vivid picture of Helen Alemeda and her glaring eyes washed into his mind. Again, anger bubbled in him, when he remembered the things she had said. But something else inside him churned strangely for a moment, as if it recognized something in her that lived in himself too. It was like a driving, blue-black rhythm that didn't fit anywhere properly: they were both out of step with things.

Sam shook his head to get Helen Alemeda out of it. Firmly he told himself, if she didn't want anything to do with him, then quite frankly, he felt the same way!

Chapter Three

Tap, tap, Tap, tap. Helen Alemeda's angry feet crunched over the pavement.

Every step dragged her closer to the horrible house where they'd be living from now on. No more Salzburg, no more Vienna. And now her father would be rehearsing around the clock to get this ridiculous new orchestra on its feet.

Her fury rose. "Ill-educated, dirty, *stupid!*" That uncombed, loud boy who had bothered her at lunch was a perfect example of everything gone wrong in her life. Everything important, powerful and unique had been taken away and replaced with people like Sam Garretson. How could you not know who Beethoven was?

When Helen stepped into the cool of the entranceway and threw down her new school bag, a voice suddenly bounced through the foyer like a hunting horn. It forced merriment into the house, as if there wouldn't be any joy otherwise.

"Is that you, young Miss Helen Alemeda?"

It was bumbling Mrs. Williams. She was the house-keeper, hired after the death of Helen's mother, when Helen had been scarcely older than a baby.

Once, Helen had looked forward to seeing Mrs. Williams each day, but that time was quite finished.

Helen would never trust Mrs. Williams again. Mrs. Williams needed to know that, so Helen took every opportunity to make it very clear.

She neatly removed her shoes, while Mrs. Williams wiped her floury hands on her apron. Helen tried to ignore the way that Mrs. Williams was peering at her.

"I've baked peach tarts. They're cooling on the rack."

There was a pleading quality to Mrs. Williams' voice. Helen felt satisfaction at that. Good! Let the traitor worry that Helen would never forgive her.

"Enjoy them," said Helen, with as much dignity as she could muster. "I've got *homework* to do. From my first day at *regular school*." She began to climb the winding staircase to her bedroom, leaving Mrs. Williams standing like a large, floury stump in the foyer.

She waited for Mrs. Williams to call something after her, something hopeful and needy that Helen could reject. But Mrs. Williams was silent, so Helen continued climbing the rest of the way.

She slammed the bedroom door and threw herself onto the bed. She glared at the picture of Beethoven hanging on the wall. He glowered back, broodingly.

Slowly, Helen's muscles began to relax.

They might have taken everything else from her, but she still had the Beethoven Game. She might never be stupid enough to write any of it down again, but it was alive and well inside her head.

"Good morrow, little maid," she mumbled to herself.

She had been playing the game for a couple of years now. In the Beethoven Game, she could actually *talk to Beethoven*. Beethoven helped her to sort out the ridiculous things that were going on in her life. He helped her to see that neither of them needed anybody besides each other.

Last summer she had taken the game a step further. Her father had gone to Bavaria for the Wagner Festival in Bayreuth, leaving Helen alone with Mrs. Williams and the tutor. It was a lonely summer. Helen had started wishing that the game was *realer*, somehow.

So she began writing letters to herself that she signed, with a mighty flourish, Ludwig van Beethoven. That way she could read and reread what he had to say.

She busily wrote and read Beethoven's letters for most of the summer, until the day that everything crashed down around her like a demolished building. Helen kept playing that day over and over in her mind, like a broken video, wishing she could step into it and change some details so that none of the bad parts had ever happened.

But they had happened. The day before Helen and Mrs. Williams were to travel to Bayreuth to join Mr. Alemeda, Mrs. Williams went up to pack Helen's things. As she was rustling amid some of Helen's dresses, she came upon Helen's letters, neatly tied up in yellow ribbon.

When Helen entered the room to find her book of sonatas, she discovered horrible Mrs. Williams, leaning over the open suitcase, reading everything!

"Those aren't for you!" Helen shrieked. "You're supposed to be packing!"

That was the end of everything worthwhile in Helen's life.

Suddenly her father had arranged a permanent engagement back home. Suddenly they were moving into this house again, where they hadn't been since Helen was a baby. Suddenly they were all talking about how she had been alone too much, needed the company of people her own age, needed 'normalcy'—whatever that meant, Helen thought bitterly.

They had thought they could weed the game out of her. But Helen knew something they didn't know.

"Ha!" Helen growled at the portrait of Beethoven, hanging on her bedroom wall. The letters might be gone, but the game was alive and well.

As she concentrated, the room around her disappeared.

She was sitting on a rock by the river. Just as she was wondering if he'd ever arrive, Beethoven stamped into the clearing.

"Good morrow, little maid!" he roared heartily, settling on a rock beside her. "You're a long way from town. Does anyone know where you are?"

She snapped, "They don't need to know where I am. I've just completed the most horrible day of my life, going to that stupid school, being bleated at by that ridiculous teacher."

"You and I, we suffer the same malady!" Beethoven boomed. "We are in danger of being smothered by the world and those who labor in it!" He took off his hat and ran thick fingers through wild hair. "That is why we cultivate the inner life—nobody has any control over that."

"They're all talking so much about stupid things, I can't cultivate anything," Helen snapped.

"A wise musician," said Beethoven, "can filter out the useless noise."

"It's all useless at the moment," said Helen.

"Then you must filter out everything!" Beethoven roared with laughter and leapt to his feet. "Come! Let us walk through the forest and I shall tell you about a new sonata I am composing. Perhaps, little maid, you will do me the honor of unveiling it for Vienna." He bowed to her, and reluctantly she rose to her feet and curtsied back.

Arm in arm, they strolled through the forest....

"Helen!" Mrs. Williams's voice boomed up the staircase. "Dr. Weiss is here."

Her eyes snapped open. When she was in the game, she lost all sense of time. She could smell the forest scents—pine needles, earth beneath her feet, flowers and weeds growing by the river.

"Coming!" she shouted.

Dr. Weiss was the piano teacher her father had hired to come on Mondays, Wednesdays and Fridays. At least Mr. Alemeda had recognized that it would be unwise to tamper with her music.

When she entered the studio, Dr. Weiss was already seated in the armchair beside the piano, with a lined notebook in his lap. He was a long, thin man, with gray hair and thick glasses. She remembered from their first meeting that he spoke quietly, as if setting a trap for a shy animal. *I'm the animal*, she thought. *But he doesn't know what he's in for.*

"Hello, Helen," he said, in his peculiar, husky voice. "It's nice to see you again. Why don't you have a seat at the piano?"

Helen settled herself precisely on the bench and gazed sternly into the white and black of the keys. It was time to show this piano teacher what he was dealing with.

Without giving Dr. Weiss a chance to speak, she launched into the opening of the first movement of Beethoven's *Pathetique* Sonata. *Crash!*. If this didn't impress him, nothing would.

Helen played with half an ear for his responses—even the subtlest shifting in his chair. He didn't interrupt her at all during the first movement. Good!

When the movement growled to an end, she stopped abruptly. Did he need the second and third movements, or had he learned enough to start with? She waited for his remarks.

But there was silence. It went on and on.

"Very impressive," said Dr. Weiss, at last. "Showy, technical. It didn't grip me, though."

Helen blinked.

"Not much sorrow," said Dr. Weiss. "Not a lot of joy either. Mostly a charge of the light brigade, from beginning to end."

Helen didn't know what 'charge of the light brigade' meant, but she sensed it wasn't something Dr. Weiss liked very much.

She began to despise Dr. Weiss intensely.

"I think we need to back up a little," said Dr. Weiss, folding his hands peacefully. "I think we need to begin with a nice, clean scale."

"Begin with a *what?*" snapped Helen.

"C scale. Four octaves, please. At this tempo." He clapped his hands to show her the speed.

"C scale is for babies," said Helen.

"Correction. C scale is the seed, and Beethoven is the tree that grows from it," said Dr. Weiss. "Let's go back to the seed."

They stared each other down. At last, Helen placed her hands on the keyboard and executed a perfect scale: four octaves, at Dr. Weiss's tempo. There!

"As I suspected," said Dr. Weiss, coolly. "Young lady, a scale is not merely a mathematical formula for everyone to admire. No, it is a majestic sweep that builds to a climax and falls away from it again. It is a beautiful balance of precision and drama. I can see we have our work cut out for us."

The fury in Helen began to bubble. "That's not what my father says." She could usually shut people up by saying that. The great Frank Alemeda was admired and feared by everyone.

"I would be very surprised if that were the case," said Dr. Weiss, calmly. "He and I recently had a most interesting conversation."

Alarm flooded Helen. "What conversation?" she muttered.

"You won't play any more little games about being a musician. Now you are old enough to start thinking like one," said Dr. Weiss.

Helen was too furious to reply. She turned her red face away. She wanted to die.

"Perhaps I'm being a little harsh," said Dr. Weiss. "But *showiness* is for babies; *interpretation* is for artists. And that begins with scales. C scale again, please. This time, show me the full range."

And as Helen's angry fingers clawed up and down the scale, she did sense a strange power in shooting to the top and falling away again. But she was not about to admit it to Dr. Weiss.

Chapter Four

"No, no, no! A verb is not a describing word! A verb is an *action* word!" Mrs. Jones' face was beginning to bloom like a tulip in early spring. She scraped a hand through her hair, and the class obediently wrote it down.

But in Sam's mind, actions and descriptions began quietly to dance together. They formed a strange new creature that described actions with colors nobody had seen before. A complicated rhythm sprouted from it and scattered over his notebook.

"Sam Garretson, I don't know how many times I will have to ask you *not* to pound on your desk. This is not music class," said Mrs. Jones, severely.

Sam flushed red. He tried to find the correct spot on the page.

"And *Helen Alemeda!*"

The whole class turned to look.

"This is not silent reading time!"

Helen closed her book with great calm. "This book is about Ludwig van Beethoven, the most important composer of music in history. I'm learning a good deal more in these pages than I am from you."

Mrs. Jones stared at Helen, appalled. The class waited, fascinated. Then Mrs. Jones snapped, "Bring it here."

Helen stared back at Mrs. Jones. Then slowly, lazily, reluctantly, she rose from her desk, slipped neatly up the aisle and handed the book to the teacher.

Mrs. Jones placed it on her desk. "When you can prove to me that you are concentrating very hard on what we are doing in class, you may have your book back."

Like a simmering black pudding, Helen's face gave off furious heat. She seated herself again neatly. Sam stared at her impossibly straight back, and could almost hear her rage hissing in green-red jagged lines. It was the same anger he sometimes felt.

But then he remembered Helen's rudeness toward him. He decided he didn't care what she was feeling.

Mrs. Jones composed herself. "We are each going to read sentences aloud, and we are going to figure out where the verbs can be found in the sentence." She handed out sheets with sentences neatly typed and numbered.

And then it happened.

Pete Gower wrapped his sheet partly around Sam's head. "Look at the little alien baby!" he said. "Little baby wearing his bonnet.""

Furiously, Sam shook the sheet off, and twisted in his chair to confront Pete.

"Samuel Garretson, turn around!" Mrs. Jones roared.

Sam twisted back, frozen.

"Peter Gower, your behavior is part of a *pattern!*" Mrs. Jones flushed even redder, if it was possible. "It is time that someone got to the root of this, and that someone is the principal. We are going to speak to him *together, this minute.* Class, underline the verbs in these sentences and be ready to recite them when I return."

Astonishingly, Mrs. Jones and Pete left the room.

For a moment, there was smothering silence. Then, as excited voices erupted throughout the class, Helen

Alemeda shot efficiently to Mrs. Jones's desk and lifted her book from the pile of papers on top.

Not looking at anyone, she returned to her place and slipped the book into her desk. "It belongs to me," she announced, not looking up. Then she began to underline verbs precisely.

Again, despite himself, Sam's admiration for Helen billowed inside like smoke. He wished *he* had been the one to talk back to Mrs. Jones so powerfully. He wished *he* had stolen back the book, in front of everyone.

Maybe he could actually be like that himself one day. Maybe all the chaotic sounds and rhythms in his head would somehow fuse into a single purpose, and he would do something truly remarkable!

When Mrs. Jones returned, her face was white with a neat red dot in each cheek. She did not notice that Helen's book had vanished from her desk.

"I hope that you are ready to recite," she said warningly to the class.

After lunch, Sam wandered through the playground, keeping a wary eye out for Pete. He was also curious to see where Helen Alemeda had gone. Pete was nowhere to be seen, but at last Sam located Helen, reading alone in the corner of the east wing doorsill. Even with her head buried in her book, Helen had a strange power that seemed to echo the tumbling patterns in Sam.

Then he stiffened.

Pete Gower and Troy Smith sidled across the parking lot toward Helen. They stopped in front of her.

They intended to steal the book from her. He didn't know how he knew—it was a flat, gray understanding.

Sam thought about watching quietly from a distance.

It was the safest thing to do. None of this was really his problem. Besides, he reminded himself for the hundredth time, Helen Alemeda had laughed at him and told him he was stupid. But suddenly the voices in his head were murmuring and grumbling.

A vivid picture of the first day of school shot into Sam's mind. He had hidden in the foursquare line and watched as Helen stopped Pete from bullying the little kid. Helen had stood up against Pete and Troy. She had done exactly what she wanted, and they hadn't been able to stop her!

Suddenly Sam was on his feet, half-eaten sandwich in his hand, racing toward the school. He had no idea what to do, but two outcasts against two bullies meant things were evenly matched.

As he drew closer, Sam heard their singsong voices.

"So you said you're going to be a famous piano player," Pete was remarking in silky tones. He ran a hand luxuriously through his hair. "I'm going to be famous too. I play lead guitar in my band. After we get good, we're going to do gigs."

"Why are you telling me this?" said Helen.

"One musician to another," said Pete suavely. He arched his back and scraped at imaginary chords.

Sam stopped in the grass and waited for Helen's response. He knew it would be devastating.

"Quite frankly," said Helen, after a moment, "I don't feel like watching you play an invisible instrument. I'm reading about real instruments, and a real composer, Ludwig van Beethoven. Why don't you join the drama club and leave me alone?"

Even Troy snickered until Pete sent him a dirty look.

Pete turned back to Helen, a dangerous glint dancing in his eyes.

"What's that thing, anyway?" said Pete. Casually, efficiently, he tore the book from her hands.

Helen leapt to her feet. "Give that back immediately!"

"Give that back immediately!" Pete simpered. "What does a famous musician need with a book? Shouldn't you be playing the piano somewhere?"

Then Pete pranced, holding the book over his head, daring her to jump for it. "It's right here. Don't you want it? I thought you really wanted it."

Helen lunged. At the same moment, Pete bent his arm back, took aim and released. The book soared over Helen's head, up, up, until—

"Guess you'll have to be good at climbing walls," said Pete.

The book's corner peeked over the edge of the roof, far out of reach.

"You—are—an—animal!" Helen shouted. Like an advancing bull, she knocked Pete onto the pavement before he had time to react.

Then Helen tore around the side of the school, toward the south doors, with Pete and Troy gaining on her. As Mrs. Jones stepped from the south hallway into the sunshine, Helen blasted past into the school. Mrs. Jones' hand neatly halted Pete and Troy.

"Boys! Simmer down."

Gasping for breath, Pete cried, "She knocked me onto the pavement! I wasn't doing anything!"

"I don't want to hear it," Mrs. Jones snapped. "Both of you, sit under that tree and don't get up until the bell rings."

"But—"

"MARCH," said Mrs. Jones.

Sam wiped his moist forehead and tried to decide what to do. He was filled with electric, confused determination. Should he confront Pete and Troy now? No. They were safely under their tree, watched by Mrs. Jones. Could he retrieve the book? Not without something to climb on, and he'd get in trouble for trying.

But Helen was storming through the school, alone and angry. Sam made his decision. He would run after her, find her, and then tell her—what?

I was ready to help!

Somehow, weirdly, he wanted her to know. He hadn't been planning to hide this time. He was the same kind of person she was. He was worthwhile.

When the teachers were looking the other way, he slipped through the south doors into the stuffy hallway. It was empty. He peered into their classroom, but Helen was nowhere to be seen. Good thinking. Pete and Troy would have looked there first. Next he searched the library and the gym. No sign of Helen.

When he tried the doors to the auditorium, they were open—which was unusual, since the auditorium was kept locked to prevent kids from banging on the baby grand at the front. The custodian must have slipped up.

Baby grand! Helen was going to be a famous pianist. Of course that was where she would be.

He eased open the big, soundproof doors.

Then he stopped as if someone had hit him.

A soft tendril of melody curled toward him, high and wandering and astonishingly sweet. Then a second tune wrapped around the first in complicated ways that stirred the colors and shapes and sounds always tossing in Sam. Together the sounds wove a peculiar whole.

The awakening patterns in his head and the music from the piano suddenly came together to create a vivid picture in Sam's mind. He saw a rainforest where the animals, birds, insects and plants sang in their own mysterious voices—separately, yet in a chorus that included everyone. It practically knocked him over, it was so alive.

He had to get closer.

Keeping low, Sam sneaked along the right aisle toward the stage, up the side stairs, and behind the stage curtain, making sure that Helen couldn't see him. But he could see her, hunched at the piano like she was growing out of it.

Over and over, she played the same melody. Each time, she changed it a little; as if she was searching for something inside it that she couldn't quite pinpoint. And every note was answered by a sound-pattern in Sam, complicated, hopeful, soaring. Somehow, the music spoke a raw language he recognized. Helen, or the music itself, was talking to him. *And he understood.*

Dimly, suddenly he felt that he was staring himself in the face—

But just then the school bell pealed out.

Helen rose instantly from the piano. Face pinched and tight, she rushed down the stairs on the other side of the stage, and raced up the center aisle. The big door closed gently behind her, and silence fell in the auditorium.

Sam waited another minute or so, trying to clear his head and sort out what had just happened. *This is important*, whispered the rhythms. *This is what we want. Try to figure it out.*

The ideas had flowed from Helen through her fingers into the air, and the piano had been a gateway, a kind of code she had learned that released the music into the empty auditorium.

That was how you satisfied the rhythms—you learned to play them out!

All afternoon he could scarcely sit still. He didn't see how anyone could expect him to pay any attention at all to math and geography when something so unbelievable had happened. He stared at the back of Helen's head. How had she learned to unlock the piano's secrets so it would play what she wanted to say?

By the end of the day Sam had come up with a plan.

When school was over, he hid in the bushes by the door until all the kids were gone. When he was sure nobody was left, he sneaked back into the school—he needed something to stand on, and something to reach with.

Sam slipped into the empty classroom, heavy with school smells—chalk, kids, dust. He heaved the desk nearest the door into the hallway, grabbing Mrs. Jones' pointer on the way out. Puffing, he dragged them to the exit, pulled the door open and yanked them outside.

When the desk was in position, Sam climbed cautiously onto it. It rocked a little. Balancing carefully, he stood on his toes. With the pointer he caught the edge of the book, pushed up a little to create resistance and then, with great care, began dragging it forward.

Only a few more inches—

The book tumbled, at last, past Sam's head to the ground.

Then Sam returned the desk and pointer to the classroom and pelted home, the book hidden inside his school bag. The book surely held answers to some of his questions; tonight he would read it.

And he knew just where he would do it. The ravine, of course.

Chapter Five

The sun slid over the sky. Shadows stretched across the ravine, but Sam couldn't stop reading Helen's book about Beethoven. He sprawled in the half-built fort until he could hardly see his hands, and night crickets chirped in the grass around him

He heard a pounding in his head—*boom, boom, boom*—like mighty drums.

By the time the sun was completely down, Sam had finished the first chapter of the book. He closed his eyes to concentrate on the dancing images. He had thought that maybe Beethoven was going to be like a rock star. But Beethoven was nothing like that.

Instead, Beethoven was a boy. He reminded Sam of himself. Just like Sam, Beethoven had sounds and rhythms tumbling around in his head. He was tangled and angry and fierce. His father drank constantly, like Mr. Epp in apartment 2D.

Sam wondered what was worse: a father who drank all the time, or a father who wasn't there at all. They were both bad, he decided.

When life got really horrible, Beethoven tried to fix things, using the talent that he had. He found a job playing an organ in a church to make money, though he probably wasn't much older than Sam.

Sam pictured Beethoven glaring fiercely through his

bedroom window, thinking somebody had to keep the family going. He wasn't going to sit back and let other people control things.

When it got too dark to see at all, Sam heaved the book up the ravine. Fortunately his mom was working late; she had told him about it that morning. So Mrs. Hatch was there—and she was easy to get around.

Sure enough, Mrs. Hatch was stirring a big pot of something on the stove when he crept in. Clouds of steam hung in the air above.

"I'm making chowder," Mrs. Hatch said matter-of-factly. "Little late for you to be getting home, isn't it?"

"I had to go to the library—school project," Sam mumbled, reddening a little. He waved the book vaguely, as evidence.

"I like a hard worker," Mrs. Hatch grumbled, approvingly. "But boys need fresh air too."

"I know," said Sam, because he couldn't think of anything else to say.

Then he raced into his room and hid the book under the bed.

The chowder looked and tasted like salty paste, with strange blobs of fishy stuff in it. Mrs. Hatch sat across from Sam and ate methodically, not speaking. Sam decided that he definitely preferred it when his mother ordered in pizza.

After dinner he announced heartily, "Well, I have to do my homework now!"

Mrs. Hatch nodded.

Sam crept into his room and closed the door. He slid the big book from under the bed and sprawled on the floor.

Sometimes, Beethoven's father burst into Beethoven's room in the middle of the night after staggering home from the tavern. Sam pictured him shouting, "Get up, kid! We've got company and you're going to entertain them!"

Sam saw red-faced laughing men who probably weren't listening to the music because they were too busy drinking. He pictured Beethoven blinking sleep out of his eyes, trying to focus on the piano when all he wanted to do was to crawl under the covers. That would make you angry, Sam thought. And if you were Beethoven, who was going to grow up to be a famous writer of music, you'd create powerful rhythms and melodies to tell everyone all the different ways you were angry.

Sam figured he would have to find some of this music somewhere and listen to it. That was before he learned how to play it, of course.

When he fell asleep, strange images and sounds darted through his dreams—music that had turned into vivid lasers shooting from Beethoven's fingers.

The next morning, before he could tell himself not to, Sam sneaked into his mother's dark room. He shook her gently. "Can I take piano lessons?"

His mother opened her eyes and gazed blearily at him. "What time is it?"

"It's five-fifteen. Can I take piano lessons?"

His mother sat up in the bed, the worried expression on her face. It was a combination of the are-you-sick and the money look. The money look was usually followed by, *You know we can't afford that!* It usually resulted in a bad mood too—sometimes lasting for hours.

"What put that crazy thought into your head?" she

asked, yawning and plumping the pillow behind her back.

"I don't know," Sam muttered. He suddenly realized she had only had a few hours of sleep. Extremely bad timing.

"I took piano lessons when I was your age," said his mother sleepily, "and believe me, they weren't fun. Miss Finlay was my teacher. She was about ninety-nine, she ate biscuits at the piano and sprayed crumbs all over me when she talked. She used to hit my fingers with a ruler when I made mistakes. Taking piano lessons was one of the worst experiences of my whole childhood."

"I wouldn't have to take lessons from Miss Finlay!" Sam said, in a slightly too-loud voice. "We could find somebody else." He twisted with frustration. His mother just wasn't the kind of person who would understand, but somehow he had to make her see. The problem was, how did you put into words the *coming home* feeling of learning to release the sounds?

"Trust me," said his mother, her voice rising to match his, "be glad I'm sparing you the experience. The time I wasted playing scales over and over.... Sam, honey, I honestly need to sleep if I'm going to be any use to anyone today. You know better than to wake me up at this hour." She began pounding her pillow into the shape she wanted.

"I *want* to play scales," said Sam, not even sure what they were. The conversation was not going to be over until she understood what he meant. He sat down on the side of the bed.

His mother sighed gustily. After a minute, she spoke using her trying-to-be-reasonable voice. "Well, I want you to concentrate on your schoolwork. I want you to think about what's lying down the road, because it'll be here

42

soon enough. If I say that piano lessons are a waste of time, then you'll just have to trust me—leaving the money issue aside altogether, which makes them out of the question to begin with. They're a luxury. *Plus* we don't have a piano."

"I could get an after-school job now, to pay for—"

"You're only eleven years old!" his mother groaned.

"I bet I could get a job bagging groceries at the store." Sam glared. It seemed like a perfectly good solution.

But his mother's expression looked like he'd asked for a job at Top-Notch Business Systems. "I want you to focus on school so you'll avoid the stupid mistakes I've made. Piano lessons are a complete waste of your time. They will have no bearing on the rest of your life. I don't want to hear anything more about them, and I want you to close the door behind you!" Her voice became harsher and harsher, as if she were trying to turn her words into granite.

Sam couldn't sleep anymore, so he began washing dishes ferociously. He tried not to slam them around but it was hard not to. She never allowed him to have anything! All she ever said was, he had to get a good job later. *But what about right now?*

By the time he left for school, he had made up his mind. He had rescued Helen's book, so Helen would have to help him find piano lessons.

The trick was to get a chance to explain this to her.

But all morning it was impossible. One thing after another seemed to be happening to her.

When Helen walked down the aisle to her seat, Pete tripped her. She tumbled awkwardly to the floor, squeaking with rage. While she was down, Troy Smith emptied

43

his pencil sharpener on her head. Shavings fluttered through her hair. Furiously Helen swiped at them. She slapped Pete hard across the shoulder as she rose.

Helen could give as good as she got—just like Beethoven.

The class roared with laughter.

Mrs. Jones twisted around from the blackboard, where she was writing language arts exercises for them to read aloud. She shouted, "Peter Gower!" as she did so. She didn't even know it was him yet.

"She just slapped me!" said Pete, with assumed outrage. "Why am I to blame if *she* slapped me?"

"Right," cried Mrs. Jones. "To the office! March!"

When it was time for art, Mrs. Jones handed out brushes and paint. They were to create a still life of a can of pencils, which she placed on her desk where everyone could see it. A low babble of voices filled the room as everyone began to paint.

This was Sam's opportunity finally. But when he gathered the nerve to say something, Helen was glaring at her painting. It looked like a demented space alien, with a stocky green body and pointed tentacles writhing around its head.

"That's a terrible painting," said Sam, without thinking. Then he wanted to kick himself. She wouldn't help him if he insulted her.

But she surprised him by answering.

"It looks," said Helen, serenely, "like an upside-down octopus. But I'm doing what they suggest a student does, so please leave me alone."

This was it.

Gathering courage, Sam blurted, "I have to tell you

something. You have to listen."

"I don't have to do anything," said Helen Alemeda.

"I heard you—in the auditorium—I was behind the curtain."

Helen turned to look at him dangerously. She was silent.

Sam struggled to find words to show her what was inside him. He stammered, "I could—I could tell what you were saying. I could hear the rhythms, I could tell the codes." His voice sounded ridiculous in his ears.

But it was too late to turn back now. Intensely he blurted, "I need to know how to make the rhythms and the patterns. I haven't been thinking about anything else since yesterday."

Helen continued to stare at him.

"Well—what are you going to say?" Sam demanded.

There was a strange expression on Helen's face, as if Sam had just said his first words in a language she actually understood. She looked surprised.

"Lots of people want to play the piano," she answered at last, in a superior voice. "Most of them fizzle out early on. Playing the piano isn't just fingers on keys. It's *nuances*, not just *charge of the light brigade*."

"I could learn," said Sam, utterly convinced.

"I doubt it," said Helen.

"You don't know!"

Helen looked up from her monstrous painting. "So why don't you take piano lessons then?"

Sam swiped at his artwork roughly before speaking. "Long story," he said gruffly. He wasn't about to explain about his mother.

"That's not my problem," said Helen.

45

Then a plan began to form in Sam's mind. The more he thought about it, the more perfect it was.

"Your problem is bullies throwing your book on the school roof and stuff," he said, slowly. "You don't know how to solve it, but I do."

"I don't have a problem with bullies," Helen snapped.

A wonderful thing happened just then. Troy Smith leaned past Sam and tipped Helen's can of red paint over. "Oops," he said. "Mess."

Paint dripped across Helen's painting and onto her skirt. She leapt out of her chair.

"Mrs. Jones!" Troy shouted, "Helen knocked her paint over!"

"Clean it up, Helen," said Mrs. Jones. ""You have to be more careful."

Eyes like midnight, Helen grabbed some paper towels, got down onto her hands and knees and sopped up the red paint.

When she had finished, Sam said under his breath, "I've got your Beethoven book. If you want it back, you'll agree to my terms."

"That's blackmail," snapped Helen. "It's a Federal crime, I'm sure you're aware."

"I know," said Sam, staring back at her. *Don't blink*, he thought.

Helen gazed at him with something resembling admiration. "What would I have to do in return?"

"Teach me," said Sam, promptly. The words were out of his mouth before he could think.

"I don't think so," Helen snapped. "I have a very busy social life."

"So I see," said Sam, eyeing the paint blotches meaningfully. "It's probably going to get a lot busier too."

Helen thought this over for awhile. Finally she said in a businesslike voice, "I have piano lessons on Mondays, Wednesdays and Fridays. You can come on Tuesdays and Thursdays for a half-hour only. But the deal is, I get my book back, and you arrange it so that Pete Gower and Troy Smith never bother me again. And you do this prior to the first lesson. Those are the conditions. Take them or leave them."

"I'll take them!" said Sam, immediately.

The mighty Beethoven drums pounded in his head again. He, Sam, had just arranged his own lessons, and they weren't going to cost anything at all! His mother had tried to keep him from learning anything, but he had figured out how to do it just the same.

"Tomorrow's Tuesday," said Helen. "The book is in my hand and the bully situation is solved by the end of school tomorrow, or no piano lesson."

"No problem," Sam promised.

After school he tore like a madman into the ravine. When he reached the half-built fort, he battered a triumphant rhythm on each board. He felt like his head would burst.

"Gentlemen!" he called to his band of explorers. "We are entering new territory!"

And with rustlings and loud trumpets of sound, he and his explorers rushed madly through the undergrowth, while the mighty Beethoven drums pounded.

But when the excitement died down and he lay staring through leaves to blue sky above, the terrible thought weighed on him.

How on earth was he going to deal with Pete and Troy?

Chapter Six

Later that afternoon, when it got too dark in the ravine, Sam staggered home, cradling the giant Beethoven book in his arms.

His mother was cooking spaghetti when he fell inside the door.

"You're home!" said Sam, startled. He had expected to see Mrs. Hatch. She was used to him coming in late, and she hardly ever asked questions. His mother, on the other hand, tended to ask a lot of questions.

"I'm home," his mother agreed, turning around to stare at him. "The question is, where have you been?"

Sam's mind whirled quickly. "I'm—I've been at the library," he stammered, remembering his code—'library' meant 'ravine'. "History project!" He held up the book as evidence.

"When's it due?" his mother asked immediately.

"It's..." If he said it wasn't due for awhile, then he could use this excuse again. "...It's a term project. It's not due until Christmas." Then he had a brilliant idea. "And—and a group of us are going to start meeting every Tuesday and Thursday after school to work on it. Till around five-thirty or so."

That would explain why he was late on the days when he had piano lessons. *If* he had piano lessons. First he had to solve the bully problem.

"I see," said his mother, doubtfully.

"Lots of work to do," said Sam with gusto.

"You can get to it after dinner," said his mother. "Wash your hands."

Later that evening, his mother sprawled in front of the TV, and the light danced on her tired face, creating shadows where the creases were beginning to deepen. Sam took the Beethoven book into his bedroom and closed the door. Maybe if he read some more, he could figure out the answer to the question rolling in his mind until it exhausted him—*How are you going to get rid of the bullies, smarty?*

He found the page where he had left off reading. Slowly the spell lowered over him, and he entered the world of the book.

Things got so bad in Beethoven's home that he finally had to make a decision. He couldn't look after his family anymore, not if it meant giving up the chance to explore the music simmering inside him. His family would have to solve their own problems! Beethoven was going to Vienna, where many famous people were making music.

As Sam slept that night, his dreams were filled with a young and booming Beethoven galloping through the mighty city of Vienna on an enormous stallion, knocking Pete Gower down with Helen's book.

By lunch the next day, Sam was tired of heaving the problem around in his mind. There was no solution. What an idiot he had been to think he could get rid of Pete and Troy.

"Three hours left," said Helen ominously as everyone filed out after lunch.

"Don't worry," said Sam, trying to sound more confident than he felt.

"*I'm* not worried," Helen stated flatly. "But no book and no bully solution equals no lesson. Plain and simple."

"Here's the book." Who knew, maybe it would soften her up a bit. It was *half* the bargain. Reluctantly he reached into his backpack. "I got it off the school roof. I was—I was reading it." Part of him didn't want to give it back, now the time had come.

Helen grabbed the book from him. "How did you get up to the roof?"

"Dragged a desk outside, climbed up on it, used a pointer," said Sam, with some pride. "Pretty easy, really."

"Stupid use of your time," said Helen. Then she pelted across the grass, leaving Sam standing alone.

A little hurt, Sam trudged to the poplar tree, flopped down uselessly and began to try to work out the problem for the ninetieth time.

"HEY!"

Sam's eyes snapped open—it was Helen. And Pete Gower was dancing in front of her, waving the Beethoven book.

The solution wasn't going to take place at three-thirty. It was going to be right now. *What was he going to do?*

"Leave her alone!" he shouted. He charged across the field toward them. Everything tingled with adrenaline. Maybe the answer would be clear when he got there.

"Scram, kid," said Pete, and knocked him down. Sam hit the grass hard. Painful, sparkling lights danced behind his eyes.

"I'm disappointed in you," Pete remarked to Helen, waving the book. "Didn't we already have this conversation? Big piano player doesn't need books when she's got her *music*." He imitated her voice. "Let's see what you've got in here, anyway."

He opened up the book to page one. "Pay attention, Troy, because then you'll be a famous musician like Helen."

Helen and Sam waited, tense.

Pete began in a bored, singsong voice: "The story of Beethoven." He pronounced the name as Helen had, the first day he had bothered her. "This man was a famous singer. Many people came and listened to his famous songs. Soon, he was famous all through the land."

He smiled up at Helen. "This is such an exciting book. We should use it in language arts."

A pestering thought slowly dawned upon Sam. That's not how the book starts, he thought. *Pete isn't actually reading what's on the page, even though he's pretending to. Why is he pretending?*

Could it be?

Rhythms piled in his head so rapidly Sam could hardly finish one before jumping to the next. Why was Pete always thrown out of language arts before he had to read aloud? Why did he hate Helen's book so much? Why did he hate Helen for reading it?

The answer was suddenly obvious.

Pete can't read!

There was no time to question whether he was right.

"That's not how the book starts," he shouted, scrambling to his feet.

"Shut up," said Pete, pushing with his free hand. Sam tottered backward but held his balance.

"Read what's *really* on the page—if you can!" said Sam, swimming with amazement and terror at his own daring. "I bet you can't!"

"I'll make you shut up!" Pete shouted, throwing the book to the ground and lunging. But Sam lunged at the same time. They locked shoulders, although Pete was taller. Sam staggered backward, but stayed on his feet.

He hissed at Pete, "I know your secret. You can't read. You never could. If you don't leave Helen and me alone, I'll tell everyone."

"That's a lie!" Pete shrieked. He squeezed Sam's arms until his circulation was cut off.

But Sam pushed back, ignoring the pain. Blood sang triumphantly in his veins. He would get his lessons. Pete wouldn't stop him! Like Beethoven, who left an alcoholic father to storm Vienna, Sam would make something glorious out of something horrible.

Helen held the book out to Pete. "So read something. Read the first paragraph. The first sentence, for that matter."

Pete pushed away as if Sam was repulsive. He glared hysterically from Sam to Helen. "I don't have to prove anything to you."

"I'll tell everyone you can't read," said Sam in a steady voice he had never heard before, "unless you promise to *leave us alone forever*."

Troy was looking at Pete strangely, as if for the first time. Sam almost felt sorry for Pete.

Pete tore the book from Helen's hands and hurled it across the schoolyard. It landed by some girls' trading cards. They looked up, surprised.

"You stay out of *my* way from now on," Pete shouted. "I don't want you coming anywhere *near* me! Come on, Troy."

Troy was still staring, as if Pete had developed a third arm.

"*I said, come on!*"

Slowly, Troy sauntered toward Pete. Pete broke into a hysterical run. Troy walked steadily, refusing to catch up.

Sam retrieved the book, crowing inside. He had done it! He had done it! For a golden moment, he felt like hurdling over a mountain or plunging into the ocean with a splash that would soak the whole world.

But he had to pretend he had known all along. He strolled back and handed the book to Helen, saying lazily, "They shouldn't bother you anymore."

Helen stared at him with undisguised interest. "How did you know he couldn't read?"

"I keep my eyes open," said Sam, scuffing dirt with his sneaker and trying not to jump up and down. "But now you keep up your end of the bargain."

Helen glowered dangerously. Sam could tell she had hoped he would fail. She also probably thought he would make a lousy piano player. "After school," she promised, shortly. "But don't expect any miracles."

Chapter Seven

Sam gnawed his pencil. Time stretched and yawned and refused to move. Meanwhile Mrs. Jones droned, and the clock on the wall hummed. Just like Christmas Eve, Sam thought, when it felt like Christmas would never come.

Finally the bell rang and Sam slammed his books in the desk. Before Mrs. Jones could say, "Please leave in an orderly fashion," he was on his feet, school bag in hand, impatiently waiting for Helen.

Helen was in no rush. She collected her pens and pencils neatly, placing them just so in her expensive pencil case. She tidied up stray pencil shavings. She arranged some papers in a folder. Finally she stretched, slipped to her feet and said darkly, "Well, come on, then."

Helen's house wasn't any bigger than the others on her block. But that wasn't saying much, Sam thought, since each house was nearly as big as Sam's whole apartment building. The house gave off a feeling of preened wealth. On either side of the carefully swept front walk, amid trimmed grass and molded bushes, someone had planted pockets of pink and yellow flowers. It was like a photo in a magazine.

Sam suddenly felt strange about his old schoolbag and dirty jeans. He smoothed his hair. *You're here to learn the codes. It doesn't matter what you look like.*

When Helen opened the door, Sam stared at the shiny floor, the windows draped with rich curtains, the carved bench under an ornate mirror. He felt even smaller and dirtier.

"Don't bother looking around. The piano's downstairs," Helen was just saying briskly when a large and radiant woman burst into the hallway.

"I saw you coming up the walk!" the woman cried in an impossibly booming voice. She extended a hand to Sam, beaming. "I don't believe I've had the pleasure, sir."

"Sam Garretson," said Sam in a small voice. This woman was so big and merry, like a hot-air balloon bobbing at a fair. Could she be Helen's mother? They were exact opposites. Of course, he and his own mother couldn't be much more different.

"Sam Garretson. How nice to meet a new friend of Helen's. I'm Mrs. Williams, and I look after things around here. Let me take that—"

She scooped up his bag before he could speak, and deposited it on the bench under the mirror.

"Sam isn't a friend," said Helen coolly. "I'm giving him piano lessons on Tuesdays and Thursdays. It's a business arrangement and it's not permanent."

Sam stared at his scuffed shoes, trying not to feel ridiculous.

Mrs. Williams glanced from one to the other. She said, "Playing the piano is hungry work. Sam, follow me. Helen, no arguments."

As Helen was protesting, Sam trotted after Mrs. Williams into the kitchen. He decided that, after you settled down to the shock of her, Mrs. Williams was pretty kind.

"Apple muffins, fresh this morning." Mrs. Williams began rummaging in the fridge. "I take it you'll have a little something, Sam Garretson?"

"Yes, please," said Sam, his mouth watering suddenly.

"Polite too!" Mrs. Williams boomed. "Could you teach Helen how to behave that way?" Placing a muffin on each plate, she handed them over the bar. Two enormous, cold glasses of milk followed. Then she sat to watch them eat.

Helen neatly picked apart her muffin and glared at each piece. Mrs. Williams apparently didn't notice.

"Where do you live, Sam Garretson?" she asked, resting her ample chin on her arms. "Nearby? I have always maintained it is good to have a friend in the neighborhood."

"He's not a friend," Helen said again, a little more sharply. She shoved pieces of muffin to the edges of her plate.

"Lovett Co-op," said Sam, in a low voice. He looked at her briefly, nervously, before biting into his apple muffin. Although the taste was beautiful—rich, moist, with pieces of tart, soft apple—he suddenly felt sick. Maybe she wouldn't want Helen talking to him, now she knew. People like Helen didn't live at the Lovett Co-op.

"If I'm not mistaken," said Mrs. Williams softly, as if she felt what was inside him, "there is some lovely countryside around that area. Have you explored the ravine?"

"Yes," said Sam, surprised. How could she possibly know his ravine? And then, because she seemed like someone you could talk to, he found himself telling about his mother and Top-Notch Business Systems. He also told her that his mother mustn't find out about these lessons, because she said they were a waste of time...just in case Mrs. Williams might want to call his mother about anything.

Then he stopped suddenly. Had he told her too much?

"I think," said Mrs. Williams, smiling right into Sam's eyes, "you are a very responsible and enterprising young man. I am filled with admiration. I would like to meet your mother sometime."

"You should know," Helen said suddenly in a loud voice, "that you have exactly half an hour for your piano lesson, as of this minute. Tick, tick, tick. You are eating into your lesson time, literally."

Sam wolfed down the rest of his apple muffin.

The music studio was white and stark, impossibly clean. Sam stood in the doorway. Suddenly he felt that he shouldn't enter. People who belonged in a room like this, with that great, black grand piano in the center, knew more than he could ever possibly learn.

But a familiar face glowered from the wall—Beethoven. Sam blinked, suddenly noticing he was everywhere you looked—pictures, carved heads, even a medallion hanging on the wall.

"You have enough Beethovens for a baseball team," he said, trying to make a joke. His voice sounded small in the large, terrifying space. He pictured uniformed Beethovens running the bases, hair flying in all directions. All of them scowling. Like Helen.

"Sit down," said Helen.

Sam crossed to the grand piano and stared at it. It was so shiny that he could see his face, pale and scared. Slowly, with trembling hands, he pulled out the great black bench and eased onto it. He forced his hands into fists so they wouldn't shake so much.

This was it.

"All right," said Helen. "It's not going to bite you. Look at the keyboard. Tell me what you see."

Sam stared at the keys all neatly lined up, side by side. He forced himself to relax, tune out everything else. "Black ones and white ones," he said, softly. And there was more, when he looked closer. "Three black keys, then two, then three, and on and on all the way along." Like houses on a street, like important dates in a year. The first code broken.

"You recognized the pattern," said Helen briskly. "There is also a low end and a high end to the keyboard. Can you find the low end?"

Sam stared hard at the keyboard for clues. But they were silent masks, hiding the answer.

"You have to make some sounds, stupid," said Helen. "Press the keys!" She sighed explosively, as if Sam was unlikely to amount to anything.

Sam gulped. He reached out a finger toward the keyboard, thinking, This is the first time. I'll remember about this later on, when I'm grown up. He reached to his left, to the very end. He hovered for a moment, then slammed the keys down with three fingers together.

Crash!

An angry, dangerous, thunderous sound boomed around the walls of the studio. It was like bashing down an ancient door, or the heavy step of a giant. It felt like waking up.

"That's the low end," he said with satisfaction. Then, without thinking, he reached to the other end of the keyboard and crushed the last three keys. Sound-icicles clattered in the room.

"That's the high end."

Helen tapped her foot impatiently. "I'll tell you what to do and when."

"Sorry," said Sam.

"Time to learn the names of the notes," said Helen. "Pay attention. I don't want to have to keep explaining it." She pointed to a group of two black keys. "See the white key to the left? That's C. Get to know it very well."

Sam peered closely at the note she pointed to. He tried to memorize its shape, the exact rise and fall of the black keys around it, the horizon of shadow and light. It was like trying to memorize your home so you could find your way back later.

"Now find me every C on the piano."

Without hesitation, Sam's hand shot along the keyboard, discovering each C in turn, and capturing it. With each added C, he felt an increase in power. Nobody could stop him!

Helen taught him all the white-key notes on the piano. She showed him what they looked like when they were written down—little circles on lines and spaces. Then they played a game. "Right," said Helen, "I'm going to name a note, and you're going to play it. Ready?"

"Ready."

As she called each note and he fumblingly found it, he marveled at how the keyboard was starting to shape itself into a familiar place. It was a road map, and the notes were addresses!

Sam imagined a tunnel through time. At one end, very far away, Beethoven looked forward; from the other end,

Sam looked back. Once, Beethoven had learned these notes too.

"Well, you're not entirely stupid," said Helen, at last. "I guess it's time to start reading music around here." She rummaged in a filing cabinet, removed a tattered book. "This was my first music primer. Play the introductory song, based on what we've learned."

"Okay," said Sam, humbly. He stared at the page and scrambled his fingers into position. He took a deep breath—this was it, the first song ever. If he failed, she might never teach him again.

But with every correct note, he began to gain confidence. Suddenly he felt he was building a ladder and climbing it, high above everything. He thought he could see the whole world.

When he finished, he was glowing.

"Now what do we do?" he exploded.

Helen said abruptly, "Now I'm going to practice, so you'll have to leave." She turned back to the filing cabinet and rummaged through one of the drawers.

"That's it?" said Sam. His fingers were tingling with what he had just done. "We just got started."

"And now we're finished," said Helen. "The door's upstairs. See you later."

He had to think of something so it wouldn't end.

Gathering his courage, he said loudly, "Beethoven."

""What about him?"

"I want to hear something he wrote. Play something he wrote."

"Oh, for goodness' sake," Helen snapped. "I freely give of my time, and then you won't leave."

"I'll leave right away if you play me something."

60

Reluctantly, she moved to the bench. "'Moonlight Sonata', first movement. Mushy, but *you'd* probably like it." She placed her fingers lightly on the keys, seemed almost to hover for a hanging moment, and then began.

Sam tried to picture moonlight, but mostly he thought of a swirling, late autumn sky where clouds threatened the first snow. Occasionally, briefly, the moon pierced through, lighting up the silvery-gray landscape. That was when the melody could be heard, above the slow rumble of the bass. The patterns inside him glittered and glowered and tumbled—because they *recognized* it.

Suddenly a voice shook him from his dream.

"There's your Beethoven for today." Helen stood up abruptly from the piano. "Leave now, please and thank you."

Sam raced home along streets that were beginning to be covered with brown leaves. The 'Moonlight Sonata' rumbled in his head. It was the first words from Beethoven to Sam. It was their first conversation! One day he would learn to play it.

But as he neared the Lovett Co-op, the hugeness of the situation dawned on him. How was he ever going to be able to play the 'Moonlight Sonata' if he didn't have anything to practice on?

He needed his own piano.

But if his mother didn't even want to buy him school supplies, she would hardly agree to a piano. Besides, if he asked for a piano, he'd have to tell her about how he had organized piano lessons for himself.

By the time he was home, Sam had hit on a brilliant solution. Grabbing his pencil crayons, he trotted down the steep, rocky path leading to the ravine. Wind sliced through his clothes—it was almost time for a warmer coat—but the ravine was the only safe place for what he was planning to do.

He selected a board from the pile beside the fort, and settled down cross-legged to work. Groups of three and two black keys, with white keys in between and underneath. Once he had sketched it in, he began to color the black keys with his black pencil crayon. When the tip snapped off, he switched to dark blue, and later to dark purple.

We make do with what we have, Doyle.

Very good, sir, said his second-in-command.

The board roughly resembled a keyboard. It wasn't nearly as long as Helen's keyboard, but it was enough for him to be able to practice the notes that he had learned.

As the wind whistled around the boards of Sam's half-built fort, and the shadows crept across the dying underbrush, Sam played the notes one by one: A B C D E F G. He couldn't hear them with his ears, but inside his head they thundered with Beethoven's own mighty voice. He could hear the patterns between them, just like colors.

Chapter Eight

Helen attacked her grapefruit with precision. She held the Beethoven book in front of her face, ignoring her father with his stupid paper and porridge. They had nothing in common anymore, since he had obviously decided her future was unimportant.

In her mind, she slipped effortlessly into the Beethoven game.

It was a busy market square in Vienna. Horses and carts clattered by on all sides of her. But she scarcely heard them, because she was waiting for him. At last Beethoven stormed around the street corner and stamped through the heavy traffic, unafraid of being trampled.

"Good morrow, little maid!" he bellowed, waving his hat.

"Good morrow."

"What's wrong?" said Beethoven.

"Now I have to teach this stupid boy piano lessons," Helen snapped. "It's his fault that I can't concentrate on the important things."

"So, don't teach him," said Beethoven.

"It's too late. We made a deal. At least, he made a deal. He forced me to go along with it."

"There are so many fools in the world," said Beethoven, philosophically. "We ignore as many as we can, and we endure the rest, until opportunity arises."

Mr. Alemeda spoke at last. He had been watching Helen for the last several minutes, while she had been in her daydream.

"After last night's marathon rehearsal," he finally rumbled, "I think the orchestra may actually pull together. Who knows? Perhaps they will actually play a piece of music from beginning to end. If the second violins come to recognize what piece we are attempting to play, that is."

Helen said nothing.

"Perhaps the dress rehearsal tomorrow night will not be an utter disaster," he continued, eyeing Helen.

Helen continued to eat her porridge without speaking.

Mrs. Williams, hateful in a bright-flowered dress, juggling an overloaded bowl of porridge, plumped into the cushioned chair beside Helen. She sighed loudly and comically.

"My dear Mrs. Williams, you seem exhausted," boomed Helen's father.

"I'm worn to a rag, Mr. Alemeda," she hooted.

Helen recognized the signs. They were going to try to behave like buffoons, to force her out of her mood. Well, they could try all day.

"And what will you be performing in your concert, Mr. Alemeda?" chirped Mrs. Williams, heaping brown sugar on her porridge. Helen scowled even more furiously. Everyone knew what he was performing. In this house they lived, ate and slept her father's schedule.

"The *Pastorale* Symphony, among other things." They waited, both looking at Helen. "Beethoven, of course."

Deliberately, Helen turned a page, examining the illustration with interest.

"You have a new friend, I understand," said her father at last.

Helen continued to read, putting on a serene expression.

"Oh, yes, I was very impressed with Sam Garretson," Mrs. Williams bleated. "Very polite, interested in music, just the sort of friend for our Helen."

"Perhaps," Frank Alemeda said, "you'd consider inviting this Sam Garretson to the dress rehearsal tomorrow night."

Without thinking, Helen slammed down her book. "I've already said several times *to anyone who would listen* that Sam Garretson is not my new friend!" she exploded. "He's just part of a business transaction. And no, he wouldn't find a dress rehearsal even remotely interesting."

Her father and Mrs. Williams exchanged glances.

Mrs. Williams cleared her throat. "I got the impression," she said in a mild voice, "that it might be the closest Sam has been to a real concert. Not everyone has been as lucky as you, you know."

"Poor, suffering Sam," Helen snapped.

"He's an enterprising child," Mrs. Williams informed Helen's father pleasantly, "when you consider he's organized piano lessons for himself. The Alemedas' kind of person, I would have thought."

That was it—the last straw. Mrs. Williams, of all people, had no right to tell her who was and wasn't her "kind of person!" Mrs. Williams had no idea what was inside Helen.

And suddenly Helen was standing on her feet, her spoon clattering in the bowl. Words tumbled out that she had been wanting to say for a long time—angry, hateful words she hoped would wound Mrs. Williams.

She cried, "You are a fat nobody who couldn't find middle C with a serving spoon! You will never amount to anything! You went through *my private things* and you ruined my life because you don't have a life of your own. I will never forgive you, and I wish you'd leave us alone!"

Mrs. Williams looked down, red-faced, at her bowl heaped with porridge and sugar.

Hah! Helen thought. *Hurt your feelings for a change.*

"Helen Olivia Alemeda!" her father thundered, dark eyebrows gathering over his eyes. He stood up too, and faced her. "You'll apologize to Mrs. Williams instantly, because you do not understand what you are saying."

"I understand *everything!*" Helen shouted back. "And if anyone owes anyone else an apology, it's her. And you!" Then she grabbed her backpack and tore out the front door.

As she pounded to school, emotions tumbled inside her—elation, fury and fear. Nobody spoke to her father that way. Not his orchestra, and certainly not his daughter.

"I still remember all the notes!"

Sam Garretson trotted up as soon as she hit the playground.

Helen marched past him savagely, head held high, but he trotted into step beside her. With his hair curling all over the place, he almost looked like a sheep that hadn't been clipped in awhile. Docile, horrible little sheep. And there was a faint orange stain on his shirt, as if he had spilled spaghetti on it once and not washed it properly.

He was everything useless and drab.

"A B C D E F G," Sam continued, following behind. "Good memory, huh?"

Helen twirled around haughtily. "Let's get something straight. The piano lessons stay in the studio. When we are at school, we don't talk—we don't even look at each other. Now leave me alone."

She marched off, ignoring the look on his face.

When she glanced back, Sam was still staring after her.

As if to drive home the fact that Helen's life was really and truly over, they had Music that morning with Miss Spence. Miss Spence had a high, thin voice like a piccolo. She rolled her eyes to make everyone excited about singing properly.

"Pretend—" the eyes rolled— "pretend there is a string coming out of your head, going up to the ceiling. You are all marionettes. Now, breathe from the diaphragm, and let's reproduce this sound. Aaaaaahhhh!"

"Aaaaaahhhh," they repeated obediently. Somebody hurled a crumpled paper when her back was turned, and everyone laughed. Helen's hands were fists. It was an insult to place her in this class.

"Lovely! Now, let's all try to maintain the same pitch and support the sound. A supported sound will always be in tune. Aaaaaahhhh!"

Then, blessedly, Miss Spence's music class faded away, and Helen slipped into the Beethoven game, to the one person who could understand her.

"Good morrow, little maid!"

"Hello." Discontent stained her voice. *"I hate this*

67

music class. Right now, Miss Spence is telling us to sup-
port the sound."

"Miss Spence," said Beethoven, raising a bushy eye-
brow for emphasis, "could not find a supported sound if
she were to seat herself upon it."

They laughed together, and Helen felt a little better.

"—Helen? Could you demonstrate?" Miss Spence and
the class were staring at her. Some people were giggling.

"Please repeat your instructions, Miss Spence," said
Helen calmly, shaking the daydream out of her head. "I'm
afraid I was paying no attention whatsoever."

After school Helen eased open the front door as quietly as she could. Slipping off her coat, she gently lowered
her school bag to the ground. Maybe she could make it up
to her room before anyone knew she was home.

But as she inched up the staircase, Mrs. Williams
swung open the kitchen door.

Helen and Mrs. Williams stared at each other.

"Did you ask him?" Mrs. Williams said.

"Ask whom?"" said Helen, trying to put the blank
expression on her face.

Mrs. Williams cocked her head to one side, so that she
looked like a flour bag with the top flopped over.

"Oh, ask *Sam*," said Helen insolently. "Your best
friend. I'm sorry, he said no. I regret having to disappoint
you in this way."

"Come into the kitchen right now," said Mrs.
Williams. "We are going to talk."

Helen's heart dropped, but she couldn't let it show.

When they were seated at the counter, nobody said

anything for a long time. Helen sneaked a glance at her watch. This was getting uncomfortable, and Dr. Weiss would be arriving shortly for another oh-so-exciting lesson.

"When I began working for this family ten years ago," Mrs. Williams said, very formally, as if she had been practicing all afternoon, "my job was to help out around the place—cook, clean, baby-sit. I think—I hope—I also helped make things a little easier for your father and maybe even for you, after your mother's accident."

"I know that," said Helen promptly, wanting to shut her up. The last thing she needed was for Mrs. Williams to go on and on about her mother. And she didn't need Mrs. Williams to outline all the ways she was more than simply a housekeeper, because Helen already knew that.

But Mrs. Williams was not finished.

"When your mother died, it was tutors and boarding schools for you, and plenty of engagements for him. Less and less time spent together. It broke my heart to watch. Do you know," said Mrs. Williams, slapping her hand on the table, "I am *glad* I found your letters and I am *glad* I read them—because it made your father look at you hard for the first time in awhile!"

"You had no right!" Helen snapped, the familiar resentment returning.

"No, I didn't," said Mrs. Williams in a firm, strange voice. "But I'm still glad I did."

They eyed each other.

"And about Sam Garretson," said Mrs. Williams. "You actually have the opportunity to do something generous. But can you stop thinking about yourself long enough to do it?"

Just as Helen was trying to gather the haughty words to make it clear that she was not always thinking about herself, the doorbell chimed.

Dr. Weiss! She jumped up. This was the first time she was glad to see him.

But it wasn't to be quite so easy.

"One last thing, in reference to your remarks of this morning," said Mrs. Williams.

She rose to her feet. She crossed her arms. Helen waited tensely for what she knew was coming. And she knew she deserved it.

Mrs. Williams spoke slowly and clearly. "I may be fat, and I may be a housekeeper, but I am certainly not *nothing*. After my years of support of this family, an ill mannered, rude little girl trying to hurt the very people who care about her will not insult me. I can sleep at night, thank you very much, knowing I've done something good during the day. Can you?"

Helen blinked.

"I'm aware of everything you're saying," she said—in her most scornful and haughty voice—to hide the fact that Mrs. Williams had, just for a second, pierced through.

Chapter Nine

Inside the tiny apartment, Sam packed his lunch carefully. But in his mind he was rehearsing A B C D E F G. C is beside the two black keys. F is beside the three black keys. Middle C is in the very middle of the piano.

In his head he could easily hear which note was which, C or F or B or A. He could move from one to the other, creating little melodies that tumbled like a circus troupe in crazy patterns.

Helen had not talked to him since yesterday, and he had kept his distance, not wanting to push it. But today he hoped it would be different. Today was the next piano lesson.

"Aaaghkk..."

A muffled sound came from the darkened bedroom, halfway between a yawn and a cough. Sam jumped guiltily. The world swam into focus and he was just Sam Garretson, standing before a kitchen sink, looking out through a dirty window.

"Sam? Are you leaving soon? Come here and say good-bye."

His mother's voice was plaintive, tired, and brownish-gray. She had been up late, typing and collating a portfolio for a client who needed three hundred copies sent right away to individual companies—all with personalized letters. Sam couldn't imagine how you kept three hundred copies straight, much less made sure each letter got to the right place.

"Mmmfff," mumbled his mother sleepily, when he gave her a kiss. "Got your lunch?"

Sam patted his school bag. "Yep. Your breakfast is on the table, whenever you get up, except for the milk. But why don't you sleep a little more?"

He wanted to make some of his guilt go away by being extra nice to her. He hated lying and keeping secrets from her. But she had forbidden piano lessons—she had said they were no way for a person to live his life—so he had no choice.

He looked down at her huddled form, and he could hear Helen's voice saying scornfully, "And this is a better way to spend your life?"

But he knew he shouldn't think about it too much. Otherwise, anger like sewage could back up in him. Fury at being in this apartment while Helen rattled around her huge house. Enraged that his mother hated the thought of piano lessons while Mr. Alemeda conducted an orchestra and allowed Helen to have lessons three times a week. Angry with himself for sneaking around while his mother worked crazy hours to keep the rent paid.

"Have a good day at school," his mother murmured.

"I will."

He closed the bedroom door carefully and quietly, picked up his book bag and tiptoed out of the apartment.

In the hallway Sam noticed the dirty, peeling wallpaper more than usual. His nose wrinkled at strange odors he didn't recognize. He suddenly felt like the co-op was trying to swallow him—especially his own brown apartment and his mother's airless bedroom.

As he walked by Pete Gower's apartment door, Sam could hear a baby crying and a woman's voice raised. He walked faster. The sounds seemed to represent everything useless about the building—and Sam's life.

The knob to Pete's door squeaked and turned.

Sam raced down the stairs. So far Pete had kept away from him, but that was probably because Sam had been sneaking around the Lovett Co-op, trying his best not to be seen. He had a dark feeling that if they met, things might not go well. If he were Pete, he'd be pretty angry that Sam had learned his secret.

School passed in a dark blur, but it helped take his mind off things. Finally, blessedly, it was over and they were entering Helen's house again.

"Take your shoes off," Helen said. It was raining outside.

Obediently Sam removed soaked sneakers, while his hair dripped in his eyes. Then a towel dangled and he glanced up, surprised. Mrs. Williams beamed down. "Take it!"

"Thank you," he mumbled awkwardly. He began to rub his hair.

"We were so sorry," said Mrs. Williams, "to hear that you weren't interested in attending the dress rehearsal tonight with Helen. I had hoped you might find it exciting."

"Dress rehearsal?" said Sam, blankly. He didn't even know what that was. An image of a fashion show shot into his mind—haughty models on a runway. He hadn't thought Helen liked that kind of thing, but rich people had strange interests.

"I was going to tell you," Helen snapped.

73

"Downstairs, when we started our lesson."

"I wondered if that might be the case," said Mrs. Williams, and shot a funny look at Helen.

Nobody said anything for a minute.

"All right," snapped Helen at last. "Do you want to come to the dress rehearsal tonight? Yes or no?"

Sam was silent. He was too ashamed to explain he didn't know what it was. He looked from Mrs. Williams to Helen and back again to Mrs. Williams, hoping the answer would materialize. He didn't want to say the wrong thing.

"Well?" said Helen, exasperated. "Is that a no?"

"It won't be quite the same as the real concert," said Mrs. Williams, then, and he knew she had guessed his problem. "Only the orchestra, of course, in its last rehearsal before the concert. But you would hear Beethoven's Pastorale Symphony, and see Helen's father conducting. Meet the orchestra. Casual clothing, of course. It's actually quite an honor, Sam. Many people would like to be invited to something like that."

He shot her a grateful look, his mind reeling. A real symphony orchestra? Going as a guest of the Alemedas? Everything was happening so quickly, he couldn't keep up.

"I would—I would like to!" he said, hardly believing they actually wanted him.

"That's settled then," said Mrs. Williams, giving Helen another peculiar look.

He forced himself to climb calmly and normally down the stairs to the studio. What he really wanted to do was hurl himself down like an acrobat, but he had to get into the right frame of mind for his second lesson. He intended to learn even more than in the first.

"Have a seat," said Helen. She had a funny quality Sam couldn't put his finger on. As if she couldn't look at him straight. "Let's review what we learned last time. I will call a note name and you will play it."

Sam geared up for the moment of truth. Had his silent rehearsing on the wooden-plank keyboard really worked? Or would today prove, once and for all, that he wasn't cut out for lessons?

The game began.

"C."

Sam found it right away—right beside the two black keys, just as she had taught him. Miraculously, he remembered all of the other notes too, the first time he was asked to play them. After two days of thinking of nothing else, Sam felt he knew each note personally.

Helen pulled out her old lesson book again and placed it on the piano. Carefully, fumblingly, Sam's fingers found the right homes and pressed the right notes. This was a little harder, because he hadn't had the music to practice from at home.

Still, the vibrations from the piano tingled in each finger like a promise.

Helen assigned three new songs in the music book, and Sam slowly worked his way through them, numb amazement covering up his other feelings. He could do it! It sounded like real music!

"Well," she said grudgingly when they had finished. "At least you didn't forget absolutely everything from the first lesson."

Sam didn't reply, just quietly glowed. She hadn't thrown up her arms and cried, Make way for the genius!

But it was better than nothing, especially from Helen.

Then, the horrible thing happened.

"Now that we're finished, I would like to discuss tonight's dress rehearsal," Helen said, closing the piano lid. "If you're coming, then you're coming, but I have a simple ground rule. Do not talk to me. I will be there to listen only. If you want the truth, it wasn't my idea for you to come anyway. Not that I mind you being there. Only don't disturb me. And please don't wear the shirt with the spaghetti stain on it—it's a bit much."

She sat like a queen, untouchable.

Suddenly Sam's stomach did a lurch, as if he was going to throw up. It was as if the boat he was in had plunged from the crest of a wave into the darkness at the bottom. Worse, he felt ridiculous. Tears unexpectedly, impossibly, prickled behind his eyelids. But it would never do to cry in front of Helen.

"Okay," he whispered, not daring to say more.

"Oh, don't go and get all crushed," said Helen.

"I'm not," said Sam. Then a tear escaped and he had to swipe at it. He saw himself squarely through her eyes and it was like a physical pain.

"I have to leave now," he said in a stronger voice. "And I don't think I can come to the dress rehearsal tonight. I have a lot of homework to do." He gulped, then forced himself to say it. "This is our last lesson too. I've wasted enough of your time."

Helen stared curiously as Sam rose to his feet.

"Well, I didn't say you couldn't go," she said. "And I didn't say anything about your piano lessons. You should—" she seemed to be wrestling with herself— "You should definitely keep up with your lessons. In fact, I insist. Your teacher says you should, so you should."

She seemed to be waiting for him to say everything was all right. She looked vaguely surprised with herself.

It wasn't all right, Sam thought. And the intense feelings from that morning—anger at his mother's sleeping form, hatred of his falling-apart building, frustration at Pete Gower—threatened to drown him.

"I was an idiot to think we might end up being friends or something."

He left her sitting in the music room, while he climbed back to the entrance way, tiptoed to his wet sneakers so Mrs. Williams wouldn't see, squeezed them on his feet, and slipped into the rain, which had slowed a little but not stopped altogether.

And Helen sat in the piano studio, staring after him. She sat very still, but inside, she ranted at Beethoven.

"Trying to make me feel guilty for laying some basic ground rules!" she cried. "It's not my fault he's never been anywhere! Who put me in charge of his education?"

Beethoven nodded, slowly and reluctantly. He seemed to wrestle with an idea inside himself. Finally he spoke, his voice sounding as though he wished he didn't have to speak the words. "But he shows some small promise, little maid. There is no doubt he seems a backward fool, but some said the same of me. Perhaps he could learn how to sound not entirely like one."

Helen simply glared at Beethoven.

Sam was almost two blocks down the street, trying not to think, when a voice shouted, "Sam!"

Helen pelted after him, hair streaming behind. She pounded up and stood panting. Finally, she gasped, "Well, I'm sorry then."

Sam didn't know what to say back. He stood there and looked at her.

"I don't believe in friends,"Helen panted. "I don't even know what a friend does," she continued with grim relish, as if she were writing somebody's death sentence.

"Well, neither do I," said Sam. He thought about his own experiences with disgust. Days spent alone, working on his fort and dreaming about leading explorers into exotic lands.

"Anyway, a true musician is self-contained. But if we get you up and running as a musician," said Helen, "we could communicate with each other occasionally."

"Me—a musician?" said Sam.

"If you kept at it, you might have a meager amount of talent," said Helen, glaring. "But no, not you. You'd rather stop just when you're getting started."

"I don't want to stop."

"Then, it's settled," said Helen severely and briskly. "Part of your education involves attending the dress rehearsal as arranged. We will pick you up at six thirty, and you'd better be ready. What's your apartment number?"

They stared at each other through the rain.

Chapter Ten

Sam slammed the apartment door in his excitement. He hurled wet sneakers to the shoe mat and tossed his keys in the basket by the door. Then he checked for messages on the answering machine. She'd better be working late.

"Hi, Sam. It's mom. I'll be here until around nine, finishing up a mass mail—again. Sure hope this guy gets a job soon. Anyway, Mrs. Hatch will be over around five-thirty, and she'll heat up the leftover chicken in the fridge, with some veggies."

Sam groped for a plan. He'd have to attack this from several angles. He would tell Mrs. Hatch that he had to work on his history project with a partner this evening. They would be working on it at his partner's home, and the parents would be picking him up. That way, maybe Mrs. Hatch would let him go without many questions.

But his mother was a different matter, of course. She'd want to know who he'd been with, and Sam wouldn't put it past her to call and introduce herself. So Sam would have to be back before she got in. That would mean catching the bus home, because the rehearsal probably wouldn't be over before nine o'clock.

He checked his watch. Only an hour until Mr. Alemeda picked him up.

The hour flew. Mrs. Hatch arrived and heated up the

dinner. She accepted Sam's story without questions, and didn't notice as Sam scooped change for the bus out of the hall basket. Before he knew it, he was running to the corner where his lane met Richmond Street Mr. Alemeda would see him there. Helen and her father didn't need to look too closely at his building.

He leaned against the rusted streetlight. Its glow fell all around him, as if he was in a charmed, magic place that was separate from the ordinary world. For a moment he felt that everything was going to turn out as it should.

Then, out of the darkness beyond the glow of the lamp, a familiar voice murmured, "Are you waiting for the aliens to pick you up?"

Sam jumped and twisted around.

Pete Gower stepped forward, the light creating strange lines on his face. He must have seen Sam from his apartment window, and come down to investigate.

Sam's stomach danced inside him. This was their first real meeting since he had learned Pete's secret.

And they were alone.

"None of your business," said Sam nervously.

"Everything's my business," said Pete. "Just like you. Everything's your business, isn't it? You like to find out secrets about people, and then you like to tell. You think you're better than everyone else."

Sam didn't answer. But he could feel his face pulsing with embarrassment and fear.

"Guess you won't mind if I wait out here with you then?" said Pete. He slipped in beside Sam. Sam inched away, closer to the lamppost. "Yes, I would mind."

"Why? What's so secret?" Pete's voice suddenly took on a new, watchful tone.

"Nothing!" said Sam, a little too loudly.

The car slipped around the corner at that moment—sleek black. Helen gestured coolly—it might have been a wave. Gratefully, Sam crossed the street, wrenched open the back door and clambered inside. A few moments more, and things would have become dangerous.

He realized suddenly that his secret was as precious as Pete's.

Helen's father appeared to be in no hurry to drive away. Instead, he leaned around from the front seat to shake Sam's hand. He boomed, "Sam Garretson, I am Frank Alemeda. Very pleased to have you with us tonight. I understand that you are a music aficionado."

"Is this a *date*?" Pete shouted through the window.

Mr. Alemeda turned very slowly, like a dangerous animal. He gazed through the window at Pete. He rumbled, "I beg your pardon, young man? Are you also a friend of Helen's?"

Pete stared back for a moment defiantly, then looked away. Mr. Alemeda's stare was formidable.

"No," he muttered at last.

"Good night to you then," said Mr. Alemeda. And he pulled away from the curb, leaving Pete standing and staring after them.

Sam and Helen could not help bursting out laughing. The great Frank Alemeda had silenced Pete Gower! Then they glanced at one another uncomfortably. Sharing laughter was almost too friendly.

It was not far to the hall, which was a relief. That meant the bus ride would not take long—maybe only fifteen or twenty minutes, which left a good ten before his mother pulled in. As long as the bus was on time.

Before Sam knew it, the car was parked and they were climbing mountainous steps to the concert hall. Then, through massive doors, they entered a lobby of glass, polished metal and mirrors.

It was a city-made fairyland.

Suddenly, Sam didn't care how he would get home. His neck creaked as he tried to see everything. Chandeliers, two curving staircases. Cascading beads down one wall, like falling water.

Mr. Alemeda boomed, "A little ostentatious, I think. If it packs them in their seats, however, I'm highly in favor of it."

Sam could scarcely speak, but he nodded jerkily. He was a little in awe of Helen's father.

Mr. Alemeda had to meet the orchestra backstage, so he left Helen and Sam to find seats that they liked. They had the whole place to choose from, since it was not open to the public tonight.

Helen led Sam through the doors into the hall.

If the lobby had strained his neck, the concert hall made his jaw drop nearly to his knees. Two balconies towered above them and a white stage yawned—huge, like a wolf's mouth. "Orchestra or balcony?" said Helen briskly.

"What?"

"Do you want to sit down here or upstairs?" The impatience was barely disguised, but at least there was a new quality to it now. It was exasperation with someone who badly needed educating, and was going to get what he needed.

"Upstairs."

So they pelted up the curving lobby staircase and

dragged open heavy doors to the first balcony. Steep stairs plummeted toward the first row. Sam felt dizzy.

"C'mon," said Helen, leading fearlessly down the steps. "First row is the best."

They sat in the center, just as orchestra members began to file onstage. They carried instruments of all shapes and sizes. Sam recognized violins. Other instruments looked like violins but were much bigger—you sat down and held them between your knees. Some were bigger yet—those you had to stand behind.

When Sam pointed them out to Helen, she said dismissively, "Oh, the medium one's a cello, and the biggest is a double bass."

There were also big, shiny brass instruments—trumpets and tubas and trombones, Helen told him—and flutes and piccolos, and interesting-looking drums like big kettles.

"Timpani," said Helen, when Sam asked about the big kettledrums.

Just then, a haunting and peculiar sound rose, like mist, from the orchestra. Gentle pipings and wailings, musical scales drifting upward and down again. It sounded like gates opening to a forbidden land. Excitement, wonder, and—strangely—a little fear flooded Sam.

He shook his head to clear it.

Helen was gazing at him with a small smile.

"The instruments are tuning," she said.

Sam could only nod.

Finally Mr. Alemeda strode onstage, and the tuning stopped. In its place was heavy silence. Time hung in the air, almost visible, halfway between night and day.

The house lights dimmed, but rose to brightness on

the stage. The orchestra was bathed in an unnatural, feverish light.

Sam realized that his hands were trembling. He sat on them.

Mr. Alemeda raised his arms, and the orchestra obediently raised its instruments. Violins slipped under chins, flutes to lips, and bows slid silently into position.

"This is it," Helen whispered.

After another hanging moment, Mr. Alemeda gently, graciously gestured the pulse of the beat, and then it began.

It was nothing like what Sam had imagined. There were no crashes of sound, no angry bellows from timpani or double bass or tuba. Instead, Beethoven opened the gate to Sam's ravine and gestured humbly for them to enter.

The first playful notes fluttered like wind through goldenrod. The concert hall disappeared and Sam could see that gentle, fair-weather clouds scudded overhead, propelled by a good-natured wind. Birds sang their hearts out. A whole day waited.

"This symphony is supposed to mirror the sounds in nature," Helen whispered. "Can you hear the bird calls?"

Sam nodded violently. "And wind and water and grass moving."

"Exactly."

They nodded at each other in the half-light.

Sam was amazed that Beethoven got it so right. He felt Beethoven speak directly to him. *See, Sam, here's where the breeze wraps around your fort. I felt this once, and now you can feel it too.*

"What is so amazing," Helen whispered, "is that a deaf person could so completely capture the sounds of the natural world. Still, he didn't need to hear anything. He didn't need anyone. He was complete in himself."

Sam nodded, not really listening. Then what she had said sank in. "What?"

"I said, I find it intriguing that someone who—"

"What did you say? Did you say Beethoven was *deaf*?"

"Yes," said Helen snappily, "He went deaf in adulthood."

"He was *deaf*?"

"For the third time, yes."

Sam was stunned. He stared ahead, scarcely seeing the orchestra.

Beethoven *couldn't* have been deaf!

"Are you sure?" he whispered urgently to Helen.

"I thought everyone knew that."

"I didn't." He hadn't read far enough in the book to learn about that. In fact, every time he thought about Beethoven, he imagined the boy whose father treated him badly. He imagined Beethoven looking at the night through his window—in an apartment not unlike Sam's—insisting he would do something extraordinary all on his own.

"How did it happen?" he whispered.

"Nobody knows for sure. But, as I said, he didn't really need to hear. He had it in his head. He was complete. He didn't need anyone, and he didn't want anyone." She spoke fiercely, and Sam had a strange feeling that she wasn't simply talking about Beethoven.

Just then, the music soared into the original theme, but mighty, triumphant. Helen was wrong! Every note said Beethoven wanted to reach out to *everyone*, to share exactly what he felt. He wanted you to hear the sounds of that meadow, under that sky, even though he couldn't hear it himself.

The first half of the rehearsal flew by, and then it was time for the orchestra's break. Suddenly Sam was shaking himself out of a half-dream. Helen peered at him with mild interest, as though examining a peculiar insect.

"C'mon," she said. "We'll meet the musicians. I suppose you'll enjoy that."

They scrambled up the impossibly steep stairs, then through the velvet hallway and down the great, curving staircase to the main lobby. Helen pushed open a small, barely noticeable door labeled "Stage". They hurried along a plain, white hallway.

Sam heard voices talking and laughing.

Then they came upon the musicians.

"Here's the *wunderkind*!" said one of them, waving to Helen. "Tossed off many concerti lately? And who's your friend?"

"He's the *enfant terrible*," said Helen, with a wry smile.

Several people laughed. Sam blushed. He felt they were laughing at him. Suddenly the spell of the marvelous night was broken. He glared at his scuffed shoes and wondered what he was doing there. Here they were speaking languages he couldn't even understand.

A tall woman—he recognized her as one of the three double bass players—put her arm around him. "It's a compliment," she said. "*Enfant terrible*—somebody who stirs things up, changes the system, won't be contained. Beethoven was an *enfant terrible*, you know."

Sam looked up into her kind face and smiled back, suddenly feeling much better.

The musicians bought Sam and Helen each an apple juice from the vending machine. Sam sat, rapt, sipping the sweet liquid and gazing around him, marveling.

Then suddenly the break was over and they were racing back to their seats. The person in the lighting booth waited until they were sitting again, before dimming the lights.

Much later, Sam remembered to check his watch.

Almost nine o'clock!

Scrambling out of his seat, he whispered to Helen, "I've got to go."

"Well, wait until it's finished. Then my father will drive you."

"No. I can't. I have to go!"

He felt like Cinderella, racing from the ball before her dress turned to rags and her carriage to a pumpkin. And he couldn't tell Helen why, because he was embarrassed at the difference in their parents. Helen would never be able to understand a mother who forbade piano lessons and sneered at the whole idea of people coming together to make music.

"Well, I'll come with you to the door anyway."

She followed as he pelted through the building to the main lobby. Then Sam paused at the huge glass doors. Awkwardly, he turned to Helen.

"Thank you," he said shyly, emotion welling up inside him. "This was the best night of my life."

"It was just a rehearsal," said Helen, shrugging.

"It was my first rehearsal ever," said Sam. He tried to think of how to put what he felt into words. That he could see the order of his life laid out before him and he badly wanted to be part of this.

"Well," said Helen finally, "I guess you'd better go, since you're in such a big rush."

Then he ran through the dark night, thankful the rain had held off, practically soaring over the black pavement toward the bus stop.

He made it home before his mother, and the triumph was complete.

Chapter Eleven

As autumn scuttled into pale mornings, brittle after-noons and crisp evenings, Helen tolerated Sam's presence on Tuesdays and Thursdays after school. The pattern was always the same: she kicked purposefully through dry leaves, away from the repulsive school and toward home, with Sam trotting behind. Once they were inside the house, Rice Krispies squares, brownies, cupcakes, date and fig bars appeared magically from Mrs. Williams' bottomless oven. When every crumb was finished, they trooped downstairs for Sam's piano lessons.

Sometimes, when she felt restricted by Sam's presence, Helen shouted at Beethoven, *"He will not leave me alone: he is to blame for us coming to this horrible city!"*

At first Beethoven had agreed completely. Sam *had* organized all of the worst details of Helen's new life. But over time, Beethoven's answers began to change. Helen wasn't sure exactly when that happened.

At first Beethoven simply murmured, *"Little maid, I suspect that this boy did not make your travel arrangements."* Even Helen had to admit that was true. As time went on, Beethoven went further. *"This one seems to have a spark, little maid. I recognize it. Don't you feel it too?"*

Helen had been grudging at first. But as Sam soaked up every word, imitated perfectly each thing she commanded, she began to relax—even to enjoy their sessions. Occasionally, she smiled, even laughed. And when she did, her face lit up, as if sunshine splashed her skin, turning it golden. And each lesson got longer. And longer. Sometimes it tumbled into dinner.

Sam memorized scales, and worked on ever more complicated songs, using both hands at once. His swelling pride and wonder scarcely could be contained. When his fingers pressed into the accepting keys and created the sounds he wanted—clean harmonies, recognizable melodies—it was beyond everything.

But at home he was silent. When his mother returned from work, he limited his conversation to TV shows he had watched or funny stories from school. She told him about her clients—those who had found work with her résumés, those who kept returning for revisions and who would probably never find work in that field.

It looked as though everything was ordinary, but underneath nothing was normal at all.

Then one morning, as wind blew leaves against the window of the classroom, Mrs. Jones sat on her desk and called for attention.

Everyone settled down.

"The school is going to hold a fundraiser to pay for new athletic equipment. A talent show." She beamed around at the class. "We have many very talented people in our class, and I hope you will all want to be involved. If you are interested, please put your name on the sheet I'm passing around."

Helen gazed meaningfully, dangerously at Sam.

"What?" Sam whispered, amid chatter erupting

around them.

"You will be performing, my young pupil," she muttered out of the corner of her mouth.

"No, I won't!" Alarmed timpani thundered in his head. Taking piano lessons or going to a concert was one thing. But performing all by yourself—in front of real people, real minds judging—was another.

"You will." Her voice purred menacingly. "I have not wasted all of this time teaching you, so that you could slide out of a performance opportunity. Musicians perform."

"I'm not exactly a musician. Plus I don't have anything to perform. Not really. Just those little songs in the book."

"You're not exactly an *anything* if you don't seize chances when they come along. And don't worry about what you're going to play. I'll worry about that for you."

Helen had a point. You couldn't say you wanted to do extraordinary things then hide when opportunity came bouncing along. If Beethoven had done that, nobody would have heard of him.

When the sheet came around, he wrote his name after hers.

He felt a little numb. Silly idiot. He had signed up to be in a concert! He remembered the first day he had heard Helen play, while hiding behind the curtain. Could he really share the same stage with her? Did he actually dare?

He couldn't concentrate for the rest of the day. But Helen immediately bent over a sheet of paper, writing. Sam couldn't see what she was doing: her shoulder blocked his view.

At lunch, he asked, "What are you working on so hard?"

"You'll find out later," she snapped.

All afternoon, Helen scribbled. When the bell finally rang, she slipped three sheets to Sam as if they were secret documents to be seen by nobody else. "Here. It's rough still, but it's a start."

"What are these?"

"Well, what do you think they are?" She glanced around to make sure nobody was looking.

Sam stared at the pages. It was music, drawn neatly in Helen's handwriting. At the top of the first page she had written, "An arrangement of Ode to Joy, from Beethoven's Ninth Symphony, by Helen Alemeda."

Helen had written a piece of music. He was astounded.

"Why did you do this?" he asked.

"Well," said Helen, sharply and a little awkwardly, "It's for you." She glared at him. "You need something to perform in the concert. And stupid Dr. Weiss has me working on composition. He says it'll help me recognize the nuances of music."

Sam held the pages as if they were diamonds.

"Are you going to say something, or just keep staring at it?"

"I want to learn it!" said Sam.

They hurried to Helen's house. Sam couldn't wait to sit in front of the Alemedas' patient grand piano and place his hands on the keyboard. Now that his own fingers had grown in strength, he seemed to be able to make the keys do more. His softs were more whispering now, his louds more resonant.

He picked cautiously through the music while Helen watched with a funny, pink look on her face. At one point Mrs. Williams peeked in and said, "That's very nice, isn't it? Is it Beethoven?"

"Ode to Joy," Helen said sharply. "From the Ninth."

"Helen wrote it for me!" Sam flushed. "I'm going to play it in the school talent show."

"I didn't write it, I arranged it."

Mrs. Williams gave Helen a warm, loving look. Sam glanced away, embarrassed. How it must feel to have someone look at you like that!

"We're very busy right now," said Helen, by way of dismissal. "Sam's lesson isn't finished."

Before Mrs. Williams closed the door, she leaned in again. "I bet your mother would love to know what you're doing, Sam. Wouldn't she be proud to hear you in the concert?"

"Yes," said Sam automatically. Mrs. Williams often mentioned his mother, and he had learned to simply agree.

By the time they had finished, Sam was already stumbling through all three pages. He couldn't play steadily yet, but there was time for that.

When he left the Alemedas' house, he bounced through the leaves, past the Co-op, past the other buildings nearby, over the hill and then down, down into the ravine. His keyboard waited there as usual, the answer to an itching question.

Sam threw himself into a corner of his fort and drew the keyboard out from under a pile of boards. Carefully he placed the pages of Helen's arrangement of *Ode to Joy* on the ground in front of him, guided his fingers into position on the keyboard, and began to play. The notes exploded in his head.

Sam was so captivated by the sounds his fingers were making that he did not notice the figure crouching in the clump of trees nearby, watching curiously.

When the first stars began glinting high above, the figure watched Sam gather his pages together, wrap them in a garbage bag to keep them dry, hide them under three boards and place his keyboard on top of the pile. Then, the figure stayed motionless under the clump of trees, as Sam tore along the path back to the Lovett Co-op.

Finally, the shape slipped from his hiding place, and drifted toward Sam's half-built fort. Pete Gower gently pulled out the pages of Helen's arrangement and turned them over carefully to see what they were about. He had begun collecting his evidence, and he was prepared to take his time. At the right moment, he would reveal what he knew. Then, finally, he and Sam Garretson would be even.

Chapter Twelve

The days slipped past, and slowly the air grew crisp. In Helen's neighborhood, people bagged their rose bushes to protect them until spring. In Sam's building, heat grumbled to life, cranking and creaking warmth through the hallways and apartments. The Lovett Co-op felt almost festive, a warm oasis amid ice. People greeted one another cheerfully.

But Sam continued to tread carefully in the hall of the co-op, especially when he inched past Pete Gower's apartment door. Since the night of the dress rehearsal, he had been lucky enough not to end up alone with Pete. But he didn't want to take any chances.

This morning, the day before the fundraiser concert, he slipped more cautiously than usual down the hallway. But as he tiptoed past Pete's apartment, the door suddenly swung open.

Sam froze.

Pete stood in the doorway, school bag in hand. From inside the apartment, Sam could hear a loud television, and somebody screeching.

"What a surprise, seeing you here," said Pete. "Look at this, we can walk to school together. You can help me practice my ABC's, because you're the expert."

Sam didn't answer. He began to inch along the hallway, hoping that Pete would not follow.

But Pete slipped easily beside him. "It's going to snow soon," he said, conversationally. "Any day now. Maybe today. Maybe tomorrow."

Sam continued to say nothing. He walked faster along the hallway.

"But what I'm wondering," said Pete, slowly, "is how you're going to play on your little piano board once it starts to snow?"

Sam blinked.

The world seemed to stop spinning.

"What are you talking about?" he asked carefully.

"Your little piano board!" Pete said, heartily. "Your little fort!"

"How do you know about that?" Sam stammered. He tried to calm down. It wasn't going to help anyone if he got upset. He had to breathe normally.

"Yep," said Pete, eyeing him with satisfaction. He nodded deliberately, and began talking to himself in a thoughtful, pondering way. "It's definitely a secret, no question about that. Now, who is Sammy keeping it a secret from? Is it the kids at school? Is it your mommy?" He nodded. "I think mommy doesn't like keyboards, for some reason."

Sam didn't answer. There was a strange, uneven pounding on each side of his head. It made thinking difficult. It kept getting louder and louder. Sam knew he was going to explode any minute.

Pete would not take this thing from him!

"What is a secret like that worth?" Pete wondered aloud. "Maybe I've got a new helper. Maybe little Sam isn't better than everyone after all."

Then Sam exploded.

"Ho, yes!" he cried. The rage overwhelmed him, like flames. "All you think about is who you're going to control! I can tell you why, because I know!"

He began to advance on Pete, who stepped back involuntarily.

"You are ignorant!" Sam shouted. As the cruel words spilled out, he felt cold triumph. "You don't care if you never learn anything! You don't care if you grow up into a stupid adult and you're stupid your whole life!"

He pushed at Pete's stomach. Pete didn't push back—Sam's eyes were too dangerous.

"Let me tell you every detail about my secret, so you'll REALLY have some power! That's what you want, isn't it?"

Pete didn't answer, so Sam continued, in a voice that didn't even seem to be his own.

"I'm learning how to play the piano. I'm learning how to read music. I'm learning how to do something you'll never be able to do. You can't even read words!" He could not keep the green disgust from spilling over his anger. "When I get older, I'm going to do this for a living, and you still won't be able to read or write your own name!"

Pete let out a strange squawk, and Sam pushed past him in a blur of fury and pain. He did not even remember how he got to the stairs and out the front door of the co-op. He scarcely remembered arriving at school.

All he knew was, he had to calm the electric shriek inside him. The secret was out, and Pete Gower knew about it.

Pete did not come to school.

Sam fidgeted and worried. He kept playing the fight over and over in his mind. He kept wishing Pete's door hadn't opened, that Pete hadn't learned Sam's secret, that Sam hadn't shouted those things at Pete. He wished he had never found out that Pete couldn't read.

In the afternoon, long-awaited snow finally swirled from the gray sky. It fluttered against the classroom window, and people stopped their tasks to exclaim, "It's snowing!" Then it came harder, to make up for heavy days of waiting.

Finally, Sam couldn't see across the schoolyard for the swirling mass of white. But he couldn't feel the same excitement as everyone else. The whirling flakes only seemed to echo the confusion tossing inside him. He couldn't see through that either.

That evening, it helped to sit at Helen's piano again. Everything made more sense when he looked at the keys. They decided to pretend that it was the night of the talent show—only a day away. Sam performed his piece, then began to shamble back to the makeshift "wings" they had created to resemble the stage.

"No!" Helen shouted, pointing to the piano. "Get back there immediately. You have to bow first."

"I have to what?"

"Concert etiquette. You bow to the audience. With one hand on the piano, like this." She showed him, bowing humbly to the chair in the corner. "You try."

"I'll feel stupid."

"Be grateful I don't make you bow at the beginning too. Some people do, but I think it's overkill."

So Sam bowed to the chair, from the waist, as Helen had done.

"Now you," said Sam. He had waited a long time to hear her play again. She had never performed a complete solo since the first lesson.

"The first movement of the Pathetique Sonata," said Helen. "Beethoven, of course." She paused to center herself, as she had often told Sam to do. At precisely the right moment, her hands raised to the keys gracefully, efficiently.

And then she attacked, from the shoulders, into the opening chord. BOOM!

As he listened to the grim, thrilling notes, Sam's head swam, and again he imagined a future he scarcely dared to dream about. One day he would study Beethoven seriously, maybe in a university. And he would teach other people about him.

The slow part came to an end with a long scale winging effortlessly, painfully down the keyboard, finally pausing. Then, viciously, the fast part pounced. Helen's left hand blurred into action; her right hand jabbed.

Suddenly the last chord resounded and Helen's hands dropped, exhausted, to her sides. Standing, she placed a hand on the piano, and bowed perfectly.

Sam clapped wildly. "Bravo!" he shouted.

"Oh, well," said Helen, looking away. "No. Not really. It's getting better." She looked oddly embarrassed. "But it'll do for the fundraiser."

Sam's stomach filled with fear. Tomorrow—tomorrow! —he would be sitting on that stage.

Meanwhile, who knew what was going on right now at the co-op? Maybe Pete had changed the rules. Maybe he'd called Sam's mother at work to tell her about everything.

There was too much inside his head.

"Oh, not again!" said Helen. "Right: look, let's have

this out." She sat again fiercely on the piano bench. She seemed to be trying to pull her thoughts together, to say just the right thing.

Finally, Helen spoke, very slowly.

"It's natural to be nervous," she said. "That never goes away. But you learn to control it, instead of it controlling you. You turn it into something else."

"Do you get nervous?" asked Sam, astonished. "I don't believe it." Not dangerous, haughty Helen!

She seemed to struggle with herself. It was as if she wanted to tell him something and keep it to herself at the same time.

"It may surprise you," said Helen at last, in a slow, strange voice, "that even I, Helen Alemeda, occasionally am a little wary about things, although I seem always in control. Coming here, for one thing, to this city. Going to a regular school. Meeting horrible people like yourself."

"Thanks," said Sam.

Helen grimaced. It seemed like something huge was trying to come out of her.

At last she said, "You play little games with yourself to get through." She shook herself, and nodded. "I've got a game."

"What kind of game?" asked Sam, leaning forward. He could tell this was important.

"You can't laugh, or I'll never teach you another lesson."

"I won't laugh."

"Well," said Helen, coldly and reluctantly. "It's a kind of fantasy game. I pretend I'm—talking to Beethoven. He gives me advice and I tell him things. It's a private world, with just the two of us."

She glared at him ferociously.

Sam said slowly, "I led an army of explorers. I usually did it down in my ravine."

They stared at each other.

Sam added, "I don't do it much anymore, though. Now I just go to the ravine. It's—how did you say it? — It's the most peaceful place I know."

Abruptly Helen leapt to her feet. "Show me."

"What?"

"Show me this ravine! If it's peaceful, it's peaceful."

"No. Not today. We shouldn't," said Sam. He had to check in with Mrs. Hatch at five-thirty, and it was almost that time now. Also, Helen would see his wooden keyboard, decorated in pencil crayons. It was so different from her grand piano, from her studio covered with pictures of Beethoven. It was babyish.

"Too bad. I want to see this so-peaceful place."

There was no stopping Helen when she had made up her mind. They pulled on coats, boots, mitts, scarves and hats. Like tubby aliens, they ventured into tossing snowflakes.

It didn't take long to travel snow-covered streets to the Lovett Co-op. Sam led around the back, filled with foreboding. The path was difficult to see against the snow, and it was beginning to cloud with ice.

"Be really careful," he said. "It's getting slippery."

"Thanks for the advice," said Helen, from behind.

They picked down the path, avoiding boulders and roots. Snow was collecting in ruts and dips. Helen nearly tripped, but Sam caught her. She shook his hand off.

As they neared the fort, Sam's insides melted horribly. Something was wrong. Something was completely wrong.

The boards had been wrenched off and lay scattered in the snow, rusty nails bent at awkward angles.

"Your building skills need work," said Helen.

As they drew nearer yet, through the silence of the swirling snow, they both saw a dark figure inside, bent over a board, arm working madly across it.

Sam stopped being Sam for a few minutes—his mind ripped apart.

"GET AWAY FROM THAT!" he cried, in a voice that didn't even sound like his. He tore across the threshold. With strength he didn't know he had, he ripped Pete Gower backward, away from the precious keyboard. But it was too late. The white and black keys had been covered in a scrawl of crayon.

It was ruined.

Then Pete and Sam were tumbling over the snow, locked in a fury of flailing arms. Helen tried to grab at them, to pull them apart.

"You can make another!" she was shouting. But Sam scarcely heard her.

Pete pulled away at last, and pelted off across the swirling white. Sam leapt to his feet and tore after him.

By now, the trail was scarcely visible at all, so Sam had to guess where it curved and twisted on the steep hill. Ahead, Pete's gray figure, barely visible amid the dancing snowflakes, climbed upward. Helen stumbled behind. Then the wind began to blow in unpredictable gusts. Sam could scarcely see ahead of him.

He did not notice that Pete had turned to face him, but he heard Pete's strangled voice screaming something. Then Pete shoved him hard. Sam tumbled backward, his balance lost. Crazily, the ground swung out from under him, and he felt himself falling.

Helen broke his fall. He managed to grab at some underbrush to steady himself, but now she stumbled and hurtled backward, into the swirling white.

Crack!

He heard a twig or root snapping, a slithering noise, a shriek. And silence.

"Helen!"

He couldn't see where she had fallen. She wasn't answering!

"Helen! Where are you?"

Only howling wind. Sam felt lost in the world. Nearly frantic, forgetting Pete who stood in front of him, he began to try to stumble back down the ravine.

"Helen! Answer me!"

A weak voice came to him over the wind. "I'm here. My arm won't move. And I've cut my head, I think."

Panicking, Sam clambered down the weed-and snow-covered hillside, searching for her. At last he saw her, crumpled against the rock that had stopped her fall.

"It's okay! I've got you!"

And somehow he helped her to her feet. Then they staggered painfully, slowly, back up the path toward the shimmering lights of the apartment complex.

Pete fell brokenly in behind, not speaking.

Chapter Thirteen

Later, Sam couldn't remember how they got to the co-op. His memory held an anxious jumble of snowflakes, wind, cold and terror. And a guilt that could not express itself yet. First he needed to call for help. Then he could examine the dark thing waiting.

He left her slumped on a couch in the lobby, left arm resting at a funny angle and a bruise blossoming, multi-colored, on her forehead. Pete sat dumbly beside her. Sam attacked the stairs, nearly falling as he spun around the landing of each flight.

He banged on Mrs. Hatch's door, then squirmed with desperation as each lock and chain squeaked. Finally the door crept open.

Sam pushed inside. "Mrs. Hatch!" he shouted. "My friend—Helen—she's hurt, and we need to take her to the hospital. I think her arm's broken. We have to hurry!"

"Well, now," Mrs. Hatch mumbled, "What have you been doing? I'd better take a look."

"No!" Sam cried. "Get your keys! We have to go now!"

Ordinarily, he wouldn't have spoken to an adult that way. But Mrs. Hatch needed to understand. He stammered out some more details, and then waited for her to find her car keys. Finally he stumbled back down the stairs, with Mrs. Hatch stamping behind.

When they arrived in the lobby, Helen was trying not to cry and looking blackly murderous, like a cumulus cloud. Sam and Mrs. Hatch helped her to her feet.

"I'm fine," Helen snapped, as they led her through the snow to the car. But when her arm twisted, she cried out in pain. In the car Sam kept his eyes anxiously on her. She did not make a sound, just stared ahead sullenly while uncontrollable tears seeped down her face.

When they reached Emergency, things sped up. A nurse hustled Helen through some doors while Mrs. Hatch and Sam tried to answer questions from the admitting nurse.

Then, after they had finished with the nurse, Mrs. Hatch growled, "Best to call your mother. We'll let her figure out how someone breaks an arm at the *library*."

But his mother mustn't know! Sam protested, suddenly terrified, "My mom can't leave work early, and I'm fine. It's Helen who's hurt."

Game over, kiddo, said a nasty voice inside Sam. *How do you plan to hide your lessons now?*

And then Sam burst into tears too.

Then, he sat in the crowded waiting room with sick people. Time began to circle as if it had no beginning or end. Sam felt he had always been sitting here.

What if she can't play the piano again? whispered the voice. *How will you live with yourself then?*

"Shut up," Sam whispered back. "Shut up, shut up."

Mrs. Williams was the first to arrive. She scooped Sam in her arms. "Are *you* hurt, love?"

He shook his head, unable to speak. Mrs. Williams wouldn't care about him after she learned how Helen got hurt. Everything was ruined. He blurted, "I did it. I took

105

her to the ravine. It's all my fault." If he had not allowed the frenzy to consume him, he would not have begun the fight with Pete. He would not have chased after Pete, and he would not have tumbled backward into Helen.

But he could not say these things aloud.

"Don't worry," said Mrs. Williams, squeezing his shoulders. "Promise me!"

Much later, it seemed, Sam's mother arrived in a flap of overcoat and briefcase. She raced toward Sam. He expected her to yell, but, like Mrs. Williams, she enveloped him in a hug. Mrs. Hatch stood to one side, waiting.

"Are you all right?" Sam's mother cried, seeing his dirty and tear-stained face. "What happened?"

"I'm fine," said Sam dully. It was all over now. He should never have rescued Helen's book from the school roof, never hidden in the auditorium to hear her play. Then he wouldn't have wanted—and destroyed—this thing for himself.

"What happened?" his mother repeated.

"He hasn't been at the library, I'm quite sure of that," said Mrs. Hatch. "People don't get hurt at the library. I'd like to know what he *has* been doing."

"M-my friend," Sam whispered, "We went into the ravine, and she fell and I think her arm is broken. Oh, it's my fault! I was selfish, and I was undisciplined, and I hurt her!"

He expected his mother to scold him. But instead she hugged him.

"Mrs. Garretson?" The voice echoed through the waiting area. Mrs. Williams slipped past Mrs. Hatch and extended a hand to Sam's mother. "May I introduce myself? I am Alicia Williams, housekeeper to the Alemedas. Sam has become quite good friends with Helen, their daughter. I have been hoping for a chance to meet you. Of course, I would have wished for better circumstances."

Sam's mother shook Mrs. Williams' hand in the polite, distant way she had with strangers. "I had no idea that Sam had made a friend."

"Just so. Perhaps we could talk for a moment? In private?"

"No!" shouted Sam.

But Mrs. Williams ushered Sam's mother toward the entrance, before she could protest. Sam and Mrs. Hatch stood silently, side by side, waiting for what would happen next. Then Mrs. Williams' enormous voice hushed so that Sam couldn't hear. She spoke for a long time. Once she pointed at Sam and made a strange gesture as if she could not believe something.

Sam's mother turned to stare at Sam as though she had never seen him before.

This was it, the end of everything.

Just then a nurse emerged from the swinging doors. "Mr. or Mrs. Alemeda?" she said.

Mrs. Williams sprinted across the waiting room. "I represent Mr. Frank Alemeda," she said. "Alicia Williams, housekeeper. How is Helen, please?"

Sam raced over too. He couldn't bear to sit and wait any longer.

"This is Helen's very good friend Sam," said Mrs. Williams, patting him on the shoulder.

The nurse smiled briefly at Sam. "Helen has a clean break in her right arm. She'll be wearing a cast for six weeks, and then she'll be good as new."

"She'll—she'll be able to play the piano?" Sam whispered.

"Only if she could play it before," said the nurse in a flat voice. "That's a joke."

Suddenly a sluice gate burst open inside Sam. Everything spewed out in grateful release.

"Thank you," he breathed.

"Shall I see her now?" Mrs. Williams asked in a voice that wouldn't tolerate a negative answer.

The nurse nodded. "This way, please." She put out a hand to stop Sam. "Only family for now, I'm afraid."

"Come and see us tomorrow, Sam," said Mrs. Williams. Then they disappeared behind the swinging doors that led to Helen. Suddenly Sam felt entirely alone. Everything that mattered was on the other side of the doors.

His mother placed a firm hand on his shoulder, startling him. "Let's get home, young man. Right now."

He followed her meekly to the car. It was not going to be a pleasant evening.

Mrs. Hatch marched through the snow to her own car.

All the way home they were silent, except for his mother hissing at drivers. Streets were slippery with new-fallen snow, and people hadn't figured out how to maneuver properly yet. The car rattled and grumbled as if it felt as annoyed as she did.

She said nothing when they entered the apartment, so Sam had a bath. Then he sneaked into his bedroom, climbed into bed and pulled sheets around his chin for safety. It was still early evening, but everything was over anyway, so he may as well go to sleep.

He lost track of time. When he woke, his mother was shaking his shoulder.

"We have to talk, Sam. Tonight, not tomorrow."

He sat up while she settled down on the side of the bed.

Then they looked at each other for awhile. Sam decided he would not speak first. Maybe he would just stop talking altogether.

"Why didn't you *tell* me about this girl?" his mother exploded at last, with a rush of exasperated air. "Since *September*, the woman tells me casually, you've been going to the girl's house twice a week after school! And she's been giving you *piano lessons*? When were you planning to tell me about this? Didn't you think I had a right to know what my own son was up to? And how could you lie to Mrs. Hatch? We both thought that you were in a history club. Instead, I had to hear the truth from the housekeeper. What must she think of me? I am very disappointed in you, Sam."

"I'm sorry," said Sam in a monotone.

"And it's embarrassing to think that they have been giving us these lessons for free. I have half a mind to reimburse them. We're not in the poor house yet!"

"No!" said Sam, urgently. "You can't! If you try to pay them, I'll—" He couldn't think of anything awful enough. But she couldn't offer some puny amount to the Alemedas, who had never asked for anything!

"Well, we don't need anyone's charity."

"It *wasn't* charity," Sam shouted. His voice echoed in the small room. "I *earned* those lessons!" Then he told her about retrieving Helen's book, and getting the bullies to leave Helen alone forever. Suddenly the rage could not be contained.

"I know piano lessons may not lead to a good job! I know you said they were a waste of time!" he exploded. "But I *have* to take them! I have to *play the sounds in my head!*" How could he explain? "I made a piano to practice on, in the ravine, and I'm playing in a talent show tomorrow—playing a song *Helen* arranged for me—and you can't stop it! If you try to make me quit lessons, I'll—I'll find some other way to get them."

He could tell that he was startling her. Good! Let her be startled.

Out of breath, he fixed her with his sternest glare, borrowing every ounce of Helen that he could muster. He thought of Beethoven, and his will stiffened even further. Nobody could have kept Beethoven from what he was meant for—not even his own deafness.

When his mother finally spoke again, it was in a quiet, soothing voice. "Let's calm down for a second. Obviously this means something to you," she said. "I can see that."

Sam didn't reply. He had to wait and see which way the conversation was going to go. He would not be talked out of this.

"A long time ago, when we talked about piano lessons, I didn't speak very clearly to you. When I told you they were a waste of time," his mother said, gently, "I said it because we can't really afford them. Sam, there is so much that we can't afford, and there is so much that I can't give to you—things that you deserve, that they say you have a talent for."

She rubbed her weary face, worn from long days of typing and answering phones. "I know I rely on you more than I should, and I know you are a good son who helps out more than you should have to. I wish I could give you everything on the planet!"

And then, shockingly, Sam's mother began to cry.

After awhile, Sam said, awkwardly, "Helen *wants* to teach me." At least, she had wanted to before. He didn't know how she felt now, but he couldn't think about that yet. "It's how we've become friends. Please don't cry. Everything is okay."

"It's not really okay," she said, blowing her nose. "It's not okay at all."

"But it is," said Sam, insistently, gently, "because this is the only thing I want."

He put his arm around her. They sat in silence. The great iceberg between them began to melt.

Chapter Fourteen

Helen was not at school the next day. Neither was Pete. Sam wasn't sure why he himself was there, but it had seemed like the only thing to do.

But he couldn't concentrate on mathematics or language arts. His mind raced over and over blurred images of snow tumbling crazily, Pete destroying his keyboard, Helen slipping down the edge of the ravine, the truth about his lessons ripping into the open. School didn't seem nearly as important.

At lunch, he left for the day. He wasn't sure where he was going, but school was definitely over.

He walked without a sense of where he was headed, until his feet carried him downtown. Here the traffic shot through brown slush, and people slithered over icy sidewalks, in and out of stores.

That's it. I'll buy her something. The gift had to tell her how important her friendship had been to him. It should also have something to do with music. He would know when he saw it. Never mind that he had no money right now—if he saw something good enough, he'd figure out how to buy it somehow.

The door to the music store, Dorlian's, jingled as he entered. Traffic sounds were smothered over by soothing classical music. Sam stood on the welcome mat and took a deep breath. Instruments of every description lined the walls. In the center were shelves and shelves of music books and CD's.

"May I help you?" A tall man gazed down at him. "Are you looking for anything in particular?"

"A gift," said Sam promptly. "For a pianist."

The man led him to a counter piled with notebooks, rulers, pencils, mugs, T-shirts, all with music pictures on them. Sam's heart began to drop ominously. Helen already had most of these things, or items similar to them. Another music mug wouldn't tell her what he wanted to say.

"How much were you thinking of spending?" the man asked, after a minute.

"Depends on the gift," Sam said gruffly.

"We have some boxed CD sets," said the man. "Let me show you."

"Thanks," said Sam. He allowed the shopkeeper to point out particularly fine new recordings of symphonies, quartets, sonatas, and concerti. Sam's mind was racing. He wasn't going to find his gift here. Even if he had all the money in the world, he was sure Helen's father probably had all of these recordings. He had probably even *made* some of them.

When it seemed like a polite moment, Sam thanked the man and said he would think about it. Then he zipped his coat and slithered back into the snow.

Marching along, he searched his mind for the perfect gift. But the only thing jumbling in his head was Helen's arrangement of *Ode to Joy*.

Which made him remember—for the first time since yesterday—that tonight was the talent concert. Sam almost laughed. Helen had intended to take his mind off it, and she had certainly succeeded. He could hardly imagine playing in the concert now anyway. Not without Helen sitting in the wings, sternly critical. Not with her arm broken, unable to play.

And so all the lessons came to this.

After a while, his shambling feet passed the library. As he realized where he was, Sam chuckled without humor. His old alibi. Maybe it was time to see what the fuss was about. He pulled open the heavy doors and slipped inside.

A sign pointed to a section marked, MUSIC. Sam's feet took him in that direction.

Row upon row of CD's stretched before him. You could hear what they sounded like on CD players lining the far wall. Sam decided to listen to something—maybe the original *Ode to Joy*. It might give him some ideas for Helen's gift.

The section marked "Beethoven" covered an entire set of shelves, with many subcategories. Sam gazed about hopelessly. *Ode to Joy* could be anywhere.

He tried to remember what Helen had told him. It came from a larger piece of music. One of the symphonies, he thought. He found a section marked, "Symphonies," with nine sub-sections. Nine symphonies! He certainly didn't have time to listen to all of them this afternoon. Sam began to think this was foolish.

A voice broke into his thoughts.

"Are you looking for something?" The librarian frowned down at him somewhat doubtfully.

She knew everything about the library. She, if anyone, could find it. "*Ode to Joy!*" he said. "It's very important. For—a project."

She lifted out Beethoven's Ninth Symphony. "The last

movement contains what you're looking for," she said. "And I'll ignore the fact that you're here during school hours. You can listen to it over there. Please try to be quiet while you do."

Sam took his CD to the wall of CD players, wondering if she spoke that way to everyone who came in. If she did, he was surprised anyone ever visited the library. He inserted the CD, found the last movement and placed the earphones over his head. He closed his eyes, trying to calm the sickening blankness inside.

From the first notes, he felt as though Beethoven was sitting there right beside him, listening too. It helped the tightness inside him to loosen a little.

Helen sometimes pretended she was talking to Beethoven. What gift would Beethoven suggest? *He* certainly wouldn't approve of a silly music mug or a pencil that didn't mean anything. Beethoven didn't believe in fancy pretending—he tried to show things as they were. And he made sense of it for other people who were listening in the right way too.

Just like Helen, Sam thought suddenly.

She had helped make sense of things for *him*—helped him find a world where people turned their feelings and ideas into music. It was the best gift. She hadn't set out to give it to him, but she did anyway, despite herself. That was what he needed to tell her.

Then the miracle happened.

A chorus of mighty voices burst in his ears, out of nowhere. They roared *Ode to Joy* as if they contained all the glory in existence. Sam gasped. The sun exploded through leaves in the ravine and birds startled in a great flock from the tree under which he had built his fort. It was the world transformed through Beethoven's own voice.

Suddenly he knew what he would give Helen. But he had to hurry.

When he got home, he dumped the contents of the hall basket all over the floor. He grabbed his mother's gardening trowel from the closet and tore back into the hallway, basket and trowel in hand.

He froze.

Pete Gower stood in the hallway, staring at him.

"Get out of my way," said Sam. Pete had done enough damage—he would not do anymore. Sam was finished with him—finished with the fights, finished with the secrets. Pete could not hurt him further: Sam was as hurt as he could be.

Pete didn't answer, just kept gaping silently, as if he wasn't exactly sure how things were supposed to go from here.

"You don't have to worry," said Sam, bitterly. "I haven't told anyone. You're safe." Pete didn't deserve to feel safe.

"Is she all right?" said Pete gruffly, unexpectedly.

"Her arm's broken. Thanks to you."

Neither of them spoke for a moment. All of the awful things dangled in the air between them.

"Let me go," said Sam. "I have to do something for her."

Pete took a deep breath, as if he wanted to say something.

Without thinking, Sam tossed the trowel to Pete. "Here. You can help dig up bulbs."

Chapter Fifteen

Snow fell numbly from the gray sky onto heaps and swirls already blanketing the Alemedas' front porch. Sam trudged up to the front door. He protected his bundle against the wind, not wanting to drop a single item he was carrying.

When Mrs. Williams answered the doorbell, Sam blurted out, "I don't care if she wants to see me or not. I have something to give her. Mrs. Williams, I'll push past you if I have to."

Mrs. Williams burst out laughing. "Sam Garretson, I'd like to see you try."

Sam did not laugh. He didn't see what was so funny.

"Well, well," said Mrs. Williams, catching her breath at last. "If you really want to see Helen, I won't be the one to stop you. Tell her you overpowered me." She burst out laughing again, wiping her eyes.

She stepped aside for Sam to enter, wisely not asking what he carried in the basket. Sam wouldn't have answered her anyway. The contents, and their explanation, were only for Helen.

When he tapped on Helen's door, nobody answered. He tapped again, a little louder. Finally he pushed the door open.

Helen lay on top of her bed, back toward him. He couldn't see her left arm but knew it wore a cast. She was reading. Sam was sure he knew what book it was.

"Helen?"

She didn't answer. At first, he thought she was asleep. But then she said in a flat voice, "Go home."

"No," said Sam, clutching the basket. "I'm here to stay."

"Then I'll go," said Helen, still in the same monotone voice. She sat up. The cast swung into view, huge and white. She stood, holding the book with her good hand. She tried to hide the cast behind her, but it was too big.

Sam immediately closed the bedroom door. He leaned against it. "I have a present for you, and I'm not leaving until I give it to you."

"I don't want a present," said Helen dully. "I don't want anything." She glared at his basket. "I certainly don't want *that*. It's filthy. You're filthy. You're covered in dirt and slush."

Sam glanced down at himself. He was dirty—it was from gathering the things for her gift.

"I should never have struck a bargain with you in the first place. You didn't keep it anyway," said Helen. "Nice job making sure Pete left us alone. It's about what I expected."

Her voice shook a little. "And now the only thing I'm good at is completely ruined."

Sam gaped and tried to think slowly.

He hadn't come here to fight. He had come to say he wished his arm was broken instead of hers. He had planned to thank her for the piano lessons and for arranging *Ode to Joy* for him. He had wanted her to see that she had introduced him to the whole world.

But suddenly he saw his basket for what it was—the

foolish gift of someone who couldn't afford anything better. He hadn't even bought it—just stolen everything from
around the co-op.

"I was going to give you this," he said awkwardly.
"But I guess it's stupid. I'm just going to take it with me."

"Do what you want," said Helen. "Please don't
assume that I care in the least." She sat on the bed, and
began to read her Beethoven book again.

Sam closed the door gently behind himself.

Then he heard the sobs.

Everyone is crying these days, he thought.

When he had re-entered the bedroom, he sat down on
the bed, waiting for her to tell him to get off her quilt.
When she didn't, he awkwardly put his arm around her.
Hot tears dripped on his shoulder. *This is Helen underneath everything.*

Then the right words began to come to him, like the
gentle tuning of instruments.

"I figure," he said, stammering, "a composer takes an
ordinary thing and turns it into something different. You
see it in a new way, sort of all mixed up with the composer too." He gasped, and the words began to come more
clearly to him. "Like the *Pastorale* Symphony. It's flowers and pastures and forests and rivers, birds and animals.
But they got mixed up with Beethoven and turned into
something completely new."

Helen sniffed rudely, but he could tell that she was
listening.

"Anyway," said Sam. He screwed up his courage to
say what he had come to say. "I think you're a composer
too. What I mean is, first I was just me. Then you turned
me into something else. I'm still me, but I'm all mixed up

with you. We both—we *mean* more now."

He put the basket on the bed. "So it's my turn. I'm going to show you the way that you look, through *me*."

Helen waited.

Sam took a deep breath. It was too late to turn back.

He lifted the first item onto the bed. It was a handful of spruce and pine needles that Pete had wrenched off the trees behind the co-op. "This is Beethoven," he said. "It may look like needles to you, but that's because you're not seeing them the way I am. Feel them."

Helen took them in her right hand.

"They're all prickly," said Sam, "like Beethoven. Like you too. Angry and mean sometimes. But in the winter they stay alive when other leaves fall and die. They're green when nothing else around has any color. Beethoven made music even though he was deaf. He didn't need ears. You don't need your arm, or even a piano, to make you a composer either."

Helen didn't answer, so he lifted out the next items.

"Here are a bunch of tulip bulbs. I—we—dug them out of the front of the co-op." He placed one in her hand. "They're not going to grow during the winter at all. People will think they're dead. Maybe they are sort of dead." He took a huge, shuddering breath. "But in the spring they'll come up like a miracle. It's kind of like when the choir suddenly sings *Ode to Joy* in the Ninth Symphony. You don't expect it." He searched for the words. "It—it *explodes!* When you arranged *Ode to Joy* for me, it was like the tulip exploding through the ground."

He peered at her anxiously. Did she understand?

Desperately he placed the final item on the bed. "This

may look like a match to you, but it's me. Kind of ugly and like a stick, with a big stupid head."

Helen smirked.

"By itself, it doesn't amount to much. But you strike it against the right thing, and *pooof!*" He stared at her earnestly. "Do you see? Do you see?"

Helen didn't answer. She simply picked up one item after another with her good hand. He waited for her to exclaim, *Aaah! I understand it now!* But she didn't.

Sam had said everything. He could think of nothing more.

Finally, he mumbled, "I have to get home now. I wish you'd come to the concert tonight. I think that's the only way I can play in it."

He pulled the door closed—and almost banged right into Mrs. Williams. She put a finger to her lips and ushered him silently downstairs. He began to walk toward his boots, but she shook her head. She gestured down the stairs to the piano studio.

Numbly Sam obeyed. He sat at the piano and stared again at keys that had become old friends.

As Helen sat on her bed, staring at the dirty bulbs and needles and matches, the music began.

First, it curled up the stairs and into her bedroom like a hesitant vine. It was unsure of itself: it was learning to feel the way, note by note. But as it grew in confidence, the tendrils strengthened and toughened. They twisted, finding strength together, and the melodies grew into a tree that bent in its own way, with its own surprised force.

As Helen listened, the tree wrenched forth surprising

new sounds that were more than leaves—they were loud, glad cries, as if someone was shouting his own name for the first time.

Helen sat frozen on the bed.

Beethoven murmured, *"I believe that he has found his voice. And can you hear the other things in it?"*

Because, mingled in the notes of *Ode to Joy* were hidden all three of them. Beethoven had written it, Helen had arranged it, and now Sam played it as if his heart had been born to do nothing else.

Chapter Sixteen

When Sam arrived home, his mother put dinner on the table. She crackled with strange excitement. Sam ate mechanically, a little bemused. How could she be so happy while his world was falling apart?

His only suit was pressed and lying on his bed, next to a tie and dress shirt. "You have to look right for your musical debut this evening," said his mother gaily. She helped him to knot the tie in place. Then she sat on the bed beside him, holding a sheet of paper.

"Do you know what this is?" she asked, with thinly concealed excitement.

"No," said Sam dully. It was a bunch of numbers.

"This is our monthly budget," said his mother. "I've been tinkering with it. Because I've been thinking. The Alemedas say you have talent. And I think we could count on you to stick to it. So...maybe you deserve something to practice on."

Sam suddenly felt he didn't have enough air.

"W...what?" he stammered.

"Don't get too excited. We certainly can't afford a grand piano. We can't even really manage an old upright. But I looked through the classifieds at lunch, and they listed some used keyboards. It would get you started at least. We could see about something else later on. With some creative number crunching, I think we could swing it."

She hugged Sam. He wasn't sure whether he was awake or dreaming. This day had been one of the strangest of his life.

"Look at the time!" said his mother suddenly. "We have to get to the concert."

Someone knocked. When Sam fumbled open the door, Pete Gower stood there, quiet and wary.

Sam said nothing, just stared at Pete, who looked as though he didn't know why he was there either.

"Where are you going?" Pete asked darkly, although Sam was sure he knew quite well.

"Talent show," said Sam. "Where do you think we're going?"

Pete shrugged and squinted and squirmed, as if there was something he wanted to say but he hadn't learned the words yet.

Finally, Sam said it for him.

"You want to come?" he asked.

"I don't care," said Pete gruffly.

So the strangest thing of all happened. Sam, his mother and Pete Gower drove together to the school.

When they arrived, lights glowed eerily from classrooms. It felt all wrong to be there at night. The halls smelled like mothers' perfumes and fathers' colognes. Voices rumbled from the auditorium. Sam's stomach did a flip-flop, as the terror flooded back.

Mrs. Jones raced toward them. "Sam Garretson, there you are! You're supposed to be backstage, young man. The concert is about to begin."

She grabbed him by the hand and led him away toward the stage door. Sam suddenly thought his legs might give out. He desperately wished Helen was there.

Backstage, kids were milling around, preparing for their performances. One girl carried a violin. Another, dressed in a tartan skirt, carried a tiny flute. One boy practiced his juggling, while three kids in the corner warmed up their voices for the trio they were going to sing.

Before he was even used to being backstage, Mrs. Jones hissed, "Places, please. The concert is about to begin!"

Then horrifying silence smothered the audience, and suddenly the first act—a little girl singing a Christmas carol—was gestured onto the stage. She was white with fear. Sam knew how she felt. She began to sing in a tiny, shy voice, "Oh, come, all ye faithful, joyful and tri-umphant..."

At the end of her performance, thunderous applause erupted from friends and family. Sam swallowed hard. There were a lot of people in the audience. What happened if you actually threw up on stage?

Several acts followed the little girl. The audience clapped wildly, even for the boy whose yo-yo snapped off and soared over the heads of the crowd. Then, suddenly, Mrs. Jones was waving at Sam to go onto the stage.

Blinking, he forced his legs to move, but they didn't seem to be working. He stumbled out, taking stock of his surroundings. The grand piano had been wheeled to the center of the stage. Beyond it, he looked for the dim faces of his mother and Pete Gower. There they were in the fifth row. His mom was beaming.

Sam sat down at the piano, grateful for the support of the bench. He looked at the keyboard.

Then the horrible thing happened.

The keys began shifting, rearranging themselves. He couldn't remember where to place his hands. A high, thin singing squealed in his ears.

In terror, he turned to the audience, appealing for support, help. Something. They were silent.

Just then, the back door opened, casting a thin light down the center aisle of the auditorium. In slipped Mrs. Williams, Mr. Alemeda—and Helen.

Helen was here! Helen was here!

Sam stared so intensely that some of the audience began turning around to see what was going on. Helen haughtily ignored the looks. She made a small gesture to Sam that could have been a wave. Or else a threat.

He realized he was grinning stupidly with astonishment and delight, so Sam turned back to the piano.

The keys swam into their proper places. He remembered where to put his hands. When he had placed them in position, he sank into the familiar white and black keys.

And then he began to play.

Ludwig van Beethoven was born in 1770 and died in 1827. During his lifetime, he wrote many kinds of music, including symphonies, chamber music, sonatas and sonatinas, an opera and oratorios. He experimented with new harmonies and new combinations of instruments. Many people therefore see Beethoven as a musical "pioneer." Some people say he helped to usher in a whole new way of composing music. He is sometimes called a "bridge" that leads the way from the classical period in music history, to a new and more revolutionary time called the romantic period.

Beethoven's childhood and young adulthood were not easy; his family was poor, and his father drank. At the age of eleven, he left school and became assistant organist at the court of Bonn, to help keep the family afloat. As a young man, however, he traveled to Vienna to study with Wolfgang Amadeus Mozart and, later, Franz Josef Haydn. These two men were considered to be among the best composers of their time.

In those days, composers were often employed by rich families to write music for special occasions. These families would then help to pay for the composers' living expenses. This meant that the composers were essentially servants to the rich; and they were sometimes treated as such. Beethoven, however, refused to be condescended to. One of his most famous sayings was, "Of Princes there have been and will be thousands. Of Beethovens there is only one."

He accepted the families' money, but composed what he wanted, and expected to be treated like an equal. He was a moody perfectionist with a bad temper, who demanded and received respect.

Around the age of twenty-seven, Beethoven began to go deaf. This was a catastrophe for any composer. But it was especially tragic for Beethoven, who found much of his inspiration in the sounds of nature; he walked often in the countryside around Vienna, carrying a notebook with him to write down his musical ideas. Beethoven's walks in the countryside inspired the symphony mentioned in this story, the *Pastorale*. Beethoven continued to write music, even after his hearing was completely gone. In fact, some of his most famous music was composed after he was deaf.

Perhaps his profound influence on music history was partly because he could "hear" sounds and melodies inside his head that were far more complex and original than any sound that could be heard with the human ear.

His ability to keep writing music after becoming deaf is also the key to one of the most fascinating aspects of Beethoven. In the face of such a terrible tragedy, he was able to create meaning. Out of something very dark, he managed to bring forth beauty; he was a revolutionary force.

Today Beethoven is still regarded as one of the greatest composers who ever lived.

BYZANTIUM AND THE ROMAN PRIMACY

BYZANTIUM
AND THE
ROMAN PRIMACY

by Francis Dvornik

FORDHAM UNIVERSITY PRESS
NEW YORK

A translation of *Byzance et la primauté romaine*
(Editions du Cerf, Paris, 1964)

LIBRARY OF CONGRESS CATALOG CARD NUMBER: 66-14187

© COPYRIGHT BY FORDHAM UNIVERSITY PRESS, 1966

PREFACE

IT WAS GENERALLY expected that after the conclusion of the Second Vatican Council the atmosphere would be favorable for dialogues between the representatives of the Roman Catholic Church and the leaders of other Christian churches; the intention being to find ways of better understanding the problems and to bring closer a rapprochement which would finally lead to reunion.

Many Catholic leaders feel that the dialogue with the Eastern Churches should begin as soon as possible, and hope for positive results, since there are no fundamental dogmatic differences between the Roman and the Orthodox Church. This may be true, but it is premature to expect a speedy agreement. There are many aspects of the historical development, constitution and spiritual life of Eastern Christianity insufficiently understood by the West. In many ways Roman Catholics comprehend the Protestant mind better than they do the Eastern Orthodox, perhaps because they live in the same environment and possess a similar mentality. In many respects the mind of the Easterners is very different from that of the Westerners, and there are few specialists among Catholic scholars who are familiar with the development of Eastern Christianity.

I have studied some of the controversial problems which are at issue between the two Churches and have discussed them in books such as *The Photian Schism: History and Legend* (Cambridge, 1948), and *The Idea of Apostolicity in Byzantium and the Legend of the Apostle Andrew*, Dumbarton Oaks Studies, IV (Washington, D.C., 1958). In both these works, as well as in other studies, I have touched on the problem, which, above

5

all, will occupy the minds of both sides in the dialogue, namely, that of the Primacy of the Roman pontiff and the attitude of the Eastern Church towards it.

I was asked to present some of the results of my research on these problems to a larger audience, and, having accepted this invitation, I published, in French, a book entitled *Byzance et la primauté romaine*. This appeared in 1964 as volume 49 of *Unam Sanctam* of the Editions du Cerf. Until now the problem of the Roman Primacy and the attitude of the Eastern Church towards it have been studied mainly by theologians, and the study has been overshadowed by the acrid spirit of the polemical literature which has imprisoned the minds of either side from the eleventh century on up to the present day.

The historical background of the problem has been generally neglected. The main object of my study has been to shed more light on this and also on the political aspect of this problem. It was important to explain first the origin and the development of the principle of accommodation of the primitive Church to the political organization of the Roman Empire, and to show how this adaptation influenced the idea of Roman Primacy in both East and West. The recognition by the Roman and Orthodox Churches of the Apostolic and Petrine character of the Roman See also had to be examined. The consequences of the adaptation of Hellenistic political philosophy to Christian doctrine, and the break with this Christian Hellenism by the West in the eleventh century, are only briefly sketched in this book. They will be studied thoroughly in my next book, *Early Christian and Byzantine Political Philosophy* (Dumbarton Oaks Studies, IX) soon to be published. Here, however, I have limited myself to the most important facts and statements to be found in Byzantine religious literature bearing on the Roman Primacy in the various periods. It would, of course, be futile to look for a clear definition of the Roman Primacy in Byzantine documents. But many official declarations appear to show that the Byzantines saw the Bishop

6

of Rome, at least on some occasions, as more than first among
equals.

I am obliged to Father Edwin A. Quain, S.J., who undertook
the translation of this book into English in order to make it
accessible to the English-speaking public, and to Fordham
University Press which accepted the publication.

The Fathers of the Second Vatican Council, particularly in
their decree on the Eastern Churches, and in many other declarations, have opened the way to a rapprochement between
East and West. The encounter of Pope Paul VI with the
Oecumenical Patriarch Athenagoras in Jerusalem, and the presence of observers from the Orthodox Church at the Council,
have furthered a spirit of friendship and mutual understanding. The annulment, pronounced simultaneously in Rome and
Constantinople on December 7, 1965, of the excommunication
in 1054 of the Patriarch Michael Caerularius by the papal
legates, and of the latter by the Patriarch, was a noble gesture.
This, however, cannot heal the schism between East and West,
completed, not in 1054, but after 1204 when Constantinople
was conquered by the Latin crusaders, and a Latin patriarch
enthroned in Hagia Sophia. The dialogue between the Christians of East and West will still have many problems to solve.
Nevertheless, these recent events have created a more favorable
atmosphere for friendly and fruitful discussion. Let us hope
that at least some of the ideas discussed in this short study will
help to form a base from which a plan for final reunion can
be established.

F. Dvornik

Dumbarton Oaks
January 6, 1966

7

CONTENTS

INTRODUCTION

TODAY IT IS quite proper to say that the only serious obstacle remaining to a rapprochement between the Orthodox Churches and Catholic Church is the question of the Roman Primacy. All other obstacles can now be considered to have been surmounted, especially those differences in rite and liturgy which played so great a role in polemic literature, both Greek and Latin, from the eleventh to the fifteenth century.

Beginning with the thirteenth century the Roman Church began to lose its attitude of mistrust with regard to the existence of different rites and the use of national languages in the liturgy. Even though the remembrance of the capture of Constantinople by the Latins in 1204 interfered with the numerous attempts at union with the Greeks, still, it had one salutary effect. It forced the Latin World to show itself more and more conciliatory, at least in regard to the existence of different rites and the use of national languages in the liturgy. The partial unions concluded with some branches of Orthodoxy after the Council of Lyons (1274) and of Florence (1439) helped this attitude to become more general.

The present-day liturgical movement which has had such salutary effects in the Catholic Church will undoubtedly contribute, not only to removing these last doubts—since it shows so well the necessity for the people to participate actively in the liturgical action—but it will surely make more understandable in the West the mentality of the Eastern Christians who have never ceased to stress the importance of the Eucharistic sacrifice in the life of every Christian above and beyond any other devotion, either public or private.

In the area of dogma, the question of the procession of the Holy Spirit from both the Father and the Son—the *Filioque*—has likewise lost much of its force. The highly emotional pre-occupation of both Latins and Greeks to find heresy in the teaching of the other—a tendency that was very strong during the centuries of controvery—lost much of its intensity especially after the fall of the Byzantine Empire.

Besides, history shows us that reasons other than theological have contributed to inflating this controversy beyond proper bounds. In this connection it is interesting to note that at the beginning of this controversy it seems that people, at least in the West, viewed the question of the *Filioque* with some detachment.

In fact a curious document of the ninth century seems to indicate this. It is the work of Anastasius Bibliothecarius, the bitter adversary of the Patriarch Photius who had himself stirred the controversy about the *Filioque*. Among the works of Anastasius we find a translation of various documents relative to the history of the Church, which is dedicated to the Deacon, John Hymmonides. Anastasius includes among them a letter of St. Maximus the Confessor (580-662) on the procession of the Holy Spirit. In his introduction[1] to the translation of these documents Anastasius writes:

We have translated also a passage from the letter of St. Maximus to the priest Marinus concerning the procession of the Holy Spirit. In it he said that the Greeks have in this matter become needlessly opposed to us since we do not at all say, as they pretend we do, that the Son is the cause and the principle of the Holy Spirit. On the contrary, in our preoccupation to assert the unity of substance of the Father and the Son, we say that the Holy Spirit, while he proceeds from the Father, also proceeds from the Son, under-standing this procession as a mission. Maximus pleads with those who know the two languages to maintain peace. He says that both we and the Greeks understand that the Holy Spirit proceeds, in one sense from the Son, but that in another sense he does not proceed from the Son. He draws attention to the fact that it is very difficult to express this precise distinction in both Latin and in Greek.

It is altogether possible that linguistic reasons have had their effect in exaggerating the importance of this dispute. The word ἐκ does, as a matter of fact, seem to mean much more to a Greek than the word *ex* does to a Latin.[2] What is significant here is that Anastasius is anxious to explain in friendly fashion this difference of opinion between Greek and Latin theologians. He wrote this commentary in 874, some years after Photius had given this latent controversy a new meaning in his appeal to the Eastern patriarchs and to the Synod of 867.[3]

Further, we also get the impression that Pope John VIII rather looked upon this question as merely a discussion among theologians on a subject which had not yet been defined as an article of faith. It is in this sense that we can explain the attitude of his legates to the Council of 879-880 confirming the union between Byzantium and Rome. Since the *Credo* was recited in Rome without the *Filioque*, it seemed quite natural for them to declare themselves as opposed to this addition to the Nicene Creed.

It is also somewhat surprising to us to see that this controversy, in spite of the efforts of Photius in his *Mystagoge* which strove to give the Greek thesis a solid theological foundation, played a relatively unimportant role in the polemics which took place between the two Churches in 1054 and immediately after the break with the Patriarch Michael Cerularius.

In the famous letter which was addressed by Leo, the Archbishop of Ochrida, at the request of Michael Cerularius, to the Latin Archbishop of Trani,[4] he does not even mention this difference between the doctrines of the two Churches. In this letter, which contains a long catalogue of bitter reproaches, Leo attacks certain innocent customs of the Latins, with especial emphasis on the use of unleavened bread in the celebration of the Holy Sacrifice of the Mass.

Cardinal Humbert, when invited by Pope Leo IX to refute

the accusations made by the Greeks, introduced this subject into the controversy when reproaching the Greeks for having suppressed the *Filioque* in the Nicene Creed.[5] This accusation which, incidentally, revealed a vast ignorance of the origin of the controversy—in fact it was not the Greeks who suppressed the *Filioque* but the Latins who introduced it—shows that this theological difference did not any longer constitute a serious cause of discord between the two Churches. It was only in the beginning of the twelfth century that the *Filioque* became the most powerful weapon in the arsenal of the Greek and Latin polemists.

Besides, it was a Latin prelate who reopened the controversy on the *Filioque*. It was Peter Grossolanus, Archbishop of Milan, an unofficial member[6] of an embassy sent by Pope Paschal II in 1122 to Constantinople for the conclusion of an agreement with the Emperor Alexius I Comnenus, who entered into discussion with the Greek clergy, notably on the *Filioque*. Seven Byzantine theologians were invited by the Emperor to reply to his arguments.[7] In his *Dogmatic Panoply*,[8] Euthymius Zigabenus took pains to furnish his compatriots with numerous arguments against the *Filioque*, drawn for the most part, from the writings of Photius.

In 1135 it was another Latin prelate, Anselm, Bishop of Havelberg, who debated the question of the *Filioque* with Nicetas of Nicomedia, the first among the twelve professors of the Patriarchal Academy. Anselm has described this debate in a work which he dedicated to Pope Eugenius III.[9]

These two debates were really rather academic, with each of the parties simply stating their positions. The two prelates spoke in rather courteous terms, avoiding anything which could be of offense to the Greeks. On his part, Nicetas of Nicomedia maintained great reserve in the polite responses which he made to Anselm.

The second phase of these discussions and controversies was opened, after 1204, by the Latins who had been victorious at

Constantinople and, on the side of the Greeks, especially by Nicholas Mesarites.[10] From this point on, it can be seen that the tone of the writings on this question, which up to then had been a rather academic matter between the theologians of the two sides, had now become a political and national matter. This is easily understandable if we remember the violent antipathy of the Greeks against the Latins who had destroyed their Empire. In this stormy atmosphere one could hardly expect the question to be discussed as a mere theological difference, when it had become a political issue.

Today, however, after so many centuries, the time has come when both Orthodox and Catholic theologians can discuss the matter without emotion.[11] We should never forget that we are here touching upon the mystery of the Blessed Trinity before which human intelligence can do no better than to bend its head and confess its incompetence.

* * *

The view has often been stated that the separation between the two Churches was really due to the different conception held of the Church and its role, in Byzantium and in the West. Ecclesiology is really a rather new branch of the tree of Christian theology and it has developed particularly since the Reformation. At the present time, all theologians—Catholic, Orthodox and Protestant—are keenly interested in ecclesiological problems.[12] Different definitions of the Church are proposed and discussed, its relation with the mystical Body of Christ is studied, and its organic evolution is explained in the light of the definitions proposed.[13]

It is not at all surprising that the specialists of this new theological discipline take some pains to find confirmation for their theories in the writings of the Fathers and in the organization of the primitive Church.[14] But these efforts could lead to dangerous deviations if we attempt to transpose ideas that were formulated recently into epochs when, in reality, such ideas did not exist at all, or if, on the other hand, we should try to interpret patristic texts in the light of these modern ideas.

This danger would exist if we should try to reconstitute an ecclesiological system which we suppose to have existed in the Byzantine Church. We must understand that Byzantine theologians never did develop an ecclesiological system in the modern sense. They were preoccupied with other problems that were much more urgent and much more essential, such as those concerning the divine nature of the three Persons in the Trinity, the Incarnation of the Second Person of the Trinity, the double nature of the Incarnate Word, the double Will in Christ, God and man, the Procession of the Holy Spirit and the participation of the Holy Spirit in the sanctification of man. These problems dominate all theological speculation in Byzantium up to the ninth century; in fact, even the very question of the representation of Christ and the veneration of his image, and those of the saints, are closely linked to Christological mysteries.

As to the conception of the nature of the Church, the Byzantines were quite content with what they found in Holy Scripture[15] and that which the Eastern Fathers had passed on to them. The Church "is the Holy City which has been sanctified . . . in becoming conformed to Christ and participating in the divine nature by the communication of the Holy Spirit." This definition by Cyril of Alexandria[16] satisfied them completely. In the conception of the Byzantines, the Church is the Mystical Body of Christ, the image of the Trinity, the work of the Holy Spirit, and its purpose is the sanctification of man. Man, in union with the Church, the Mystical Body of Christ, should sanctify himself with the aid of the grace of the Holy Spirit, which the merits of the Incarnate Word have assured to humanity. He should, in a sense, "divinize" his nature and realize a union with God. To be sure, this union will not be perfect except in the world to come but man, meantime, has at his disposal all the means necessary to attain, here in this life, a high degree of sanctification.

The necessary means to arrive at this end are to be found in the Church which distributes them by the intermediary of the priesthood: there are the sacraments, especially that of the Body and Blood of Our Lord. It is this sacrament which realizes best the union of our nature with Christ. Holy Communion brings about the union not only of the Christian with Christ but it also unites him to all members of the Church, thus representing the catholicity and the universality of the Church.

As we see, this conception of the Church finds its foundation in Christology and in the theology of the Holy Spirit. That this is so is clear from the evolution which Christian doctrine followed in the course of the first nine centuries, the time when the Eastern Church enjoyed the primary role. We realize that this conception was affected, from time to time, by the different Christological heresies: Nestorianism, Monophysitism and Monothelitism. The primitive conception of the nature of the Church, however, continued to be held as Orthodox theologians eliminated these deviations.[17] This Oriental conception of the Church, although more deeply imbued with a mystical spirit, is identical with that of the West.

Alongside of this mystical and celestial aspect, however, the Church, even for the Byzantines, had an earthly existence. It possessed a hierarchical structure, was a concrete organism, was ruled by laws that were voted by assemblies of bishops, and it found it necessary to accommodate itself to a political situation which varied and to the social structure of the communities in which the faithful lived and its priests worked. These conditions of life were, in the East, often quite different from those that existed in the West and these differences seemed to have raised problems which had their influence on the conception of the role which the Church ought to play in society and the attitude which it ought to take in the face of political authority. All of this had its repercussions on the relations which existed between the two Churches and, unfortunately, provoked a separation which developed until it ended in a formal schism.

At the same time it would be exaggerated and even erroneous to try to find an explanation of these differences in an ecclesiology which developed in different fashion in Byzantine and in the West from the fourth to the eleventh century. Along their own line, the Byzantines continued to stress the mystical character of the Church and its role in the sanctification of the faithful. The Greek Fathers, St. Athanasius, St. John Chrysostom, and St. Cyril of Alexandria continued to lead in theological speculation. Their ideas were taken up and developed, especially by St. Maximus the Confessor (662)[18] and St. Germanus,[19] and they were taught in Byzantium until the end of the Empire.[20] The differences that become clear both in Byzantium and the West in the conception of the Church and its earthly aspect, the differences which stand out also in the evolution of the organization of the two Churches, are due to the fact that the two portions of Christendom have developed under different political and social conditions. The only political philosophy which the Byzantines knew was founded on the Hellenistic political system which the first Christian ideologists, Clement of Alexandria and Eusebius, had adapted to Christian doctrine. This system, which one could call Christian Hellenism, saw in the Emperor a representative of God upon earth, almost the vicegerent of Christ. According to this political conception, the Christian Emperor not only had the right but also the duty to watch over the Church, to defend the Orthodox faith, and to lead his subjects to God. It is from this point of view that we must judge the development of Eastern Christianity and its ideas on the relation of the Church on earth to the civil power.[21]

This ideology was accepted throughout all of Christendom but the Roman Church had been able to escape its untoward consequences and the abuse of the imperial power, owing to the fact that the emperors did not reside at Rome; also important were the profound transformations which the establishment of the new nations in the western part of the Empire brought into being.

If we study the evolution of Christianity in the East and in the West from this point of view, a great number of problems become quite clear. The position of the Christian Emperor in the entire Church after the conversion of Constantine, a position which cannot be identified with caesaropapism, becomes understandable. We also see the differences which existed between the two Christian worlds, differences which inevitably developed when the Church of Rome finally divested itself of the last traces of Christian Hellenism and developed its own political system.

This system restored to the Pope his special position in the Church and stressed the idea of universality, and gave rise to the idea of the superiority of spiritual power over the temporal—a thesis which the East was never able to comprehend.

The consequences of this evolution likewise had their effect in the legislative domain. While in the Byzantine Church the Emperor continued to be the lawmaker, using the right which Christian Hellenism had granted to him, in the West it was the Sovereign Pontiff who, increasingly, became the sole lawgiver in the Church. To explain these differences, the theologian might be tempted to seek for reasons in the order of ecclesiology, but in that path, the historian will be reluctant to follow him.[22] The Byzantines did not possess the ecclesiological mentality of modern theologians.

It would be a mistake to believe that the Byzantine theologians were content to consider solely the mystical and heavenly aspect of the Church. For them, the Church was also an earthly institution comprised not only of the faithful but also having a well-organized hierarchy which should rule the faithful and preserve the true faith. With regard to the earthly aspect of the Church and its organization, there were two problems which preoccupied Byzantine thinkers. The first was the position of the Emperor in the Church. The intrusion of the emperors into the dogmatic area revealed the danger which a false application of Christian Hellenism could present for the hierarchy and the faithful. This danger provoked violent reactions and stirred up a desire to find an element strong enough to be a counterweight to these abuses and to guarantee the privileges of the hierarchy in the definition of doctrine. This element existed: it was the Primacy of the Bishop of Rome, the uncontested chief of all Christian churches in the West. In times of crisis this was remembered in Byzantium. They looked for and sought the help of the Bishop of Rome although suspicious of his growing prestige, and disinclined to allow him the right to intervene directly in internal affairs of the Byzantine Church. In Byzantium, the problem of the Roman Primacy was intimately connected with that of the imperial power. It is to this problem of the Primacy that we address ourselves in this book.

NOTES

1. See the edition of the prefaces of Anastasius in MGH, *Epistolae*, VII, 425, and PL 129, 560. For the translation of the letter of Maximus, *ibid.* 577. Cf. St. Maximus, *Opuscula theologica et polemica ad Marinum*, PG 91, 136.
2. In *Orientalia Christiana periodica*, 15 (1949) 221-22, E. Hermann makes the point that theologians today recognize the fact that the Latin doctrine could very easily sound false to Greek ears, since the Greek preposition ἐκ does not altogether correspond in meaning to the Latin *ex*.
3. It appears that Photius himself suspected that there was a semantic problem, as can be seen in a passage in his *Mystagogia*, PG, 102, 376AB.
4. PG, 120, 836ff.
5. PL, 143, 1003, in the Bull which excommunicated the patriarch.
6. On the basis of indications furnished by one of the seven Greek theologians, Nicetas Seides, V. Grumel has shown that Peter was not an official member of the embassy, but that he had been requested by the Pope to assist the legates. At this time, Gros-

solanus was on a pilgrimage to Jerusalem; "Autour du voyage de Pierre Grossolanus, archevêque de Milan, à Constantinople en 1112," *Échos d'Orient*, 32 (1933) 28-30.

7. Grumel has identified them, as follows: Eustratius of Nicaea, Joannes Phournes, Nicetas Seides, Nicholas Muzalon, Theodore of Smyrna, Theodore Prodromus and Euthymius Zygabenus. Cf. B. Leib, *Rome, Kiev et Byzance à la fin du XIe siècle* (Paris, 1924), 312. See the discourse of Grossolanus in PG, 127, 911-20.

8. PG, 130, 20-1360.

9. *Anselmi dialogi*, PL, 188, 1130ff. Cf. F. Dvornik, *The Photian Schism* (Cambridge, 1948) 345, 396.

10. See *infra*, Ch. 8, note 12.

11. In this connection, see the studies by Catholic and Orthodox theologians in *Russie et Chrétienté* (1950) 123-244, and the article by J. Meyerdorff on the origin of this controversy in *Pravoslavnaja Mysl* (Paris, 1953), 114-137 and the study of V. Lossky, *La procession du Saint-Esprit dans la doctrine trinitaire orthodoxe* (Paris, 1948).

12. See the article of O. Semmelroth, "Ecclesiologie," in *Lexicon für Theologie und Kirche*, 3 (Freiburg, 1959) where we find a short history of Ecclesiology and some useful bibliographical information. For further detail see the reviews of the conferences given at "Colloque d'ecclésiologie," organized by the Faculty of Catholic Theology of the University of Strassburg, Nov. 26-28, 1959, which were published in the *Revue des sciences religieuses*, 34 (1960) and in the collection "Unam Sanctam" (No. 34, Éditions du Cerf), under the title: *L'Ecclésiologie au XIXe siècle*.

13. Cf. especially the work of S. Jaki, *Les tendances nouvelles de l'ecclésiologie* (Rome, 1957; Bibliotheca Academiae Catholicae Hungaricae, Sectio phil.-theol. vol. 3). On pp. 99ff. there is an examination of recent Orthodox ecclesiology. The author shows at what point these new tendencies have been influenced by Protestant theology and by some elements from non-Christian philosophy.

The same subject is treated by Paul Evdokimov in *L'Ecclésiologie au XIXe siècle* (Cf. n. 12), 57-76, under the title: "Les principaux courants de l'ecclésiologie Orthodoxe au xixe siècle." See also the conference of Père B.-D. Dupuy, "Schisme et

Primauté chez J. A. Möhler," *ibid.*, 197-231., and the remarks of Evdokimov in the course of the discussion, *ibid.*, 375-92.

14. For example: L. Cerfaux, *La théologie de l'Église suivant saint Paul*, 2nd. edit. (Paris, 1948); K. Adam, *Der Kirchenbegriff Tertullians* (Paderborn, 1907); L. Bouyer, *L'Incarnation et l'Église Corps du Christ dans la théologie de saint Athanase* (Paris, 1943); G. Bardy, *La théologie de l'Église, de saint Clément de Rome à saint Irenée* (Paris, 1945); the same, *La théologie de l'Église de saint Irenée* (Paris, 1947); A. Hamel, *Kirche bei Hippolyt von Rom* (Güttersloh, 1951). On the Orthodox side, see N. Anastassieff, "La doctrine de la primauté à la lumière de l'ecclésiologie," in *Istina* (1957) 401-20.

15. Especially, Ephesians, 1, 17-23.

16. *In Isaiam*, V, 1, ch. 52, §1; PG 70, 1144C.

17. This has been outlined by V. Lossky in his *Essai sur la théologie mystique de l'Église d'Orient* (Aubier, 1944), 171-92. For the Catholic point of view, see, Yves M.-J. Congar, "Conscience ecclésiologique en Orient et en Occident," in *Istina* (1959) 189-201. See also the brief discussion in his study, *After Nine Hundred Years* (New York, 1959) 57-69. V. Lossky, *op. cit.*, reproaches Congar for over-emphasizing (in his *Chrétiens désunis* [Paris, 1937] 14), the mysterious aspect of Oriental ecclesiology and for not paying enough attention to its terrestrial aspect. It would seem that Congar has treated this point adequately in the book cited above.

18. Notably, in his *Mystagogia*, chaps. 1-5; PG 91, 663-73, 705. St. Maximus saw in the Church the image of God, but also the image of the world and of man. He here has in mind two aspects of the Church: the mystical and the terrestrial. The Church is like a temple in which the faithful occupy a place within, different from that of the priests. The Church represents the unity of the world and the universe which it is to sanctify by the communication of the Holy Spirit. On the doctrine of Maximus, see the article of V. Grumel in DTC, vol. 10, 453ff. Naturally, St. Maximus was primarily interested in Christological and soteriological problems. He only touched on ecclesiology in passing.

19. Especially in his work, *Historia ecclesiastica et mystica contemplatio*, PG 98, 383ff.

20. See, for example, Photius' ideas on the Church. For him, as well, the Church is the Bride of Christ, His Mystical Body; it is Christ, the Head, who directs the Church. On the other hand, he does not neglect the terrestrial aspect of the Church, her hierarchical structure, her right of jurisdiction over the faithful. See the documentation in Th. Spáčil, "Conceptus et doctrina de Ecclesia juxta theologiam Orientalis separati," in *Orientalia Christiana*, 2 (1923) 36-7.

21. The Hellenistic political system and its adaptation to Christian doctrine will be studied in my book: *Early Christian and Byzantine Political Philosophy, Origins and Background* (Dumbarton Oaks Studies, IX).

22. Congar, in the study cited, "Conscience ecclesiologique" (*supra*, n. 17), made the first attempt to cast a bit more light on the ecclesiological problems of the two Churches. In the first part of this interesting study, he has described very well the more mysterious aspect which the Church assumes in the Oriental and Byzantine mind. Besides, in showing the process of separation, he was constrained to adduce some facts resulting from events and ideas that belong rather more to the political than to the religious sphere.

BYZANTIUM AND THE ROMAN PRIMACY

THE PRINCIPLE

OF ACCOMMODATION

In the eyes of Orthodox Christians the problem of the Roman Primacy seems today to have become more difficult than ever to resolve because they often identify that Primacy with the administrative centralization which has developed in the West in the course of the latter centuries. In this they are forgetting that, among other causes, the fact that important groups of Christians have separated themselves from the center of unity has rendered this centralization possible and, to a degree, even necessary.

What is more, in the course of the period during which the Greeks and Latins devoted themselves to bitter and unceasing controversy, certain theories were developed which only served to obscure the essentials of the problem and rendered its solution more difficult. Was the Pope ever considered in the East as occupying a position in the Church more elevated than that of other patriarchs or bishops? Should not the foundation of Constantinople—the New Rome—be explained as a transfer of the Primacy of the Church of Rome to Constantinople? Did not the assumption of the title ecumenical Patriarch, which was taken by the bishops of the new capital of the Empire, confirm this interpretation? Did not the Byzantines, to better support their claims, invent the legend of the apostolic origin of the see of Byzantium as founded by St. Andrew, the brother of St. Peter? And, since Andrew was one of the first among the apostles, since he followed the Lord before Peter did, should not he and his successors be considered as superior to Peter and his successors at Rome?

Neither side—those who supported these ideas and those who opposed them—could win this debate. The suspicion and even mutual hostility that was caused by political divisions and by a different evolution in the administration of the Church in the West, particularly from the eleventh century on, seemed to have poisoned these discussions and made it very difficult for theologians and faithful on either side to consider this problem without bitterness.

Hence, no good purpose will be served by resurrecting arguments, for and against, which we find in the controversial writings of the past. Let us rather try another method, too often forgotten—the historical method. This will allow us to examine, in the light of the documents that have been preserved, what precisely was the position of Byzantium with regard to the Primacy of Rome, and that, from the very foundation of the Byzantine Empire up until the time of the separation of the Churches. Perhaps it will also make it possible for us to discover traces of the primitive tradition in the very period that was vitiated by mistrust and mutual hostility and, at the same time, it may open to us a way which can produce some positive results.

As far as the Petrine tradition is concerned, it is important to stress the fact that the Church in the East had never denied the fact that Peter had lived in Rome, that he died there as a martyr and that it was there that his body rests. It is clear that the primary proof of this fact, a proof which could not be contested nor otherwise explained although there are other less explicit proofs, comes to us from the East: it is a letter of Denis, the Bishop of Corinth, sent to Rome around the year

180.[1] The equally valuable testimony of St. Irenaeus is also that of an Oriental.[2]

To be sure, this is only an "argument from silence." Yet, it is important and it is corroborated by the fact that not one of numerous cities of the East visited by St. Peter, according to the Acts of the Apostles (either original or apocryphal), ever dared to pretend that the Prince of the Apostles had ended his life within its walls or that they possessed his relics. This honor was incontestably reserved for the city of Rome, and this explains why the Churches of the East have never disputed Rome's prestige which came to it from the fact that the Prince of the Apostles had lived and died and was buried there.

But, until the fourth century, the Bishops of Rome never had any need to stress this fact. They had, as a matter of fact, another title which assured them the first place in the hierarchy; their see was, at the same time, the residence of the Emperor and the capital of the Roman Empire—a reason which was then respected throughout all of Christendom. For the Church from the very first days of its existence had conformed itself, for the organization of its ecclesiastical administration, to the political divisions of the Roman Empire.[3]

This important fact has too often been neglected by Church historians who are inclined to see in it rather an anomaly and a deterioration of the apostolic tradition in the Church. In reality this principle of accommodation to the political division of the Empire had been introduced by the Apostles themselves, and there were practical reasons why they did so. Necessarily, the Apostles began their preaching in the great cities of the Empire where important Jewish communities were found. Even when they addressed themselves to Christian communities, which they themselves had founded, they had to adapt themselves to the existing political organization. Thus, Peter wrote to the communities of the provinces of Galatia, Pontus, Cappadocia, Asia and Bithynia. Paul, addressing his letters to the Christian centers, sent them to the capitals of the Roman provinces; to Rome—capital of the province of

Italy; to Ephesus—capital of the province of Asia; to Corinth —capital of Achaea; to Thessalonica—capital of Macedonia. In the second epistle to the Corinthians (1.1), he clearly indicates that his letters should be sent by the bishops resident in the capitals to the communities of the other cities of the province.

Thus, a letter communicating the decisions of the first Council (Acts 15.22-23), intended for Syria and Cilicia, was sent to Antioch, the capital of Syria. Cilicia was then an independent administrative unit. We know also that St. Ignatius, Bishop of Antioch, in his letter to the Romans (2.2), wrote that he was the bishop of the whole province of Syria, of which the capital was Antioch.

Naturally, this does not mean that the Apostles conferred upon the bishops residing in the capitals of the provinces any special rank superior to that of the other bishops of the same provinces. But since all of the economic, social and political life of the provinces of the Roman Empire were centralized in the capitals, it was altogether natural that the bishops of these cities should, little by little, come to be considered as the most important in the hierarchy of the province.

This fact became particularly clear when it was necessary for all the bishops of one province to gather themselves together for discussion of questions that concerned their churches. Naturally, they came together in the capital of the province and it was the bishop of the chief city who took the lead in these meetings and directed the debates. After this fashion regional councils were organized. The letters of St. Cyprian, who describes the African councils which took place in the city of his see, at Carthage, the capital of Africa, show us that this accommodation to the political administration went still further. His descriptions make it clear, in fact, that the bishops in their deliberations followed the protocol which guided the sessions of the Roman Senate and which was followed also by the provincial magistrates in the reunions of their diets.[4]

...ans of this region considered them as their supreme
...n the other hand, it is not sure that at the time of
...cil of Nicaea there were any metropolitans at the
...he provinces that comprised the region.[11]
...time, the rights of Alexandria which had been tradi-
...recognized, seem to have been contested by two in-
...First, Meletius, Bishop of Lycopolis, in ordaining the
...n the districts which were found under the immediate
...ion of Alexandria, had provoked a local schism in the
... Besides, the Emperor Diocletian, in reorganizing the
...in 297, had deprived Egypt of the particular position
...had been given it by Augustus, and he incorporated it
...he dioceses of the East, of which the capital was
...h.[12]

...wever, the Fathers of the Council, taking into considera-
...he fact that the position of Alexandria in Egypt was so
...g that it could not be contested either by the local
...ps or by Antioch, were led to confirm this position by a
...al canon. The events which followed only proved that
...were right in doing so. The integration of Egypt into
...diocese of the East proved in fact to be impracticable and,
...ween 380 and 382, Egypt became once again an independent
...cese.

...On the other hand, Antioch could not pretend to exercise a
...ect jurisdiction over the whole of the diocese of the East. It
...ms that its bishops had acquired the right of jurisdiction
...er certain provinces other than the province of Syria itself.
...letter of Pope Innocent I (402-417)[13] addressed to Alexander
...Antioch seems to indicate this. The Bishop of Antioch re-
...uested the confirmation of his rights which, it seems, were
...ontested by the metropolitans of the provinces in question
...nd the Fathers granted him satisfaction. The tenor of the
...canon indicates clearly, however, that these rights were more
...imited than those of Rome and Alexandria. For the other
...dioceses of the civil administration we do not possess informa-
...tion that is sufficiently precise.

34

One further important remark: not all of the bishoprics located in the provincial capitals were of apostolic origin; Ephesus for example, was the capital of the province of Asia, Corinth the capital of Achaea and Thessalonica the capital of Macedonia. This shows us that it was not apostolic origin which was the determining factor in the organization of the primitive Church. It was rather the principle of accommodation to the political organization of the Empire that was paramount. This we see in the title that was borne by the bishop of these capital cities. They were called "metropolitans" because they traditionally resided in the "metropolises," that is, the capitals of the provinces, and thus it became quite natural for the bishops of the capitals to assume the right of surveillance over the other bishops of their political districts, in accordance with the practice of the magistrates of the capital, whose jurisdiction extended throughout the whole of the province.

* * *

This form of ecclesiastical administration had been formally sanctioned by the first ecumenical council, that of Nicaea (325). In Canon IV, it was decreed by the Fathers of the Council:[5]

Each new bishop should be installed by the group of bishops resident in the province. If it is not possible for the bishops to come together because of pressing difficulties or because of the distances involved, then at least three bishops [of the province] shall come together and, after having obtained the written agreement of the other bishops, they shall proceed to the consecration. It belongs to the metropolitan of each province to confirm what has been done.

This canon definitively established the principle according to which the ecclesiastical organization should model itself upon the political organization of the Empire. This accommodation was, besides, already an accomplished fact at the time when the Council of Nicaea met. To convince ourselves of this we

31

need but consider the order followed by the Bishops when they signed the decrees of the Council and we see that it corresponded to the political division of the Eastern portion of the Empire.[6]

This principle was never contested. On the contrary, other official decrees confirmed it in even clearer fashion. The Synod of Antioch, held in 341, decreed in Canon IX:[7]

This bishops of each province should remember that the bishop resident in the capital (metropolis) should occupy himself with all of the province and should exercise surveillance over the whole. Any person with matters to be taken care of, from anywhere in the province must go to the capital. For this reason, it is decreed that the bishop [of the capital] should have precedence over all the other bishops and they shall not undertake any serious matter without consulting him. This is in accord with the ancient canons of our Fathers.

This canon also recalls the reason which made the position of the metropolitans so important: because since all the political, economical and social life was concentrated in the capital, all those who had business to conduct were obliged to go there.

The decrees promulgated by two Popes show that the principle was also accepted in Rome and in the western part of the Empire. Pope Boniface (418-422),[8] referring to Canon IV of the Council of Nicaea, decreed that each province should have its metropolitan, and he forbade metropolitans to exercise their authority over provinces other than their own. A similar declaration was made by Pope Innocent I (402-417).[9]

* * *

Further, we should note that the Council of Nicaea sanctioned a suprametropolitan organization which had already developed in the Church. From this point of view Canon VI is of great importance. There we read the following declaration:[10]

In Egypt, Libya and Pentap
served, that is, that the Bisho
all this territory, as is the ca
sesses the same power. In si
the Church of Antioch and th
to be preserved.

It is clear from this canon th
mind still another accommoda
pire, namely, that of dioceses
provinces and was administere
the title of Exarch. Canon VI n
of Italy, Egypt, and the East, wi
andria, and Antioch. These thre
portant administrative units of
especially Egypt, they intended to
andria possessed the same rights as
ordination of all the bishops of the
tion of the rights of metropolitans. F
clear. In the diocese of Italy, the B
in fact, a direct jurisdiction over all
ing obliged to pass through the metr
that it be so in view of the intimate re
tween Rome and the cities of the dio
only considered as *municipia*, whereas
the City. The tenor of the canon also
these rights of the bishop of Rome to
that there was no need to give them any

The case of Egypt seems to have been
Thanks to the immense prestige which
quired over the other cities of Egypt du
period—a prestige which had increased
domination—it was quite normal for the b
to claim a dominant position in the religious
try. It was under the direction of the bisho
that Christianity had spread in Egypt and so

It also seems that Canon VI in its primitive form did not have in view these dioceses but rather the metropolitans of the eparchies, or provinces.[14] If this interpretation is correct, the Fathers were prepared to confirm exclusively the rights of Rome and Alexandria and partially those of Antioch but they did not seem inclined to favor the extension of this practice to other dioceses lest they seem to deny the rights of metropolitans guaranteed by Canon IV.

Despite this precaution, the ecclesiastical organization adapted itself more and more to the division of the Empire into dioceses and the canon mentioned seems to have speeded this evolution. Canon VI, voted by the Second ecumenical Council at Constantinople in 381, seems to confirm this impression. It reads as follows:[15]

According to the canons the Bishop of Alexandria must limit himself to the administration of Egypt and the bishops of the East should only rule over the East—provided that the rights of the Church of Antioch, as noted in the Canons of Nicaea, are respected —and the bishops of the dioceses of Asia, Pontus and of Thrace should respectively, restrict themselves to the administration of their dioceses.

This canon, which makes clear what the Fathers of Nicaea had in mind in the canons they approved, shows also clearly that the Fathers of Constantinople were determined that the organization of the Church should adapt itself to the political division of the Empire. Canon VI of the same council which ruled on the right of appeal of a bishop condemned by a Synod of his province, confirms this impression, since it permitted him an appeal to a larger Synod, composed of the bishops of the diocese of the civil administration of which the province formed a part.

Because of a lack of documentary information it is unfortunately not possible to follow in more detailed fashion the development of the ecclesiastical organization of the East. Nevertheless, it is altogether evident that the Councils of

Nicaea and Constantinople provided a canonical base for the development of a suprametropolitan organization coincident with the division of the Empire into dioceses, an organization which found its culmination in the erection of patriarchates. The Exarchs of the dioceses—this title is often given to the bishops of the diocesan capitals—became Patriarchs. The result would have been that Ephesus, Caesarea in Cappadocia and Heracleia would have become the see of a patriarch since these cities were capitals of the diocese of Asia, Pontus and Thrace; Constantinople, however, brought this evolution to an end by assuming supreme jurisdiction over all three dioceses.

In the East, this organizational structure was accepted without any difficulty. St. Jerome, in a letter written in 396 or 397,[16] violently reproached the Bishop of Jerusalem for having addressed himself to the Bishop of Alexandria on a matter concerning his diocese instead of directing this appeal to the Bishop of Antioch. This shows very well that the metropolitan and suprametropolitan organization was generally accepted in the East.

* * *

We have seen that the principle of accommodation to the political division of the Empire was also accepted in Rome. And there is something more. When the civil diocese of Italy was divided in two as a result of the organization ordained by Diocletian, Milan became the capital of the diocese of *Italia annonaria* which comprised all of the north of Italy and the Bishop of Milan then assumed direct jurisdiction over all the provinces of the new diocese. The direct jurisdiction of the Bishop of Rome was limited to the provinces known as suburbicarian.[17] Rome seems to have accepted this situation without protest because it agreed with the principle of accommodation to the division of the Empire. At the same time the changes which took place in the political status of Illyricum caused the erection of a Roman vicariate in Thessalonica. When the primatum habeant ecclesiae civitatum ampliorum." See, C. H. Turner, *Ecclesiae occidentalis Monumenta iuris antiquissima* (Oxford, 1899), I, 121. For details, see *The Idea of Apostolicity*, 15ff.

15. Mansi, 3, 560.
16. PL, 23, 407A.
17. Cf. F. Lanzoni, "Le diocesi d'Italia dalle origini al principio del secolo VII," *Studi e testi*, 35 (1927) 1016ff.; P. Batiffol, *Cathedra Petri* (Paris, 1938), 43.
18. See the recent bibliography on the problem of papal jurisdiction in Illyricum, in my book, *The Idea of Apostolicity*, 25-30. Also, on Illyricum, see my *Les légendes de Constantin et de Methode vues de Byzance* (Prague, 1933), 248-83.
19. H. Leclercq, *L'Afrique chrétienne* (Paris, 1904) and R. Höslinger, *Die alte africanische Kirche* (Vienna, 1935).
20. H. Leclercq, *L'Espagne chrétienne* (Paris, 1906); E. Magnin, *L'Église wisigothique au VIIe siècle* (Paris, 1912).
21. For more details, see L. Duchesne, *Fastes episcopaux de l'ancienne Gaule*, 2nd. edit. (Paris, 1907-15), I, 86-146 and H. Leclercq, "Gallicane (Église)" in DACL, vol. 6, 395-403.

THE PRINCIPLE

OF APOSTOLICITY

IT IS NECESSARY to point out that in Africa, Gaul, and Spain, Rome gained a very considerable prestige from the earliest days of the Christianization of these provinces. To be sure, the reason for this was first, that the first missionaries to these countries were, for the most part, priests sent by Rome. Quite naturally, this prestige was enhanced by the fact that Rome was then the imperial residence and the capital of the Empire. Nor must we forget that the young churches of these countries had also a great veneration for St. Peter, the founder of the episcopal see of Rome, and for the bishops of Rome who were his successors.

It is quite possible that the bishops of Rome up until the fourth century drew sufficient authority and prestige from the fact that their residence was in the capital of the Empire. Thus it was unnecessary to invoke, in each case, the Petrine origin of their see. The idea that the Apostles were, above all others, the teachers and masters sent by the Lord to preach the Gospel throughout the world was equally well rooted in Rome as it was universally accepted in the East. It is for this reason that the first Christians were not accustomed to designate an Apostle as the first bishop of the see where he had implanted the faith. The one who was considered the first bishop was the one who had been ordained by an Apostle.

This custom was equally the practice in Rome. This becomes clear from the first list of the Roman Bishops which was composed by Irenaeus, Bishop of Lyons, who died as a martyr in 202. Irenaeus attributed the foundation of the Church of Rome not only to Peter but also to Paul and he wrote:[1]

After having founded and established the Church, the holy Apostles confided to Linus the charge of the episcopate . . . his successor was Anacletus and after him, in the third place from the time of the Apostles, the episcopate was entrusted to Clement, who had seen the Apostles. Clement's successor was Evaristus and Evaristus was followed by Alexander. Then as the sixth bishop after the time of the Apostles there was Sixtus and after him, Telesphorus, famous for his martyrdom. In turn there was Hyginus, Pius and Anicetus. Soter succeeded Anicetus and was followed by Eleutherius who, at the present time, occupies the episcopal see as the twelfth bishop since the time of the Apostles.

According to this list it is clear that the Bishop of Lyons did not count Peter among the number of the bishops of Rome. It is possible that Irenaeus had used as his source the list of Hegesippus which was older; all the same, it is possible that Hippolytus of Rome made use of the list of Irenaeus. In this regard, the fashion in which Eusebius, in his *Historia ecclesiastica,* treats the question of the apostolic succession in the cities whose sees had been founded by the Apostles is particularly instructive. He attributes the foundation of the bishopric of Rome to St. Peter and to St. Paul, of Alexandria to St. Mark, and of Antioch to St. Peter, but he does not put the Apostles at the head of the list of bishops of these cities.[2] For him the first bishop of Rome was Linus, the first of Alexandria Annianus and the first bishop of Antioch was Evodius.

*   *   *

The Petrine origin of the see of Rome, however, was not forgotten. Tertullian[3] is the first to make use of Matt., 16.18-19 to prove that Peter was the foundation of the Church, the possessor of the Keys of the Kingdom of Heaven and of the power to bind and to loose. The opinion according to which Callistus (217-222) was the first Pope to make use of the text of Matthew to prove that he was the heir of the power of Peter cannot be authenticated. As for the testimony of Tertullian which is often cited, it is not clear and it should be used with caution.[4] What is certain in any case is that the passage of Matt. 16.18-19 was in current use at the beginning of the third century.

It is quite possible that the transfer of the imperial residence to the East at the beginning of the fourth century contributed to speeding the development of the Petrine idea in Rome. The catalogue of Liberius, in the year 354, attests that the primitive tradition concerning the origin of Roman Christianity had already been abandoned at this time. The catalogue attributes the foundation of the Roman Church to Peter alone and places him at the head of the list of the bishops of Rome. It is possible that Eusebius was aware of this shift in the Roman tradition since in his *Chronicon* which is later than his *History*, he speaks of Peter alone as the founder of the Church of Rome.

In the Western Church it was St. Cyprian who contributed most to the removal of the distinction between the character of an Apostle and that of a bishop. He asserted that the powers of the bishop were identical with those of the Apostles.[5] Besides, he designated Rome as the "cathedra Petri" and ecclesia principalis," [6] declaring that the unity of the Church rested upon the investiture given to Peter by Our Lord.

Such categorical declarations coming from a Father who was not a Roman and who enjoyed great prestige throughout all of Western Christendom could not help but make the West forget the distinction between the functions of an apostle and a bishop. In the fourth century the ancient custom of attributing the foundation of the Church at Rome to Peter and to Paul disappeared completely. Optatus,[7] Jerome,[8] and Augustine[9] mentioned Peter alone as the founder of the Church of Rome and as the first bishop of that city.

Beginning with the second half of the fourth century the see of Rome was simply called the see of Peter. Very important for this point of view is the Synod of Sardica which invited priests to appeal to the bishop of Rome "in order to pay honor to the holy memory of the apostle Peter." [10] From then on, it is not surprising that beginning with Liberius and Damasus the Popes adopted for their see a new title, namely the *sedes apostolica*. This new title soon became very popular in all the churches of the West, in Spain, Africa, and in Gaul. They went even further in this veneration paid to Peter in attributing, in the fifth century, the origin of the episcopate to St. Peter alone. It was only in the sixth century that this exaggerated tendency disappeared.[11]

This development is easy to explain. In the West there was only one see—Rome—that could claim apostolic foundation. In vain did Arles try to take advantage of the situation by creating the legend that its first bishop, Trophimus, had been consecrated by Peter in Rome and sent to Arles. According to another tradition that is equally legendary, Sirmium claimed that its first bishop, St. Andronicus, had been one of the seventy disciples of the Lord. It seems that this city had been, during the first half of the fifth century, the residence of the prefect of Illyricum. But the invasion of the Huns brought to a sudden end all these ambitions. Sirmium was destroyed in 448 and only a feeble glimmer of its ancient glory remained.[12] The see of Rome was left as the only city of the West that could boast apostolic origin: it had been founded by the first of the Apostles, Peter.

* * *

But the question of the apostolic character of a see was viewed in quite different fashion in the East. There had been many important sees in the East which had been founded by an Apostle: this was the case for Jerusalem, Antioch, Alexandria and Ephesus. Apart from these great sees, there was a large number of other less important ones in Asia Minor and in Greece which, according to both authentic and apocryphal writings, had at least been visited by an Apostle. For this reason the principle of apostolic origin never took very deep root in the ecclesiastical organization of the East and the principle of accommodation to the political divisions of the Empire remained always preponderant.

It is in this light that we must examine Canon III of the Council of Constantinople, in 381, which gave to the Bishop of Constantinople the second rank in the ecclesiatical hierarchy.

For the Orientals this promotion was altogether natural granted the change that had taken place in the political organization of the Empire. The new capital of the Empire, the residence of the Emperor, could not remain subordinate to the metropolitan of the diocese of Thrace, Heracleia. When Constantinople became the New Rome, it acquired the right of occupying a place immediately after Rome, the ancient capital of the Empire.

It is generally believed that the reaction of Rome to this decision was manifested immediately and with considerable force. But actually this did not happen until 451 when the Council of Chalcedon not only ratified the decision of the Council of 381, but also placed under the jurisdiction of Constantinople three civil dioceses of Asia Minor and Europe, those of Thrace, Asia, and Pontus. After 381 we look in vain for a declaration from Rome which could be considered as a protest against the elevation of Constantinople in spite of the fact that Canon III had certainly been known in Rome in the autumn of 381.[13]

How are we to explain this development? We must not forget first of all that the Council of 381 did not have, at the beginning, an ecumenical character. It had been convoked by Theodosius the Great to handle the affairs of the Church of the East and only the bishops of that part of the Empire had been invited to attend. Canon III had as its object, in the first place, to reduce the undue influence which the Bishop of Alexandria had assumed in the East. Peter of Alexandria, then the first among the Oriental prelates, had extended his influence not only to Antioch where he supported Paulinus, a bishop of his own choice, against the legitimate bishop, Meletius,[14] but also at Constantinople where instead of St. Gregory of Nazianzus, he put forward Maximus the philosopher who had been secretly ordained by Egyptian bishops Peter had sent to Constantinople.

If we take account of all of this we see clearly that Canon III was in no sense voted in order to weaken the prestige of Rome but only with a view to lessening the presige of Alexandria in the Church in the East.[15] Since there was no question of doing anything but bringing about conformity to a practice that had been universally recognized as regular, this measure met with no opposition in the East and Timothy, the brother and successor of Peter in the see of Alexandria, willingly ceded the first place in the Church in the East, and the second in the entire Church to the Bishop of Constantinople and he signed the Acts of the Council in 381.

The very fact that information about this canon was not communicated to the Church in the western part of the Empire[16] is clear proof that, although it entered into the domain of ecclesiastical legislation, it was in no sense directed against Rome, and that it was only intended to straighten out affairs in the Church of the East. In the minds of the Orientals this canon did not infringe the rights of Rome which remained the first see in the ecclesiastical hierarchy. It had no other purpose but to regulate internal affairs in the eastern part of the Empire in adapting the ecclesiastical organization to the new political arrangements.

Nevertheless, this desire to run its own affairs reveals for the first time—and this fact must be stressed—a particularist spirit in the Church in the East. Unfortunately the attitude taken by the Church in the West only served to confirm the Orientals in this disposition.

Bishop Paulinus of Antioch had addressed himself to a Synod of the Church of the West which was being held at Aquileia in the same year as the Council of Constantinople. At the instigation of St. Ambrose, Metropolitan of Milan, the Synod sent a letter to the Emperor demanding that he convoke a council to deal with the schism of Antioch.

Maximus was expelled from Constantinople and he presented himself at Aquileia and, unfortunately, succeeded in persuading St. Ambrose and the Synod that he was the legitimate Bishop of Constantinople and that he had been unjustly deposed by the Council meeting in the capital. Ambrose and the bishops of the north of Italy were angered by the false rumors concerning the new Bishop of Constantinople, Nectarius, and they believed the assertions of Maximus. Ambrose in a letter addressed to the Emperor complained that the ecclesiastical affairs of two great sees, Antioch and Constantinople, had been dealt with without consulting the Church in the West and he demanded the convocation of a council at Rome to examine these disputes. The Emperor and the Oriental bishops, if one can judge from the second letter of Ambrose to Theodosius,[17] were annoyed at this intrusion of the Westerners into their internal affairs, especially since they had already been dealt with by a Synod. The Emperor refused to convoke a general council and the bishops of the East, invited by Ambrose to a Synod at Rome, responded in a very polite letter[18] in which they categorically declared that they were quite capable of running the internal affairs of their own Church in conformity with the canons.

The tenor of this letter shows clearly that the Orientals were determined to run their own internal affairs without intervention from any other Church and this also confirms our interpretation according to which the canons voted by the council concerned solely the Church of the East. Unfortunately, the mistake committed by St. Ambrose and his bishops in accepting a bishop who had been installed by fraud, unworthy of this office by reason of his private life, and canonically deposed by a synod of his Church, could not help but strengthen the bishops of the East in their isolationist sentiments and in their determination to defend the autonomy of their Church in anything that concerned its administration. This incident shows how difficult it was for the West to come to any exact idea of affairs in the East.

Since at this time the principle of accommodation to the political divisions of the Empire was still agreed to in the West, the promotion of Constantinople to the second rank in the hierarchy was passively accepted. This was facilitated by the fact that the canon did not give Byzantium anything but a precedence in honor, without expressly increasing the extent of its jurisdiction. In 381 no one could foresee what was going to happen in the future.

For this reason Pope Damasus offered no protest against the elevation of Constantinople even though Alexandria had always been, in the past, in close contact with Rome. This event, which has often been considered the first conflict between Rome and Byzantium, actually took place in an altogether friendly atmosphere. Everyone continued to regard the Bishop of Rome as the first bishop of the Empire, the head of the Church.[19]

* * *

The conflict between Byzantium and Rome which arose in 451, during the Council of Chalcedon, appeared to be much more serious. We know that the Fathers of the Council had voted in the absence of the Roman legates, the famous Canon XXVIII which not only confirmed the precedence of the bishop of the capital over Alexandria and Antioch but also placed under his jurisdiction the three dioceses of Thrace, Asia and Pontus as well as the territories which, in the future, might be acquired by their missionaries.

The legates, on learning what had taken place, protested vigorously against the vote on this canon. We know that Pope Leo I refused to sanction this innovation and in his letters objected categorically to the promotion of Constantinople to the second place in the hierarchy.[20] Attempts have often been made to see the vote on this canon as an attack directed against the Primacy of the Bishop of Rome and this opinion seems to be confirmed by the hostile attitude of Leo I. But is this explanation correct? Did the Fathers of Chalcedon really have the intention, in elevating the Bishop of Constantinople, to deprive the Bishop of Rome of his privileged position?

To give a satisfactory reply to this question and to explain the attitude of the Fathers of Chalcedon we must examine once again what had happened in the Church of the East since 381. Even though the bishops of Alexandria had accepted the decisions of this Council, they had not, in fact, abandoned their claims to predominance in the East. Everything that happened in the Church in the East from the fourth to the middle of the fifth century finds its explanation in the rivalry between the sees of Alexandria and Byzantium and the claim of Alexandria to the first place.

The position of Egypt in the East remained very powerful; its importance as the wheat basket for the two capitals, Rome and Byzantium, had the effect of enhancing the prestige which the Bishop of Alexandria enjoyed at the court. He also had at his disposal enormous riches since the heavy endowments of the pagan temples had been put at his disposal. The Bishop had always found fanatical partisans of his religious policy among the monks whose numbers had continued to increase since the foundation of the first monastic community in Egypt. He also benefitted from the great reputation which St. Athanasius of Alexandria had acquired in the East because of his intrepid struggle against Arianism, a heresy condemned at Nicaea.

Timothy, bishop of Alexandria, who had signed Canon III of the second council had already found an occasion for revenge; he took part in an intrigue which forced St. Gregory of Nazianzus, Bishop of Constantinople, to resign from his see.

Shortly after 381, Bishop Theophilus of Alexandria (385-412) used every possible means at his disposal and all his riches to frustrate the Bishop of Constantinople, St. John Chrysostom.[21] He obtained from the Emperor a decree which seriously humiliated the see of that city, and Chrysostom, who was at odds with the Emperor, was unjustly deposed and sent into exile.

The triumph achieved by St. Cyril of Alexandria (412-444) was even greater. It was due to his intercession that Nestorius of Constantinople was accused of heresy and condemned by the Council of Ephesus (431), deposed, and sent into exile. This was a great victory for Alexandria. We know that Cyril used every means to accomplish his purpose, even to sending rich gifts in order to win the favor of high functionaries at the court.[22] This struggle between Constantinople and Alexandria would appear in an even clearer light if the theologians who today defend the orthodoxy of Nestorius should turn out to be correct.[23]

The successor of Cyril, Dioscorus, thought to achieve an even more definitive victory than his predecessor in the struggle to impose the Monophysite doctrine on the entire Christian world. This doctrine was confirmed at the Second Council which met at Ephesus in 449, thanks to the support which Dioscorus was able to muster at the court. At this council the Bishop of Alexandria occupied the first place, the legates of Rome had the second, Jerusalem the third, Antioch the fourth and Constantinople only the fifth place. Dioscorus achieved his victory by means of tactics which hardly do him honor. Flavian, Bishop of Constantinople, died a few days later as a result of wounds received at Ephesus at the hands of the fanatical partisans of Dioscorus. The Synod of Ephesus was in all justice called thereafter the *Latrocinium* (Robbery). But, at the time, it seemed a victory for Alexandria over the other patriarchial sees, and particularly over Constantinople. The Coptic biography of Dioscorus shows that it was his ambition to place himself above all the patriarchs, since he seemed to have conceived the idea of pretending that St. Mark was superior to St. Peter.[24] In vain did Pope Leo endeavor to turn Dioscorus to a better path. In vain did he invoke the relationship which existed between the two sees by the fact of their connection with St. Peter. As long as the Emperor Theodosius II refused to convoke another council, Dioscorus was successful. It was only after the death of Theodosius II that the Pope obtained from his successor Marcion, with the intervention of the Empress Pulcheria, the convocation of a new council at Chalcedon.[25]

Taking all this into account we can then understand why the Oriental prelates wished to take advantage of the chance to put Alexandria back in its true place and to enhance the prestige of Constantinople in the East. Therefore, Canon XXVIII was essentially directed against Alexandria and the pretensions of its powerful patriarchs. It is important also to remember the predominant role which Pope Leo played in the council through the intermediary of his legates and the prestige which he had acquired among the Orientals, by reason of his efforts in the convocation of the council, and for his determined and courageous defense of the true doctrine. His letter to the Patriarch Flavian in which he explained the doctrine on the Trinity was read in the council and was declared a monument of orthodoxy. The atmosphere of the council was therefore not at all unfavorable to Rome, quite the contrary. This also shows once more that the Fathers, in voting on canon XXVIII had in view, above all, Alexandria.

That being the case, why was the Pope so alarmed by the vote of this canon? It seems that he shared the idea that Constantinople ought to have a pre-eminence of honor because he was also quite familiar with the principle of accommodation. His legates had not protested at all against Canon XVII which established that the Church should adapt itself, each time a change took place in the civil organization of the provinces and in particular when a new city was founded.[26] This canon was among those which Rome approved. The legates likewise had not protested against Canon IX which stipulated that the clerics of other patriarchs could appeal a judgment of their metropolitan, either to the judgment of their Exarch or to that of the Bishop of Constantinople. This was a new privilege accorded to Constantinople, a privilege confirmed by Canon XVII, mentioned above. Even though this privilege was a considerable one it did not, in the eyes of the legates, seem to change the status of Constantinople in any essential way.

The submission of three civil dioceses to the jurisdiction of the Bishop of Constantinople, however, raised it to a position without parallel in the East.[27] The legates of the Pope saw in that a danger for the unity of the Church and also, in the future, for the Primacy of Rome and that all the more, since the bishop of the capital could easily obtain the support of the emperors.

*　　*　　*

What bothered the Pope was that there was no mention in the canon of the apostolic and Petrine character of the see of Rome. The new measure was based solely on the principle of accommodation. By this time, Rome had already lost the prestige which it had once enjoyed as the capital of the Empire and the residence of the Emperor, and its bishops could thereafter base their privileged position in the Church only on the apostolic and Petrine character of their see. Leo was very conscious of this and he stressed the apostolicity of his see in his letters to the Emperor; at the council his legates insisted on every occasion on being recognized as the envoys of the Apostolic See.[28] The fact that the Oriental Fathers had asserted the elevation of Constantinople only on political grounds and their failure to mention the Petrine and apostolic character of the see of Rome appeared, in the eyes of Leo, to be full of danger.

Unfortunately, the Oriental Fathers were unable to grasp the significance of the apostolic origin of a see in the organization of the Church. They were much more under the influence of the old principle of accommodation. Nevertheless, they had not the slightest intention of denying the Primacy to Rome, and their attitude during the last session of the Council proves this. In fact, the legates, citing Canon VI of Nicaea, made use of an old Latin translation which was preceded by the declaration: "Romana Ecclesia semper habuit primatum." [29] This declaration was not found in the Greek original of the canon. The original Greek version was also read in the course of this same last session, thus the prelates were perfectly aware then that the Latins had inserted an addition to the canon in order to stress the prestige of Rome, but not one of them protested against this addition. Still, the fact that the Emperor, the Patriarch of Constantinople, and the Fathers of the Council all sought from the Pope the acceptance of this canon clearly shows that they did not see it as any diminution of the position which the Pope occupied in the Church.[30]

It is possible that they finally came to understand the reason why the Pope showed himself hostile to this canon for, in their letters, they stressed the apostolic character of the see of Rome. These assurances did not appear sufficient to Leo. The apostolic character of Rome should have been mentioned in the canon itself. If it had been done, it would have been difficult for the Pope to refuse his approval.

Because of this omission, the Pope set up in opposition to the principle of adaptation to the political divisions of the Empire, the principle of the apostolic and Petrine origin of a see. Rome held the Primacy not because it had been the capital of the Empire and the residence of the Emperor, but because its see had been founded by Peter, the Prince of the Apostles. The second place in the Church belonged to Alexandria because its see had been founded by Mark, the disciple of Peter. The third place fell to Antioch, because Peter had preached there, and his disciples in the new faith had there for the first time received the name of "Christians." Further, said Leo, the decision of Chalcedon is a contradiction of that of Nicaea, since the Fathers of this first council only recognized three principle sees, Rome, Alexandria, and Antioch.

The Pope did not advert to the fact that his argumentation contained one weak point. As a matter of fact, according to the theory of apostolic origin, Antioch should have held the second place because Peter founded a bishopric there. Besides, Canon VI of Nicaea had very much as its foundation the principle of accommodation to the political situation of the Empire and further, the Pope in his desire to introduce in the ecclesiastical organization the principle of apostolicity forgot that it was really the principle of accommodation which, in the eyes of the Byzantines, continued to assure to Rome the primacy in the Church. The Byzantine Empire, in fact, was the continuation of the Roman Empire. The Byzantines did not call themselves Hellenes or Greeks, but *Romaioi* (i.e., Romans). Rome remained the base of their Empire and in their eyes the ancient capital was always the "Imperial City." This is the title which many of the Oriental bishops gave to Rome when they spoke at the Council of Chalcedon.[31] Because of this "Roman ideology" it was not possible that the Byzantines could ever bring themselves to deprive Rome and its bishop of the privileged position which the city occupied in the life and in the political ideology of the Empire, and its bishop in the ecclesiastical hierarchy. They would never have dreamed of transferring the Primacy of Rome to any other city for this would have destroyed the base on which their Empire was established.

Bishop Julian of Cos, who represented Pope Leo at Constantinople, understood this situation very well and he suggested that the Pope accept the contested canon.[32] This could have been done in a letter in which the Pope would have declared that the apostolic and Petrine character of Rome was its sole source for the Primacy in the Church. If we take into account the friendly attitude of the Fathers of the Council toward the Pope, such a declaration would certainly have been accepted by them without any difficulty.

But Leo judged otherwise and he believed, for the moment at least, that he had won the victory. Because of his opposition Canon XXVIII was not introduced into the official canonical collections. It only appeared in the sixth century in the *Syntagma of fourteen titles*.[33] Therefore, the first misunderstanding between the Church of the East and the Church of the West had as its cause the opposition of two different principles of organization of the Church: the principle of accommodation to the political division of the Empire and the principle of the apostolic and Petrine origin of an episcopal see. The Fathers who gathered at Chalcedon did not succeed in finding a compromise between these two principles. This was regrettable, for despite the apparent victory of Pope Leo, Constantinople continued to exercise its jurisdiction over the three minor dioceses of the Empire. The patriarchs of Alexandria and Antioch were weakened by the expansion of Nestorianism and Monophysitism; also, the Patriarch of Constantinople had become *de facto*, the most important and the one that exercised the greatest influence throughout the Christian East.

It was the new Monophysite crisis, started in Alexandria, which had the effect of bringing together the Patriarch Anatolius and Pope Leo. The Patriarch, Timothy of Alexandria, discontented with the decisions taken at Chalcedon, called for the convocation of a new council. The Pope was opposed to this because he feared lest the decisions of Chalcedon be called into question. He found an ally in the person of the Patriarch of Constantinople who, on his part, feared a new protest on the part of the Pope against Canon XXVIII, a protest which would certainly find support from the Patriarch of Alexandria. Therefore a new council was not convoked, but Rome lost the support of Alexandria and Antioch in its rivalry with Constantinople.

NOTES

1. Irenaeus, *Adversus haereses*, PG 7, 849ff. The most important work on the lists of bishops of Rome is that of E. Caspar, "Die älteste römische Bischofsliste," in *Schriften der Königsberger gelehrten Gesellschaft*, Geisteswiss. Kl. 4 (1926), 206ff.
2. Eusebius, *Historia ecclesiastica*, III, ch. 2, 15, 21; PG 20, 216, 249 and 256.
3. Tertullian, *De praescriptione haereticorum*, CSEL (Vienna, 1942) vol. 70, 26.
4. Cf. J. Ludwig, *Die Primatworte Mat. 16, 18-19 in der altkirchlichen Exegese* (Muenster, 1952), 11-20; C. B. Daly, "The Edict of Callistus," in *Studie patristica*, vol. 3 (Berlin, 1961), in Texte und Untersuchungen, vol. 78, 176-182. It seems that Tertullian's attack was directed against the Bishop of Carthage, Agrippinus. Hippolytus, who seems to mention an edict of Callistus, does not cite Matt., 16, 18-19 (*Refutatio*, IX, 12, 20ff., GCS [Berlin, 1916] vol. 3, 249ff).
5. The most characteristic passages are to be found in the following writings of St. Cyprian: *Letters* 3, 43, 66 and 67 (CSEL, vol. 3, Edit. Hartel) pp. 471, 594, 729, 738; *De unitate ecclesiae, ibid.* 212-13.
6. *Letter 59. ibid.* 683. Cf. Th. Camelot, "Saint Cyprien et la Primauté," in *Istina* (1957), 421-34 and especially, M. Maccarrone, "Cathedra Petri und päpstlicher Primat vom 2 bis 4 Jahrhundert," in *Saeculum*, 13 (1962) 278-92.
7. *Libri septem*, CSEL, vol. 26, Edit. C. Ziwsa, 36.
8. *De viris illustribus*, PL 23, 663-66.
9. *Letter 53*, PL 33, 196; CSEL, vol. 34, 153ff.
10. Mansi, 3, 23. The example of Palladius of Ratiaria shows, however, that the prestige of the Roman see did not pass uncontested. Although he called Rome an apostolic see, after his condemnation by the Synod of Aquileia, in 381, he declared that the see of Peter was the equal of all the other sees. On this, see L. Saltet, "Un texte nouveau: La *Dissertatio Maximi contra Ambrosium*," in the *Bulletin de littérature ecclésiastique*, series, 2 (Toulouse, 1900), 118-29.

11. See the documentation in Batiffol, *Cathedra Petri*, esp. 95-103.
12. On Sirmium, see my book, *Les légendes de Constantin et de Methode*, 251ff. The city had disappeared completely by 582, after its destruction by the Avars.
13. For more details, see my *The Idea of Apostolicity*, 50ff. According to the *Chronicon paschale* (Edit. B. G. Nieburg, Corpus Scriptorum Historiae Byzantinae, Bonn, 1832), Constantine had already made Constantinople independent of the jurisdiction of its metropolitan of Heraclea. If that is the fact, it was done in virtue of the principle of accommodation.
14. On this local schism and its consequences, see the study of F. Cavallera, *Le schisme d'Antioch* (Paris, 1905).
15. See also, I. Ortiz de Urbina, *Nicée et Constantinople* (Paris, 1963), 216ff. (Histoire des Conciles oecuméniques, edit. G. Dumeige, vol. I).
16. This we learn from a declaration of Pope Leo the Great in his letter to Anatolius, Patriarch of Constantinople. Mansi, 6, 204.; edit. E. Schwartz, II, vol. 4, 61.
17. See these letters in the correspondence of Ambrose, *Epistolae*, 12, 13, 14. PL 16, 987ff., 993ff.
18. This letter is preserved to us in the *Historia ecclesiastica* of Theodoretus, edit. L. Parmentier, GCS, 19 (1911) 289ff.; Mansi, 3, 581-88.
19. It has been believed that the passage relating to the patriarchal sees which is found in the third part of the famous *Decretum Gelasianum* had been voted in 382 by the Council of Rome in order to protest against Canon III of the Council of Constantinople. This passage of the *Decretum* grants the second place in the hierarchy to Alexandria and the third to Antioch because of the connection these sees had with St. Peter. It is now generally recognized that this document was composed at the end of the fifth century. For more details, see P. Batiffol, *Le Siège apostolique*, 146-150. H. Marot ("Les conciles romains des IVe et Ve siècles et le développement de la primauté," in *Istina* [1957] 458) is wrong in tracing this canon back to the Synod of 382. Cf. my remarks in the next chapter, on this canon.
20. See especially Letters 104, 105 and 106 to the Emperor Marcion, to the Empress Pulcheria and to the Patriarch Anatolius. PL 54, 994-1009; Mansi, 6, 182-207.

21. The best brief account of these intrigues is to be found in N. H. Baynes, "Alexandria and Constantinople: A Study in Ecclesiastical Diplomacy," in *The Journal of Egyptian Archeology*, 12 (1926), 145-56. This paper has been re-edited in his *Byzantine Studies and Other Essays* (London, 1955), 97-115. Cf. also G. Bardy, "Alexandrie, Rome, Constantinople," in *L'Église et les Églises* (Chevetogne, 1954), I, 183-207, and H. Marot, *op. cit.*, n. 19, *supra*, 209-40.

22. For greater detail, see P. Batiffol, "Les presents de S. Cyrille à la cour de Constantinople," in *Études de liturgie et d'archéologie chrétiennes* (Paris, 1919), 154-79.

23. On this topic see the study of M. V. Anastos, "Nestorius was Orthodox," in *Dumbarton Oaks Papers*, 16 (1962), 117-40.

24. Cf. F. Haase, "Patriarch Dioskur I nach monophysitischen Quellen," in M. Sdralek, *Kirchengeschichtliche Abhandlungen*, 6 (1908), 204.

25. On the relations of Pope St. Leo with the Emperor, see P. Stockmeier, *Leo I. des Grossen Beurteilung der kaiserlichen Religionspolitik*, Münchener theol. Studien, Hist. Abt. vol. 14 (1959), 75-168. Cf. also the recent article of W. Ullmann, "Leo I and the Theme of Papal Primacy," in the *Journal of Theological Studies*, N.S. 11 (1960), 25-51.

26. During the first session of the Council, the legate Paschasinus, on learning that at the "Robber Synod" the bishop of Constantinople had been relegated to the last place, declared: "For our part, we believe Anatolius [of Constantinople] to be the first." At that, the Bishop of Cyzicum replied: "Yes, because you know the canons" (Mansi, 6, 608B). He was referring to the canons of Constantinople, 381.

27. Cf. Th. Camelot, *Éphèse et Chalcédoine* (Paris, 1963), 161ff. (Histoire des conciles oecuméniques, edit. G. Dumeige, vol. 2).

28. For greater detail, see *The Idea of Apostolicity*, 75ff.

29. Cf. C. H. Turner, *op. cit.*, ch. 2, n. 14, *supra*, I, 103, 121. See also, S. Schwartz, "Der sechste nicänische Kanon auf der Synode von Chalkedon," in *Sitzungsb. Preussichen Akad.* phil. hist. K1. (Berlin, 1930).

30. The majority of specialists recognize the fact that the canon in question does not deny the Primacy of Rome. On this point, see the well-documented study of E. Hermann, "Chalkedon und

die Ausgestaltung des Konstantinopolitanischen Primats," in the symposium *Das Konzil von Chalkedon*, edited by A. Grillmeier and H. Bacht (Würzburg, 1953), II, 459-90. See also, M. Jugie, *Le schisme byzantin* (Paris, 1941), 11-19 and J. Meyendorff, "La primauté romaine dans la tradition canonique jusq'au Concile de Chalcédoine," in *Istina* (1959), 463-82.

31. For example, during the second session, the senators Maximus of Antioch and Theodore of Claudiopolis, Mansi, 6, 960C, 1048D, 1080B; *Ibid.* 7, 12B, (Edit. E. Schwartz, II, vol. 3, part 1, p. 81; part 2, pp. 47, 71; II, vol. 1, part 2, p. 94.

32. This seems to be confirmed by a letter of the Pope to Julian; Mansi, 6, 207, letter 107.

33. Published by V. N. Beneševič, *Kanoničeskij Sbornik XIV titulov* (St. Petersburg, 1903), 155. For a history of the application of the Petrine principle by the papacy, see A. Michel, "Der Kampf um das politische oder Petrinische Prinzip der Kirchenführung," in *Das Konzil von Chalkedon* (cf. n. 30, *supra*) I, 491-562.

THE SCHISM OF ACACIUS

IT IS POSSIBLE that the collaboration beween Pope and Patriarch would have resulted in a compromise on Canon XXVIII if it had only lasted longer. Unfortunately, the period of good relations came to an end when a new conflict, called the Schism of Acacius, arose which lasted from 484 until 519. The Patriarch Acacius had accepted the decree of the Emperor Zeno, known as the *Henoticon*, issued in 482; this decree which aimed at reconciling the Monophysites by granting them some concessions, really weakened the dogmatic decisions of Chalcedon. Pope Felix refused the compromise and he excommunicated Acacius.

In the course of this controversy the idea of the apostolic and Petrine tradition was the most powerful weapon in the Roman arsenal. It was on this foundation that Pope Gelasius (492-496) developed his ideas on the plenitude of pontifical power. He not only repudiated Canon XXVIII of Chalcedon but in his struggle with the patriarch even refused to accord Constantinople the status of a metropolitan city.[1]

Taking advantage of the new political situation he boldly opposed himself to the Emperor Anastasius I (491-518). At this time, the Byzantine empire had been considerably weakened by the invasions of the Germans and the Huns. With the support of Theodoric, King of the Ostrogoths and Master of Italy, Gelasius denied the Emperor the right of intervention in religious affairs such as he claimed. Exalting the role of the priesthood, Gelasius placed it almost on the same level with the imperial power. His definition of the two powers has become classic:

Two powers govern the world: the sacred authority of the Pontiff and the imperial power. Of these two powers, the priests carry a weight that is all the more heavy in that at the last judgment they will have to render an account not only for themselves but also for the kings.[2]

It is probable that his contemporaries did not realize that the declarations of Gelasius marked a rupture with Christian Hellenism, with the political philosophy which had been accepted by all Christians since the conversion of Constantine. It is nonetheless true, however, that the words of Gelasius, as adopted by his successor Symmachus, helped the canonists of the eleventh century to develop a new political doctrine, that of the superiority of the spiritual power over the temporal, a doctrine which, without any doubt, caused the decline of the papacy at the end of the Middle Ages.

The Oriental patriarchs found the attitude of Gelasius much too rigid. The Pope complained, in his letters, that the Orientals accused him of arrogance, pride and obstinacy,[3] and controversial writings only served to exacerbate the mutual animosity. However, in spite of the bitterness which the attitude of Gelasius had stimulated in the minds of the Byzantine prelates, they were impressed by the arguments of the Pope. We notice in their replies to papal letters that they speak more often than formerly of the apostolic character of the Roman See. The principle of apostolicity so strongly stressed by Gelasius now began to take root in Byzantium.

*   *   *

It was Pope Hormisdas (514-523), who with the help of Justinian, the nephew of Justin—who was himself the successor of the Emperor Anastatius I—brought the schism to an end. We notice with considerable surprise that the Byzantine prelates, who had been so determined to defend the autonomy of their Church in the course of this controversy, all signed the *Libellus Hormisdae*, the document which defined clearly the primacy of the Roman see.[4] Here are the essential passages:

We cannot pass over in silence the affirmation of Our Lord Jesus Christ, Who said: "Thou art Peter, and upon this rock I will build my Church. . . ." These words are borne out by the facts: It is in the Apostolic See that the Catholic religion has always been preserved without stain . . . it is for this reason that I hope to achieve communion with the Apostolic See in which is found the entire, true, and perfect stability of the Christian religion.

These words were selected with the deliberate intention of instructing the Byzantine prelates, and therefore it is not at all surprising that the Patriarch John asked permission to precede his acceptance with a preface in which he attempted to place the see of Constantinople on the same level as that of Rome:[5]

I accept the fact that the two most holy Churches, that is to say, that of Ancient Rome and that of the New Rome, should be one; I admit that the see of St. Peter and that of the imperial city should be one.

We are here in the presence of one of the first efforts, made by a Patriarch of Constantinople, to reconcile the two principles, that of the apostolicity of a see and the accommodation to the political divisions of the Empire.

Another fact becomes clear from the correspondence between the Patriarch and Pope Hormisdas. In his first letter of September 7, 518,[6] the Patriarch John assured the Pope that he accepted the doctrine defined by the Councils of Nicaea, Constantinople, Ephesus and Chalcedon. We get the impression that the patriarch wished to bring the Pope to a formal recognition of the ecumenicity of the second council, that of 381. He likewise mentions the four councils in the preface to his confession which we have mentioned above and which he signed on March 28, 519. In his reply to the first letter the Pope speaks of the councils in general but mentions by name only that of Chalcedon;[7] in his second letter he makes no allusion whatever to the councils.[8] But while he expresses joy at the profession of faith of John, he passes over in silence the insistence of the Patriarch who spoke of the faith defined by the four ecumenical councils. From this we can conclude that the ecumenicity of the council of 381 had been, at least, tacitly, recognized by Rome. This appears to be confirmed by the fact that the Pope accepted the letters of Justinian,[9] those of the Bishop of Nicopolis[10] and of the Patriarch Epiphanius (520-536)[11] in which the council of 381 is counted among the four ecumenical councils.

This reconciliation with Constantinople caused Rome to forget the bitterness felt in the time of Gelasius and Symmachus. Without wishing to grant formal recognition to the status of Constantinople as holding the second place in the hierarchy, Rome was obliged to consider Constantinople as a major see, and, *de facto*, as the most important see after Rome.

*　　*　　*

It is possible that this acceptance of the ecumenicity of the second council provides us with the explanation of a curious anomaly. When we recall the opposition of Leo the Great to the elevation of Constantinople in the hierarchy of the Church and the statements of Gelasius and Symmachus which went so far as to refuse to rate Constantinople among the major sees, we are surprised to see that the first Latin canonical collection which has been preserved, the *Prisca*, also contains Canon III of the Council of Constantinople, the very one which granted to the see of the capital the second place in the

Church. There we read "[That] the Bishop of Constantinople has the primacy of honor after the Bishop of Rome, since we consider it to be the younger Rome." [12]

The author of this collection was Italian in origin and he made his compilation after the Council of Chalcedon, toward the end of the fifth century or in the first years of the sixth century.[13] It is interesting to notice that, at this time, the first ecumenical councils enjoyed such respect at Rome that the author of this collection felt obliged to insert all of their canons, forgetting that the time was not long past when Rome rejected the promotion of Constantinople.

The author of the *Prisca* made use of a Greek collection of conciliar decisions which contained the canons voted by both general and local councils.[14] His collection is older than that of Dionysius Exiguus. Dionysius, who was born in Scythia around 470, died at Rome in 550. He arrived there before 496 and it was there that he composed his three collections of conciliar canons, also making use of a Greek collection. Two of his collections have been preserved to us and in both of them we find the same canon of the Council of 381 on the privilege of the Bishop of Constantinople.[15]

The *Collectio Hispana*, the famous collection which Alexander III called "the authentic canonical collection of the Church of Spain," was composed before the Fourth Synod of Toledo (633), and it was during that Synod that it was completed.[16] Besides the conciliar canons it contained the decretals of the Popes from Damasus to Gregory the Great; to these had been added the decretals of other Popes, down to Leo II (682). Beginning with the ninth century this collection was called the *Isidoriana* and attributed to Isidore of Seville, who was born around 560 and died in 633. This attribution to Isidore is contested by the majority of specialists but we can accept the opinion according to which Isidore would have exercised an influence on its definitive edition.

The collection of conciliar canons which we find in the *Hispana* is founded on the *Dionysiana*. Hence it is not surpris-

ing that we also find, in the manuscripts of the *Hispana*, Canon
III of the Council of 381 expressed in the following fashion:
"Constantinopolitanae vere civitatis episcopum habere primatus
honorem post Romanum episcopum, propter quod sit nova
Roma." [17]

To explain the presence of Canon III in the collection of
Dionysius, M. Peitz has offered the hypothesis that the definitive reconciliation between Byzantium and Rome after the
Schism of Acacius only took place in 520-521, when the envoys
of the Patriarch Epiphanius were in Rome, as the bearers of a
letter of enthronement of a patriarch. From some declarations
of the Orientals he concluded that the Byzantines had recognized the supreme jurisdiction of Rome over Constantinople
and over the East and Rome, in recognition of this gesture, had
accepted Canon III of the Council of 381, recognizing at the
same time the ecumenicity of the Council provided the Byzantines would abandon Canon XXVIII of Chalcedon.[18]

Unfortunately, this very attractive explanation cannot be
accepted. The decisive objection against it is that we find
absolutely nothing on this matter in the contemporary sources.
The author himself is obliged to admit that no protocol was
composed on the negotiations held at Rome during the winter
of 520-521.[19] No document was prepared to be signed by the
two parties. This does not at all correspond to the traditions
of the pontifical chancery. Besides, after the experience of the
Schism of Acacius, Rome had every reason to be on its guard
against being satisfied by an oral promise in a matter so important. If there had been any agreement of this sort, if
Constantinople had been officially recognized as the second
patriarchal see, following immediately after Rome, how can we
explain that the thesis of Leo the Great, of Gelasius and of
Symmachus, which opposed this position of Constantinople in
the hierarchy, could be brought up again when a new tension
arose between East and West, as happened in the ninth century under Nicholas I and in the eleventh century under Leo
IX?

As a result it only remains for us to accept the explanation given above. Even though the position of Constantinople had not been officially recognized, the fact that the Council of 381 had been accepted as ecumenical was for the Latin canonists, sufficient reason for accepting all its canons. Nor should we forget that these collections were the work of canonists working in private who mode no pretense of imposing their works on the whole Church.

This apparent anomaly is much better explained if we consider that Pope Damasus had never protested against Canon III of the Council of 381. As for Leo the Great, he had not been bothered by this canon which only accorded to Constantinople a place of honor,[20] as much as he had been by Canon XXVIII of Chalcedon which conferred on Constantinople jurisdiction over three entire dioceses and thereby made Constantinople a dangerous rival of Rome. Even down to our own days it has been generally accepted that Rome had rejected in 382 Canon III of the Council of 381, and it is perhaps this conviction that has influenced M. Peitz and caused him to seek a satisfactory explanation of this apparent anomaly. In reality the explanation of this enigma is much more simple. The canonists of the fifth and sixth century, realizing that Rome had never raised any protest against this canon, considered it perfectly legitimate and inserted it in their collections.

* * *

One other detail should be stressed. Although the collection of Dionysius Exiguus only contains the twenty-seven canons of the Council of Chalcedon and omits Canon XXVIII, and although most of the manuscripts of these first collections do the same, still at least two manuscripts of the *Prisca* have combined Canon III of Constantinople with Canon XXVIII of Chalcedon. Further, in the manuscripts, the canons of Constantinople follow immediately after those of Chalcedon. The two collections which make up this version and which we find in the manuscript of Chieti and in that of Justel are very ancient. They date from the sixth century and they are both of Italian origin.[21]

The explanation given by F. Maassen is quite satisfactory. The two compilers made use of a Greek manuscript which first gave the text of twenty-seven canons of Chalcedon and then before copying Canon XXVIII, they numbered the canons of Constantinople. If we consider the content of Canon XXVIII, it seems that before defining it, during the fifteenth session of the Council, the Fathers began by reading the Canons of Constantinople which, at this time, had not yet been numbered. Canon III of Constantinople served, in fact, as an introduction to the decisions of Canon XXVIII. It is most interesting to notice, in any case, that two collections founded on the *Prisca* contain this canon which was so opposed by the Popes from Leo the Great until Hormisdas. From that we can conclude that Canon XXVIII must have figured, at the end of the fifth or the beginning of the sixth century, in some Greek collections of conciliar canons and that these collections were known in Italy.[22] The fact that two Italian compilers did not hesitate to recopy this canon shows that the opposition to Constantinople and its pretensions in the hierarchial order were not quite as general in Italy as has been supposed. It would seem that the misgivings cherished by the Curia with regard to Constantinople were not universally shared in ecclesiastical circles.[23]

The first great misunderstanding between Rome and Byzantium, the Schism of Acacius, thereby came to an end in a friendly agreement and the prestige of Rome was, without any doubt, considerably enhanced in the eyes of the Byzantines. Even though the declarations on the Roman Primacy contained in the *Libellus Hormisdae* had certainly appeared to be rather strong to the members of the Greek hierarchy, nevertheless, all the bishops signed it. Besides, the presence of Canon III of 381 in the first collections of conciliar canons in the West shows that anti-Byzantine feeling had decreased in the Roman Church.

NOTES

1. PL 59, 65. For more details on this schism, see E. Stein, *Histoire du Bas-Empire* (Bruges, 1949), 31-39, 165-92; E. Caspar, *Geschichte des Papsttums* (Tübingen, 1933), II, 10-81; A. A. Vasiliev, *Justin I* (Cambridge, Mass., 1950), 166ff.; A. Fliche-V. Martin, *Histoire de l'Église* (Paris, 1939), vol. 4, 291-320, 423ff.

2. We find this definition in his letter to Anastasius I, PL 59, 42-3. See my study, "Pope Gelasius and Emperor Anastasius I," in *Byzantinische Zeitschrift*, 44 (1951), 111-16. For greater detail, see *The Idea of Apostolicity*, 109-22.

3. Especially PL 59, 27-28; and, *The Idea of Apostolicity*, 118ff.

4. PL 63, 460; Mansi, 8, 467.

5. PL 63, 444A; *Col. Avel. Epist.* 159, CSEL, vol. 35, 608, 2.

6. PL 63, 429; *Col. Avel. Epist.* 146, *ibid.*, 591.

7. PL 63, 430A; *Col. Avel. Epist.* 145, 589; "Dilectionis tuae confessionem gratanter accepimus, per quam sanctae synodi comprobantur, inter quas Chalcedonem. . . ."

8. PL 63, 455ff.; *Col. Avel. Epist.* 169, CSEL, vol. 35, 624-26.

9. PL 63, 475C; *Col. Avel. Epist.* 187, 644, 2.

10. PL 63, 387CD; *Col. Avel. Epist.* 117, 523, 5, 6.

11. PL 63, 497D; *Col. Avel. Epist.* 233, 708. And what is even more revealing is the statement made by the legates of Pope Hormisdas at Constantinople. In their report to the Pope, dated 29 June 529, they say that they declared in the presence of the Emperor and the Senate: "We neither say nor admit anything outside of the four councils and the letters of Pope Leo. We accept nothing that is not contained in the Synods that have been mentioned or that is not written by Pope Leo" (*Col. Avel. Epist.* 217, CSEL, vol. 35, 678; see also, *ibid.*, 686, the letter of the deacon Dioscurus). Cf. also, Congar, "La primauté des

quatre premiers conciles oecuméniques," in *Le Concile et les conciles* (Paris-Chevetogne, 1960), 75ff.

12. See the edition by C. H. Turner, *Eccles. occid. monumenta iuris antiquissimae* (Oxford, 1907), II, 418; PL 56, 809.

13. C. H. Turner, *ibid.*, 150. Cf. F. Dvornik, "The See of Constantinople in the First Latin Collections of Canon Law," in *Mélanges G. Ostrogorsky* (Zbornik radova Visant. Inst. Belgrade, 1963), 97-101.

14. For more details, see F. Maassen, *Geschichte der Quellen und der Literatur des canonischen Rechts im Abendlande* (Graz, 1870, reprinted 1956), 87-100. On the manuscripts of the *Prisca*, see Turner, *op. cit.*, 150.

15. Turner, *op. cit.*, 419. An edition was made by A. Strewe, *Die Canonessamlung des Dionysius Exiguus in der ersten Redaktion* (Berlin-Leipzig, 1931, Arbeiten zur Kirchengeschichte, vol. 16), 61. Canons II and III (Mansi, 3,559) are there contracted into one, Canon II, in which we read: "Verumtamen Constantinopolitanus episcopus habeat honoris primatum praeter Romanum episcopum, propterea quod urbs ipsa sit junior Roma." See also, Maassen, *op. cit.*, 103ff.

16. See R. Naz, "Hispana ses Isidoriana collectio," DDC (Paris, 1953), 5, 1159-62.

17. Turner, *op. cit.*, 418. On the manuscripts of the *Hispana*, still unpublished, see Turner, 402-03. Cf. also, Maassen, 667-716 and P. Fournier-G. Le Bras, *Histoires des collections canoniques en Occident* (Paris, 1931) I, 100ff. A critical edition of the Hispana is in preparation. This collection had an equally great influence in Gaul. In the *Epitome Hispana*, it appears that the third canon of the second council was not cited (Cf. Turner, 419). M. Peitz has offered the hypothesis that Dionysius composed, at the invitation of Pope Gelasius, a collection of the canons of the Oriental councils, utilizing the protocols preserved in the pontifical archives. To these he would have added the canons of the second and the fourth ecumenical councils and the 138 African canons. To this original collection, made around A.D. 500, fifty apostolic canons were also added. According to Peitz, Dionysius modified this collection in numerous ways and augmented it by adding the pontifical decretals down to the year 384. It was this collection, still according to Peitz, which

Pope Hormisdas sent to the Spanish bishops and which became the *Hispana.* Despite considerable documentation, on which Peitz endeavored to support his thesis in his study, *Dionysius Exiguus Studien* (edit. H. Foerster, Berlin, 1960, Arbeiten zur Kirchengeschichte, vol. 33), Peitz has here constructed a theory without a solid foundation. On the canonical collections of the fifth and sixth centuries, cf. W. M. Plöchl, *Geschichte des Kirchenrechts* (Vienna-Munich, 1953), I, 251ff.

18. *Op. cit.,* 273-316.

19. *Op. cit.,* 308. The author pretends that the probity and sincerity of the Greek envoys were accepted with confidence. This is, indeed, a strange assumption which by no means supplies for the complete absence of any written documentation.

20. During the final session of Chalcedon, Eusebius, bishop of Dorylaeum, declared that in that very year, 451, during his stay in Rome, he had read canon III of 381 to the Pope, who approved of it. Cf. Mansi, 7, 449. edit. E. Schwartz, II, vol. 1, Part 3, 97.

21. Cf. F. Maassen, *op. cit.,* 94-99, 526-36. The Chieti manuscript is given in PL 56, 809-10, as follows: "With regard to the primacy of the Church of Constantinople, the holy synod declared: Conforming ourselves in all things to the decrees of the holy Fathers and having in view the canon enacted by more than 150 most reverend bishops who gathered in this royal city, this is what we have determined as to the primacy of the holy Church of Constantinople, the New Rome; since the holy Fathers granted the primacy to the see of Old Rome because of its situation as the seat of the Empire, so also, confirming the decision of the 150 venerable Fathers, we grant primacy to the New Rome since we judge it reasonable that the city that is honored with the presence of royalty and the Senate should receive confirmation of its primacy after Old Rome and it should be as honored as Old Rome in ecclesiastical affairs. We deem that it should be second after Old Rome and we also grant to its metropolitans governance over Pontus, Asia and Thrace. Also, that bishops in the territory of the barbarians are to be incardinated into the parishes by the above-mentioned see. Likewise that each metropolitan, in the parishes mentioned, should ordain the bishops as was specified in the divine canons.

22. This would appear to weaken still more the theory of M. Peitz.
23. It seems that this was particularly true for the south of Italy where Byzantine influence was quite strong. We may mention that the Chieti manuscript is of Neapolitan origin.

JUSTINIAN AND ROME

THE ARCHITECT of this agreement was the Emperor Justinian (527-565).[1] It is certain that his efforts to reconcile Rome and Byzantium were inspired by his ambitious dream of liberating Rome and Italy from the domination of the Goths and of restoring to the Roman Empire its ancient splendor. This was, to be sure, a political ambition and, in order to realize it, he needed the support of the Pope. But it would be inexact to say that his favorable attitude toward Rome had no other motive than a political one. The renovation of the Roman Empire proceeded side by side with the renewal of the ancient traditions, with the renaissance of ideas on the terrestrial monarchy as the mirror of the heavenly monarchy, of the Emperor as the representative of God, ideas which were those of Christian Hellenism. This renewal also served to put great stress on the Roman Idea, the ideological basis of the Empire.

After having destroyed the Gothic domination in Italy and the Vandal control in Africa, Justinian brought Rome and its Church back into the Empire. This was a situation which he wished to make permanent. He also felt it necessary to bring to an end for all time the rivalry existing between the two capitals of his Empire, Rome and Byzantium, and he wished to harmonize the old ideals of Christian Hellenism—which had always inspired the faithful, particularly in the East—and the new religious and political currents which were showing themselves, especially in Rome, during the schism which had just come to an end.

It is in this perspective that we should look upon the attempts at politico-religious legislation initiated by Justinian. First of all, his classic definition of imperial power—the *Basileia* (Imperium) and of the spiritual power, the *Sacerdotium*, which he gave in his Novel VI, published on March 6, 535:[2]

The two greatest gifts which God in His infinite goodness has granted to men are the *Sacerdotium* and the *Imperium*. The priesthood takes care of divine interests and the empire of human interests of which it has supervision. Both powers emanate from the same principle and bring human life to its perfection. It is for this reason that the emperors have nothing closer to their hearts than the honor of priests because they pray continually to God for the emperors. When the clergy shows a proper spirit and devotes itself entirely to God, and the emperor governs the state which is entrusted to him, then a harmony results which is most profitable to the human race. So it is then that the true divine teachings and the honor of the clergy are the first among our preoccupations.

Even though Justinian here manifests his full acceptance of the ideas of Christian Hellenism such as they had been conceived by the first political philosophers at the time of Constantine, and even though he holds firmly to his right to look after the Church and after the maintenance of the "true divine teachings," he nevertheless here makes a great concession to the priesthood in that he places it almost on the same level as the imperial power. The prestige of the priesthood had in fact grown during the crisis of the fifth century thanks to the courageous defense of its rights in the definition of the faith. We should remember the declaration of Gelasius on the relationship between the two powers.[3]

*   *   *

If Justinian wished to restore the Roman Empire he had to grant to Rome a place of honor in the Empire. The ancient city had to continue to be the center of Christendom as it had been one time the center of the Empire and the residence of the Emperor. It is this privilege of Rome which Justinian had in mind when he declared in his Novel IX of May, 535:[4]

The old city of Rome has the honor to be the mother of laws and no one can doubt that it is there that we find the summit of the sovereign pontificate. This is why we ourselves believed it necessary to honor this cradle of law, this source of the priesthood, by a special law of our sacred will.

Further, in his letter to Pope John II, the Emperor called the Church of Rome "caput omnium ecclesiarum." [5] In his letter to the Patriarch Epiphanius, reproduced in the Constitution on the Trinity[6]—a very official document—the Emperor declared:

We have condemned Nestorius and Eutyches, prescribing that, in all things, the unity of the holy Churches with his Holiness the Pope and Patriarch of old Rome should be maintained . . . for we cannot tolerate the situation in which anything that concerns the ecclesiastical order should not be reported to His Holiness since he is the head of all the holy priests of God, and since, each time heretics have arisen in our midst, it is by a sentence and a true judgment of this venerable see that they have been condemned.

In the same climate of ideas we can cite a similar declaration, an even more categorical one, which is found in the Theodosian code.[7] It is the introduction to Novel XVII, issued by the Emperor Valentinian on July 8, 445 and on which Justinian probably depended. The Novel was directed against the pretensions of Hilary, Bishop of Arles, who without the permission of the Pope wished to extend his jurisdiction outside of his own proper diocese. There we read:

Since the Primacy of the Apostolic See has been confirmed by the merits of St. Peter, the Prince and the crown of the episcopacy,

by the dignity of the City of Rome, and also by the authority of
the holy synods, no one should presume to attempt to do anything
illicit outside of the authority of this see. For the peace of the
churches will finally be preserved everywhere when the whole
Church is subject to its supreme ruler.

These statements are authentic and important, and it is in this
light that we must consider the famous declaration of Justinian
in his Novel CXXXI.[8]

We decree, in accord with the decisions of the Council, that the
most holy Pope of Ancient Rome is the first of all the hierarchs
and that the holy bishop of Constantinople—the New Rome—
occupies the second see, after the holy and apostolic see of Rome
but with precedence over all other sees.

This statement should not, in any sense, be considered as unfavorable to Rome. Justinian wished to bring to an end the
jealousy between the two sees and to stabilize the ecclesiastical
order according to the ideology of the times. This could only
be done by an act of imperial legislation.

It should be equally stressed here that Justinian had no
intention of abandoning his imperial right in religious matters.
It is equally true that this right, in principle, was not denied by
any of the Popes. Here we only have to recall the letter of
Pope John II to Justinian in which he approved of the edict of
March 15, 533, on the theological proposition: one of the
persons of the Trinity (*unus Trinitatis*) was crucified.[9] Pope
Agapitus himself expressed his satisfaction on seeing the orthodoxy of the Emperor and his desire to lead all his subjects
to the true faith; he nevertheless reminded the Emperor that
the preaching of the faith was the duty of priests.[10] Pope
Vigilius likewise, at the beginning of his pontificate, offered
thanks to God that He had given to Justinian "not only an
imperial soul but also a sacerdotal soul." [11] Still, it was necessary
for the Emperor to learn that the new currents which manifested themselves in politico-religious thought were much more

powerful than he believed and the priesthood was more determined than ever to defend its rights. His most important intrusion into the domain of theology was his condemnation of the "Three Chapters." [12] Even though he was motivated in this condemnation by his desire of leading all his subjects to the true faith as it had been defined at Chalcedon, and even though this condemnation could be reconciled with Catholic doctrine, nevertheless this imperial action provoked a veritable storm in the Church. It was the Africans who protested most violently and Pope Vigilius was obliged to tell the Emperor that he was wrong. Justinian finally realized his error and in order to bring peace to men's minds, he had to give satisfaction to the priesthood by convoking a fifth council. In his decree of convocation he thus defined the role of the priesthood and of the *Imperium*.[13]

Our orthodox and imperial ancestors, in order to combat each heresy when it arose, had the custom of making use of very zealous priests, united in council, and to preserve the peace of the Church by the proclamation of the true faith.

The acceptance of this decree of convocation by Pope Vigilius served to bring the affair to an end.

* * *

The new currents of thought which had appeared in politico-religious speculation had left another mark on the Byzantine mentality. We have seen that the insistence of Rome in defending the principle of apostolicity in the life of the Church had made an impression upon the Orientals. This explains the origin of the idea according to which the direction of dogmatic and religious affairs should be put into the hands of the patriarchal sees whose bishops represented the *Sacerdotium*. Thus was born the idea of the Pentarchy, that is to say the direction of the Church by the five patriarchs. It is expressed for the first time in the legislation of Justinian. On three occasions at least, the Emperor makes a clear allusion to five "archbishops and patriarchs," directing them that they should make known his laws and measures to all the metropolitans of their dioceses and that they should see to it that they are strictly observed.[14] From this point of view Novel CIX is particularly important, for there the Emperor seems to combine the idea of the apostolic origin of the Church with the Pentarchy.

If we keep before our eyes the Novels in which the Emperor accords a preponderant place to the holder of the see of Rome, we might conclude from that, that the idea of the Pentarchy had not, at the beginning, any anti-Papal bearing. Its appearance is due to the influence exercised in the Church of the East by the growing prestige of the *Sacerdotium* and the idea of apostolicity. This idea would, much later, help the Orientals in their struggle to limit the imperial interventions in matters of faith.[15]

Historians have often criticised Justinian for his politico-religious ideas. However, as we have seen, his ideas on the relations of the *Imperium* and the *Sacerdotium*, as well as his ideas as to the place of Rome in the Church and in the Empire, were nothing but a logical deduction from a former development. Contrary to what has often been said, the two great religious centers, Rome and Constantinople, would have been able to find in Justinian's ordinances, with relation to their place in Christendom, a solid foundation for a harmonious collaboration in the spirit of Christian Hellenism, softened somewhat by the progress which the prestige of the *Sacerdotium* and the idea of apostolicity had created in the Byzantine mentality.

*   *   *

Unfortunately, the work that Justinian set out to accomplish was frustrated by unforeseen political events. The north of

Italy was invaded by the Lombards, a Germanic tribe, and the flourishing provinces of Illyricum were ravaged by the invasions of the Avars, a people of Turkish race, and by the Slavs. Further, the Arabs had occupied Syria, Palestine and Egypt. Thus the Empire found itself reduced to Asia Minor, to Greece and the seaports of Thrace, Macedonia, Dalmatia and Italy.

Everyone is familiar with the theory of the celebrated Belgian historian, Henri Pirenne,[16] according to which it was the occupation of the eastern provinces by the Arabs and their control of the sea-lanes linking the East and the West which provoked the rupture of economic and cultural relations between Byzantium and the West. His discovery caused a sensation in the scientific world when it was announced because it seemed to furnish an explanation of the crisis that civilization underwent at this time. But other historians have pointed to a number of weak points in this thesis and they have turned to other causes to explain the phenomenon.[17] Whether the theory is true or not, we should not forget one important factor which serves as a compliment to the thesis of Pirenne and, at the same time, will satisfy the critics. I mean the destruction of Illyricum by the Avars and the Slavs.[18] In the Roman and Byzantine period, the diocese of Illyricum comprised Pannonia, Dalmatia and all the other European provinces down to the Peloponnesus, with the exception of Thrace; its population was made up of Latins and Greeks, who in the ecclesiastical structure were under Roman jurisdiction. The invasions of the Avars destroyed this bridge which existed between the Latin and the Greek world and the occupation of a large part of Illyricum by the Slavic tribes blocked for centuries this path of communication between East and West.

At the same time the Byzantines found themselves forced because of the invasions of the Persians and the Arabs to concentrate their attention more and more on the East and on Asia Minor, the only preserves remaining to them for their economic life and their military support. The inevitable consequence of this situation was that the Hellenistic and Eastern elements took a predominant position in the civilization and the religious life of the Byzantines.[19]

Besides, the invasions of the Germanic tribes in the western provinces of the Empire brought a foreign element into the very heart of Roman civilization. In Christianizing these new nations the Roman missionaries were forced to accept and to respect their national traditions, at least those that were not directly opposed to Christian principles but which, often, did not always correspond to Roman traditions. The new result was that Constantinople and Rome developed in quite different directions.

The separation which ensued could have been avoided if the bridge of Illyricum had not been destroyed. But the disappearance and the de-Christianization of the Latin provinces of Illyricum, their occupation by barbarian tribes and the loss of control of the Mediterranean sea by the Empire, all this made the mutual exchange of new ideas between the East and West almost totally impossible. It is among these facts that we must seek for the causes of the separation which arose between the East and the West at the beginning of this epoch and which, finally, proved fatal to Christendom.

* * *

This separation did not really make itself fully felt until the end of the seventh century and during the course of the eighth century. During this period, the ecclesiastical order which had been strengthened by Justinian continued to be respected. The reign of St. Gregory the Great (594-604) is particularly important in this regard. Even though he was not able to count upon the support of the Emperor Maurice (582-602) who carried on an inconclusive struggle against the Persians, the Avars, and the Slavs and although, in order to protect the rest of Italy against the Lombards, he had to act almost like a sovereign ruler, Gregory remained faithful to the

Emperor and continued to regard the Roman Empire as the political expression of the universality of the Church. Here is how he expressed his ideas on the relations between the *Sacerdotium* and the *Imperium:*[20] "In so far as it is possible for us to do so without sin, we will tolerate whatever is done by the Emperor if it is in accord with Canon Law." Holding such convictions, it was altogether natural for him to announce to the Emperor the conversion of the Anglo-Saxons[21] and to ask his permission to send the pallium to Bishop Syagrius of Autun in order to satisfy the desire of the Frankish queen, Brunhilde.[22]

The relations between Rome and Byzantium were defined by Gregory in a letter which he sent to John, the Bishop of Syracuse:[23]

Whatever one may say about the see of Constantinople, can anyone doubt that it is submissive to the Apostolic See? This has always been recognized by the very pious Emperor and by our brother, the bishop of that city.

The Bishop of Constantinople to which Gregory here refers was John IV (the Faster, 582-595), and he was the occasion of a new incident which had already arisen during the pontificate of Pelagius II (579-590),[24] the predecessor of Gregory the Great. Pelagius had been scandalized on learning that John IV had taken upon himself the title of Ecumenical Patriarch. Gregory,[25] in turn, protested and it has been said that he introduced for the first time the papal title "Servus Servorum Dei," to counterbalance the title the patriarch had assumed.[26] The misgivings felt by Church historians at the use of such a title by the Patriarch of Constantinople is understandable and some of them even think that its use must be interpreted as a pretension to universal jurisdiction. In reality, it is nothing of the kind. This title had already been given in 449 to the Bishop of Alexandria, Dioscorus.[27] At the Council of Chalcedon, on many occasions, Pope Leo was honored by the same

79

title[28] and, both Pope Hormisdas and Pope Agapitus had likewise been saluted by the Oriental prelates as ecumenical patriarchs.[29]

At Constantinople, in fact, this title had been in use since the sixth century. It had been given to the Patriarch John II [30] as well as to his successors Epiphanius, Anthimus and Menas.[31] This is the title that is generally used by Justinian in his Novels and his decrees with regard to the patriarchs he mentions. If we compare the way in which Justinian uses this title with what he says in his decrees on the Pope and on the other patriarchs, we get the impression that the title merely expresses the supreme power of the patriarch within the limits of his own patriarchate.[32]

Hence it would seem that the implication which the patriarchs of Constantinople gave to this title was merely a simple application of the principle of accommodation. The title undoubtedly expressed nothing more than the supreme position which Constantinople occupied in the East,[33] and there is no need to see in it any intention of usurping jurisdiction over the universal church or of refusing to Rome the Primacy.

Besides, Gregory himself did not see in it any attack upon the primacy of his see. He mentioned in the letter which we have quoted above that John the Faster recognized that the see of Constantinople was submissive to the see of Rome. Further, John IV gave the Pope still another proof of his submission in allowing the priest, John of Chalcedon and the monk, Athanasius, to appeal from his tribunal to that of Rome and in sending along to the Pope all the documents concerned with their case.[34] Gregory actually gave a definitive decision in the case demanding that John should be re-established in his dignity because of his innocence and recommending mercy for the monk Athanasius out of consideration of his goodwill and his repentance.

Perhaps the objection raised by Gregory against the use of the title "Ecumenical Patriarch" is best found in the ascetical character of this great saint. It becomes clear from his letters that he saw in it, above all, an expression of pride which detracted from the dignity of a priest. In his mind, only Jesus Christ is the universal Master and it is only the entire Church stretching over the whole of the world which can be called "ecumenical." He had no intention but to offer his confrère of Constantinople a kind of admonition not to go too far in his pretensions in the East. It is significant to note that the Oriental patriarchs,[35] on this occasion, did not seem disturbed and they considered the use of this title by their Byzantine colleague either as an empty formula, or as an expression of the rights that had been accorded to Constantinople by the Council of Chalcedon.

All the same, the controversy had disturbed the minds of men and the Emperor Phocas (602-610), the successor of Maurice, felt it necessary to redefine the status of the sees of Rome and of Constantinople. In the *Liber Pontificalis*,[36] we read that Pope Boniface II (607), the second successor of St. Gregory, "obtained from the Emperor Phocas [confirmation] of the fact that the Apostolic See of the blessed Apostle Peter [that is to say, the Church of Rome] was indeed the head of all the churches, because the Church of Constantinople had said that it was the first of all the churches."

This passage from the *Liber Pontificalis* is vague enough and its Latin is far from being Ciceronian. This edict of Phocas, however, contrary to what has often been implied in the manuals of ecclesiastical history, was merely a repetition of the decision of Justinian concerning the status of the two sees and a new confirmation of the Roman Primacy.[37]

NOTES

1. On the religious politics of Justinian, see E. Stein, *Histoire du Bas-Empire*, 369-417, 623-90. On his relations with Pope Agapitus, to whom, in 536, he accorded the privilege of ordaining the new patriarch of Constantinople, see the study of W. Ens-

slin, "Papst Agapet I. und Kaiser Justinian I.," in *Historisches Jahrbuch*, 77 (1950), 459-66.

2. Edit., G. Kroll, *Corpus iuris civilis*, III, 35ff. On the relations of Justinian with the apostolic see of Rome, see especially, P. Batiffol, *Cathedra Petri*, 210-13, 249-319.

3. See p. 60, *supra*.

4. Kroll, *op. cit.*, 91.

5. PL 66, 15; *Cod. Just.*, I, 1, 8. *Corp. iur. civ.*, vol. I, 11.

6. *Cod. Just.*, I, 1, 7.

7 *Codex Theodosianus, Leges Novellae* (Edit. T. Mommsen, P. M. Meyer, Berlin, 1905) vol. 2, 102. On Hilary, see E. Caspar, *op. cit.*, I, 446ff. Valentinian tried to combine, in his Novel, the principle of apostolicity and the principle of accommodation.

8. Kroll, III, 655.

9. *Cod. Just.*, I, 1, 8; *Corp. iur. civ.*, I, 10; see PL 66, 17ff.

10. PL 66, 37; *Col. Avel. Epist.* 91, 343.

11. Mansi, 9, 35.

12. For more information on this controversy see the fine study of E. Amann in DTC, vol. 15, 1868-1924.

13. Mansi, 9, 178ff.

14. Novel CIX, praefatio, *Corp. iur. civ.*, III, 518. See also Novel CXXIII, 3, *ibid.*, 597 and Novel VI, epilogus, *ibid.*, 47.

15. Cf. ch. 6, *infra*.

16. *Mohammed and Charlemagne* (New York, 1939).

17. These criticisms have been gathered by A. F. Havighurst, in the symposium, *The Pirenne Thesis, Analysis, Criticism and Revision* (Boston, 1958).

18. See my book, *The Slavs, Their Early History and Civilization* (Boston, 1956), 42ff., 118ff.

19. Cf. F. Dvornik, "Quomodo incrementum influxus orientalis in imperio byzantino s. VII-IX dissensionem inter ecclesiam Romanam et Orientalem promoverit," in *Acta conventus Pragensis pro studiis orientalibus* (Olomouc, 1930), 159-72.

20. Letter to the Deacon Anatolius, PL 77, 1167, *Epistolae*, II, ep. 47. Cf. H. E. Fischer, "Gregor der Grosse und Byzanz," in *Zeitschrift der Savigny Stiftung, Kan. Abt.* 36 (1950), 129-44.

21. *Epistolae*, XI, ep. 29; PL 77, 1142.

22. *Epistolae*, IX, ep. 11; PL 77, 952.

23. *Epistolae*, IX, ep. 12; PL 77, 957.

24. We know of this from the letters of Pope Gregory.
25. See his letter to John the Faster, to the Empress Constantina, to the Emperor Maurice and to the patriarchs, Eulogius of Alexandria and Anastasius of Antioch. Epistolae, V, epp. 18, 20, 21, 43; PL 77, 738, 745, 749, 771. Cf. Fischer, op. cit., 97-110.
26. This does not appear to correspond completely with the truth. Gregory had not invented this title and he had already used it when he was a simple monk and a deacon. See the detailed study of S. Vailhé, "Saint Grégoire le Grand et le titre de patriarche oecumenique," in Échos d'Orient, 11 (1908), 65-69, 161-71.
27. Mansi, 6, 855.
28. Ibid., 1005, 1012, 1021, 1029. See The Idea of Apostolicity, 79-80.
29. Mansi, 8, 425, 895.
30. Ibid., 1038, 1042, 1058, 1059, 1066, 1067.
31. Cod. Just., lib. I. tit. 1, lex. 7 (Edit. Krueger, II, 8); lib. I, tit. 4, lex. 34 (Ibid. 47); Novels, 3, 5, 7, 16, 42, 55, 56, 77 (Edit. Schoell, Kroll), III, 18, 28, 35, 48, 115, 263, 308, 311, 312.
32. This impression is also confirmed from the letters of the Emperor Constantine IV (669-678) to Pope Donus and to the patriarch George I in reference to the convocation of the sixth council. He uses the title "ecumenical" for both of them, and in his letter to the Pope he recognizes the apostolic character of his see (Mansi, 11, 106, 197, 201).
33. On the use of this title for patriarchs, see Grumel, "Le titre de patriarche oecuménique sur les sceaux byzantins," Revue des études grecques, 58 (1945), 212-218; V. Laurent, "Le titre de patriarche oecuménique et la signature patriarchale," Rev. des études byzantines, 6 (1948), 5-26. On the controversy, see P. Batiffol, S. Grégoire le Grand (Paris, 1928), 204-211; S. Vailhé, "Constantinople," in DHGE, 13, 643-45. See also E. Caspar, Geschichte des Papsttums, II, 366ff., 452ff.
34. Epistolae, VI, epp. 15-17, PL 77, 807ff.
35. This is seen clearly in the letters of the patriarchs of Antioch and Alexandria. PL 77, 882, 898.
36. Edit. Duchesne (Paris, 1886) I 316: "Hic obtinuit apud Focatem principem ut sedes apostolica beati Petri apostoli caput esset omnium ecclesiarum, quia ecclesia Constantinopolitana prima se omnium ecclesiarum scribebat."

37. This is the sense that Humbert of Romans gave to this imperial decree in his presentation of subjects for discussion at the second council of Lyons (1274). Enumerating the cause of the Greek schism, he said: "Sed per Phocam imperatorem, procurante Bonifacio Papa, ordinatum fuit, quod Romana ecclesia, sicut erat, sic et diceretur caput omnium" (Mansi, 24, 125).

5

THE PRIMACY IN THE SEVENTH

AND EIGHTH CENTURIES

WE HAVE ALREADY seen that the arguments which the Popes
drew from the apostolic and Petrine origin of their see had
made a considerable impression upon the Orientals. This has
led a number of scholars to think that the Byzantines, merely
to counterbalance the prestige acquired by Rome from this
prerogative, had imagined that the see of Byzantium was itself of apostolic origin. Thus, the see of Constantinople was
supposed to have been founded by the apostle Andrew, the
brother of Peter. And, as Andrew had been the first to be
invited by the Lord to follow Him and since he had been
the one to bring Peter to Christ, Andrew was therefore
superior to Peter, and his successors at Byzantium should be
likewise superior to the successors of Peter at Rome.

It has been thought that this legend of the apostolic origin
of Byzantium must have been invented after the conclusion of
the Schism of Acacius. It is found especially in the list of the
Apostles and the disciples which is attributed to Dorotheus,
Bishop of Tyre.[1] According to the author of this list, Dorotheus had suffered persecution in the reign of Diocletian. He
lived until the reign of Julian and died a martyr under Licinius.

The compilation includes also a declaration of Pope Agapitus made on the occasion of a visit to Constantinople in 525. It is there said that the Pope recognized the authenticity of the account according to which St. Andrew, going from Pontus into Greece, would have visited Byzantium and there ordained Stachys as its first bishop. The author then adds a list of twenty bishops who, according to him, succeeded Stachys in the see of Constantinople.

The fact is, that of all these bishops only the last one on the list, Metrophanes, a contemporary of Constantine, can be verified with any certitude. The voyage of Pope Agapitus to Constantinople in 525 is merely legendary. We do possess exact information about the visit which Agapitus made to Constantinople in 536 but the account of this visit which is contemporaneous[2] with him reveals absolutely nothing of that which is described in the legendary account. The author of this document knows nothing of any of the bishops who were thought to have succeeded Stachys. He only mentions the bishops who succeeded Metrophanes, using as his source for this the official list which he could consult in the archives of the Patriarch of Constantinople.

It is well known that the tradition of the voyage of Andrew from Pontus to Greece, his activity in Achaea and his death at Patras is considered legendary by a large number of specialists. Eusebius, the first historian of the Church and a contemporary of Constantine, who has passed on to us all that was known in his time of the activity of the apostles, places the apostolate of Andrew in Scythia,[3] here depending upon the authority of Origen. This is the only historical information which we possess as to the work of Andrew. From it we can only conclude that Andrew died in the country in which he carried on his mission, in Scythia. It is well known that there were numerous and flourishing Jewish colonies[4] in the cities of Crimea and along the shores of the sea of Azov and that the Jewish religious propaganda had been particularly fruitful among the pagans of these cities. This will perhaps explain why Andrew had chosen this country for his mission. It is interesting, besides, to note that Syriac tradition knows nothing of Andrew's activities outside of Scythia even at that time when it was believed in Greece that he had died at Patras. It is therefore quite possible, even likely, that a saint bearing the same, or a similar name, and buried at Patras, had been substituted for the Apostle Andrew. Since in the neighborhood of ancient Scythia there was a barbarian tribe called *Achaioi*, which the ancients had often considered as a colony founded by the *Achaioi* of Greece, it is possible that this circumstance helped in the substitution.

The account attributed to Dorotheus of Tyre is based upon the apocryphal Acts of Andrew. Very probably these Acts were composed at the end of the third century, in Achaea, by an intellectual Greek, an orthodox Christian but imbued with rigorist and neoplatonizing tendencies.

The original version of these Acts has not been preserved. In it, there must have been mention of Byzantium and of a visit there by the Apostle; otherwise the legend would never have been created. Fortunately for us, St. Gregory of Tours (538-594) provides us with a very valuable hint for the reconstitution of these Acts in their original version, because they constitute the principle source used by Gregory in his book on "the miracles of Andrew." Describing the voyage of the Apostle from Pontus into Greece, Gregory mentions expressly, among the places visited by Andrew, not only Thrace but also Byzantium.[5]

*   *   *

Hence it was quite easy for the one who invented this legend to find an apparently authentic foundation for his discovery. All he had to add was an account of the ordination of Stachys, the "disciple" of Andrew. The name, Stachys, is found in the Epistle to the Romans (Rom., 16.9). We have long known how the lists of names of the disciples of Christ were established.

Since their names were quite unknown, selections were made from people mentioned in the letters of St. Paul and the Acts of the Apostles and they were inserted into the lists. Thus it was that Stachys was promoted to the rank of the first bishop of Byzantium and that of a disciple of Andrew.

As to the origin of this legend, we find no trace of it before the end of the seventh or the beginning of the eighth century.[6] It is found for the first time in the list of the disciples of Our Lord attributed to Epiphanius of Cyprus, who died in 402.[7] But this list could not have been composed before the end of the seventh century.

Even though the legend was invented in order to pay honor to Byzantium, it was not generally accepted at this time. The author of the legend had certainly been impressed by the apostolic and Petrine arguments provided for the see of Rome. The idea that an apostolic origin for a see was of the highest importance and that the ecclesiastical organization had to respect it was actually very widespread in Byzantium in the seventh century. However, official circles there had found a much better base for the apostolicity of Constantinople. According to the ancient Syriac, Armenian and Coptic traditions[8] we know that the "apostolic" character had been attributed to Byzantium for the reason that Byzantium had become the heir of the see of Ephesus, which had been founded by the Apostle John, when the diocese of Asia, administered by Ephesus, had passed under the jurisdiction of Constantinople. Even in the ninth century when the legend of Andrew had begun to spread its roots in official circles in Byzantium, the Patriarch Ignatius stressed that his see was of apostolic origin, deriving this character from the fact that his see was that of St. John and St. Andrew.[9] It was rather at the end of the eighth century or the beginning of the ninth that the catalogue of bishops from Stachys to Metrophanes was composed and it was inserted into the compilation of Pseudo-Dorotheus. After 811 there was added the list of the disciples of the Lord, based upon the list of the pseudo-Epiphanius.[10]

At least two lives of St. Andrew were composed at this time in which we find mention of the activity of Andrew in Byzantium. However this legend was not officially accepted until the tenth century for it was only then that there was instituted the feast of St. Stachys, first bishop of Byzantium. Thus it is clear that up to the tenth century this legend had never been utilized against the Primacy of Rome. We shall see later[11] the role which it played in the Greco-Latin controversies.

*　　*　　*

It is evident that the conception of the imperial power which had been enshrined in Christian Hellenism could become a great danger for the Church and could destroy the harmony which, according to Justinian, should exist between *Sacerdotium* and the *Imperium*. Thus it was that a new crisis was provoked by Heraclius (610-641). He was carrying on an inconclusive struggle against the Persians who had invaded the eastern provinces of the Empire and he believed that he had, at all costs, to win to himself the fidelity of the Monophysites of Syria and Egypt who could easily turn towards the Persians as their liberators. In his *Ecthesis* of 638, a dogmatic decree which declared that Our Lord, after the Incarnation had only one will (the Monothelite doctrine), he made an important concession to the Monophysites who admitted only one nature —the divine, in the Incarnate Christ.

The imperial decree, generally accepted at Byzantium, nevertheless set off intense opposition in the West. Alarmed by the violence of this opposition, the Emperor Constance II (641-668) replaced the decree of Heraclius by another, called the *Typus*, in which he forbade to the faithful any discussion of the problem of whether there were one or two wills in Christ. Pope Martin I (649-655), protested against this ban and, after having defined the Catholic doctrine on the two wills of Christ, condemned Monothelitism. Constance, suffering for a long time from a sense of injury inflicted by the Pope who had neglected to await his approval at the time of his election, immediately undertook the duties of his office [as he conceived them], ordered the arrest of the Pope, brought him to Constantinople, and there condemned him as a traitor. The poor Pope died in exile, in Crimea. This brutal intervention of the part of the Emperor profoundly shocked the whole of Italy.

In truth, it must be said that at the beginning of this dogmatic quarrel when the patriarch Sergius, the promoter of Monothelitism, had asked advice of Pope Honorius I (625-638) on this doctrine, the Pope who, of course, professed the orthodox doctrine gave in his rather evasive reply the impression—which was false—that he was favorable to the thesis of Sergius. On the other hand, the attitude of his successors, John IV, Theodore and Martin, was much more resolute and they all condemned this doctrine.

There had been protests raised not only in the West, in particular in Africa[12] but also in the East, demanding that the popes should make use of the supreme authority which they held in the Church for the condemnation of heresies. We may cite especially Sergius, the head of the Church in Cyprus, in his address to Pope Theodore in 643.[13] He calls the see of Rome "the pillar constructed by God of unshakable solidity, the tablet whereon the faith is clearly written." After having stressed the apostolic character of the Roman see he writes, "Yes, thou art Peter, as the divine Word has truly said, and upon your foundation the columns of the Church are supported." Inviting the Pope to use the power of binding and loosing which Christ had granted to him, the Archbishop called the Pope "the Prince and Doctor of the orthodox and immaculate Faith." No less expressive is the declaration of Sophronius, Patriarch of Jerusalem, who sent a messenger to Rome giving him orders as follows:[14] "Go, therefore to the Apostolic See where are found the foundations of orthodox doctrine." At the Synod of 649 in Rome, his delegate, Stephen of Dora, made declarations which make abundantly clear the respect held in Palestine for the authority of the apostolic and

Roman see. He denounced the Monothelite heresy before "the higher and divine chair [of Peter] so that the wound may be entirely healed." This see, he insisted, had made a practice of doing this "because of its apostolic and canonical authority." Finally he called upon Peter to whom the Lord had confided the keys, who was, "the first, charged with feeding the flock of the entire Catholic Church," and who was charged with the confirmation of his brethren. It is well known that St. Maximus was one of the most intrepid defenders of the orthodox doctrine. We find in his letters categorical statements on the supreme position of the see of Rome. This chair, he says, is the foundation of all the Christian churches of the world. This chair has received not only from Christ but also from the holy councils, "the power to issue commands to all the holy churches of God in the entire world." He invited the Monothelites to betake themselves to Rome, to renounce their doctrine and to ask for pardon.[15]

* * *

Obviously these statements cannot be considered as the official voice of the Byzantine Church. However, even at Byzantium the situation was to become much clearer on the accession of the Emperor Constantine IV (668-685). After the brutal intervention of Constance II at Rome there had been other irritating incidents stirred up by the Emperor or by the imperial exarchs of Ravenna. Italy, exhausted by the penetration of the Lombards to the interior of the peninsula, lost, little by little, that very spirit of solidarity with the Empire which Justinian had tried to strengthen. Pope Agatho (678-681) assumed the role which had at one time been enjoyed by Leo the Great and in his dogmatic letters sent to the East, prepared for the convocation of the sixth ecumenical council (680-681).

When defining the faith the Fathers of the council extolled the merits of the Pope. In announcing to him the results of their deliberations they declared that there was a need for very special remedies to cure dangerous maladies and

for this, Christ, our true God, the primordial force and the ruler of the whole of the universe has given us an eminent physician—your Holiness, honored by God, who can diagnose this illness and courageously provide the remedy of orthodoxy, thus bringing health to the universal Church. We now present to you that which must be done, to you who occupy the first see in the universal Church, to you who rest upon the firm rock of the faith. This we do after having read the letter outlining the true faith addressed by your paternal beatitude to the most pious Emperor, a letter which we recognize has been written with divine help by the highest authority there is among the apostles.[16]

Sometime later they added that they had condemned the heretical doctrines, "illuminated by the Holy Spirit and instructed by your teachings." In their letter to the Emperor, they said:[17]

It was the chief, the first of the Apostles who fought beside us. We have, to fortify us, his disciple and successor who in his letters explained to us the mysteries of God. This ancient city of Rome has sent to us a confession written by God . . . it is Peter who has spoken through Agatho.

These words are important but there is no need to exaggerate their weight. This very same council, at the same time as it condemned the Monothelites, condemned Pope Honorius, since the letters which Honorius had sent to Sergius had been wrongly interpreted as favorable to Monothelitism. It is interesting, also, to note that this condemnation was recognized even in Rome, and inserted in the profession of faith which the Pope recited and signed after his election. Of course, in Rome, no one attributed to Honorius the paternity of the condemned heresy. They merely censured his lack of vigilance.[18]

The peaceful climate which followed the conclusion of the Monothelite controversy was soon disturbed again by a very serious incident. Justinian II (685-695, 705-711) had convoked another council in 692 which met in the same hall of the imperial palace called *Trullos,* and which proposed to complete the work of the two preceding councils by voting some disciplinary canons. Among the 102 canons voted by this assembly were found a number condemning certain liturgical uses in the Latin church. We see appearing here the sad beginnings of the estrangement of two Churches which, for the reasons mentioned above, began to make themselves felt.[19]

Besides, the attachment of Italy to the Empire also began to decline. Pope Sergius I (687-701) refused to accept the decisions of this council and when the Emperor attempted to have the Pope arrested and brought to Constantinople to be judged there, the Italian militia revolted and prevented the execution of the imperial order. The ambassador of the Emperor only owed his life to the personal intervention of the Pope. The successor of Sergius, John VI (701-705), had to intervene again and calm the militia when the Emperor Tiberius III sent an expedition to Rome to punish the rebels.

The incident only came to an end in 710. Pope Constantine I at the invitation of Justinian II came to Constantinople. According to the enthusiastic account of the *Liber Pontificalis,*[20] he was well received by the Emperor and the people. The incident was closed and it is said that on this occasion the Emperor had "renewed all the privileges of the Church." These words are to be understood in the sense that Justinian II confirmed the privileged place occupied by Rome in the hierarchy, thus renewing the decrees of Phocas and Justinian I.

*　　*　　*

The controversy which arose over the subject of the veneration of the images of the saints is of the greatest importance for understanding the development of the idea of the Roman Primacy in the East. The condemnation of the veneration of images by Emperor Leo III was the last direct intervention of an Emperor into ecclesiastical affairs. The imperial order, which was sent to Pope Gregory II in 726 demanding the acceptance of the decree under pain of deposition and severe punishment, opened a controversy which lasted for a long time and was particularly dangerous not only for the *Sacerdotium* but also for the *Imperium*.

Supported by Italy and all of the West, Gregory II sent to the Emperor a very courageous reply condemning the step that he had taken. Should the Emperor send a whole fleet, and, should his soldiers approach the walls of Rome itself, the Pope had only to take refuge in the country to be in perfect safety. The prestige of the Pope was very great, continued Gregory, not only in Italy but throughout the West.

The whole of the West turns to our humble person and although we are in a perilous situation, they have, nevertheless, great confidence in us and in him whose image you have threatened with deposition and degradation, the Holy Leader Peter, whom the kingdoms of the West continue to regard as God upon earth.[21]

This correspondence is most interesting from the point of view of politico-religious speculation. In the first letter the Pope, while refusing to obey the Emperor, lets it be clearly understood however that he is not giving up Christian Hellenism. He stresses the fact that the orders of the Emperor were always communicated to the nations which Rome had converted and that the Popes exhorted the new kings to remain faithful to the Emperor. This shows that the idea of a universal Church in a universal Empire had still remained alive in Rome.

When the Emperor took up the matter again, reminding the Pope that it was his right since he was "Emperor and priest," [22] Gregory II did not deny the sacerdotal character that was attached to the imperial office. He admitted that this title had been rightly given to the emperors who in perfect accord with the priests had convoked the councils so that the true faith might there be defined, but it was Leo, himself, who had transgressed the decisions of the Fathers.

Dogma is not the business of the Emperors but of priests . . . just as the priest does not have the right to look into the affairs of the palace and to propose the distribution of imperial dignities, so also the Emperor does not have the right to supervise the Church and to judge the clergy, nor to consecrate and distribute the blessed sacraments . . . We invite you to be a true Emperor and priest.[23]

The defenders of the cult of images in the East found their only support in the papacy. It was quite natural for them to stress the apostolic and Petrine character of the see of Rome just as the Iconoclast emperors invoked the sacerdotal character of their office. On many occasions in his letters, St. Theodore of the Monastery of Stoudios, simply calls the Pope *apostolicus*.[24] This was the title which he was normally given at this time in the West. St. Theodore certainly had knowledge of this from the Greek monks and the Greek monasteries in Rome.[25]

Theodore acknowledged the right of the Emperor to convoke councils, according to ancient usage, but he insisted on the preponderant role which the Popes had enjoyed on the occasion of certain councils.[26] When a difficulty arose as to dogma and the Emperor did not think it useful to convoke a council, Theodore recommended that the affair should be brought to the Pope so that a decision might be given. At the same time, he attributed the apostolic character to all of the patriarchs, as well as to that of Constantinople, since they were all the successors of the Apostles.[27]

Another courageous defender of the cult of images, Stephen the Younger, in 760 rejected the Iconoclast Council of 754. Naturally, he mentioned the patriarchs who had likewise rejected it. Speaking of the Pope, he says "according to the prescriptions of the canons, religious matters cannot be defined without the participation of the Pope of Rome." [28]

The most eloquent and the most telling testimony on the Primacy of the Pope is given to us by the intrepid defender of the cult of images, the Patriarch Nicephorus. In his work in defense of the cult of images he exalts the importance of the decisions of the seventh ecumenical council when he says:[29]

This Synod possesses the highest authority. . . . In fact it was held in the most legitimate and regular fashion conceivable, because according to the divine rules established from the beginning it was directed and presided over by that glorious portion of the Western Church, I mean by the Church of Ancient Rome. Without them [the Romans], no dogma discussed in the Church, even sanctioned in a preliminary fashion by the canons and ecclesiastical usages, can be considered to be approved, or abrogated; for they are the ones, in fact, who possess the principate of the priesthood and who owe this distinction to the leader of the Apostles.

Nicephorus also manifested a great respect for Pope Leo III in his synodical letter, sent after his election. After having expressed his orthodoxy in the faith, he insistently besought the Pope,[30] "so that by your decisions and your teachings we may remain firm in this faith, without failure or mixture of error."

The declarations made by the defenders of the cult of images and the confidence which they manifested in the bishops of Rome opened a new stage at Byzantium in the recognition of the Roman Primacy. But here again we must be careful not to go too far. Official circles in the Church of Byzantium remained ever faithful to their ancient traditions and were careful not to exceed them. This is made very clear in the Acts of the seventh ecumenical council which condemned Iconoclasm. Pope Hadrian (772-795) had addressed a letter to the Empress Irene and to her son, Constantine, which was read during the second session of the council.[31] It is very significant that many passages of this letter, which expressed very clearly the Primacy of the Roman see, are not to be found in the Greek version which was read before the Fathers of the council. In particular the citations of the promise of Our Lord to Peter (Matt., 16.18ff.) were suppressed in the Greek version. All that remains is a brief allusion to these words of Our Lord. Wherever the Pope mentions Peter as the founder of the see of Rome, the Greek version adds the name of Paul. The protest which the Pope made against the use of the title "ecumenical" by the patriarch of Constantinople was also suppressed as well as his remarks criticizing the elevation of Tarasius from the lay state to the patriarchate. The Greek translators likewise made some changes in the letter of the Pope to Tarasius, as was remarked by Anastasius Bibliothecarius in his translation of the Acts. However, the passage of Matt., 16.18 is found there.[32]

To be sure, this obviously does not mean that the Primacy of the Pope was denied in the Greek versions. There remain sufficient expressions which indicate this Primacy. The fact is, however, deserving of note, for it would seem to show that the Byzantines, although quite ready to recognize and to accept the principle of the primacy of the see of Rome, remained solicitous in preserving the autonomy of their Church, and found it difficult to accept the direct intervention of the Pope into their internal affairs. The addition of the name of Paul to that of Peter shows that the patriarchal chancery remained faithful to the ancient tradition which Rome had also recognized, and which it had followed up until the fourth century.[33] We shall see that in this matter the Byzantines did not accept the new Roman usage until the ninth century.

This solicitude of the Byzantines to preserve their autonomy should not be forgotten. It had already been manifested, as we have seen, on the occasion of the second ecumenical council.[34] And it prevented the Byzantines from coming closer to a Rome whose pretensions they did not always understand.

NOTES

1. There is a critical edition by Th. Schermann in his book *Prophetarum vitae fabulosae, indices apostolorum discipulorumque Domini* (Leipzig, 1907), 151ff. See also, PG 92, 1060-1073.

2. This account is quoted *in extenso* by Baronius in his *Annales*

ecclesiastici, ad annum 536 (Edit. A. Pagi [Lucca, 1738-1759], nos. 59-63).

3. Eusebius, *Hist. eccles.*, 3, 1; PG 20, 216.
4. Cf. F. Dvornik, *Les légendes de Constantin et de Méthode*, 171.
5. *Liber de miraculis beati Andreae apostoli,* edited by M. Bonnet, in MGH, *Scriptores rerum merovingicarum*, I, 821-46.
6. I have examined this problem in all its details in *The Idea of Apostolicity*, 138-264.
7. Cf. Schermann, *op. cit.*, 107-26.
8. For details, see *The Idea of Apostolicity*, 242-44. There exists a history of Armenia, written by the Catholicos John VI and some apochryphal canons of Nicaea which were used by the Nestorians and the Monophysites, and preserved in an Arabic version.
9. In the course of an interrogation by the Roman legates at the Synod of 861, Ignatius declared: "I am in possession of the see of the apostle, John, and Andrew, the first to be called an apostle." Cf. Wolf v. Glanvell, *Die Kanonessammlung des Kardinals Deusdedit* (Paderborn, 1905), 603.
10. See *The Idea of Apostolicity*, 178-80.
11. See p. 158, *infra.*
12. See the Acts of the African Synod of 646, Mansi, 10, 920-21.
13. Mansi, 10, 913.
14. *Ibid.*, 893, 896.
15. See, especially, the letter he wrote to Rome, to the illustrious Peter (PG 91, 137-40, 144) and the *Acta Maximi* (PG 90, 153). Martin I is referred to as "The supreme and apostolic president of all the hierarchy, the true ecumenical leader," in the letters of the monks Theodosius and Theodore of Gangrae (PG 90, 193, 197, 202). We should mention that St. Maximus stressed the fact that the supreme power which the bishop of Rome holds over the Church has been confirmed by the councils: "[Apostolica sedes] quae ab ipso incarnato Dei verbo, sed et omnibus sanctis synodis, secundum sacros canones et terminos, universarum, quae in toto terrarum orbe sunt, sanctarum Dei ecclesiarum in omnibus et per omnia percepit et habet imperium, auctoritatem et potestatem ligandi atque solvendi" (Mansi, 10, 692). While he was not unaware of the

fact that the source of this power was the Divine Word, he particularly insists on the confirmation by the synods. These words reveal the Byzantine mentality. This very insistence shows, perhaps, the way in which certain circles, at least, in Byzantium, interpreted the decisions of the councils of Nicaea and Chalcedon and the decrees of Justinian (sacros terminos) concerning the first see. Even the patriarch, John, in addressing himself to Pope Constantine in 712, proclaims that the Pope is the head of the Church according to the canonical decrees (Mansi, 12, 196).

16. Mansi, 11, 684, 685.

17. Mansi, 11, 665.

18. This profession of faith is found in the *Liber diurnus*, a collection of formularies and prescriptions of the pontifical chancery. It was revised after the sixth council. It has been edited by H. Foerster, *Liber diurnus romanorum pontificum* (Berne, 1958), 155. This profession, with certain changes, remained in use in Rome until the eleventh century. See my remarks on it in *The Photian Schism*, Appendix I, 435-47.

19. On this progressive estrangement, see Congar, *After Nine Hundred Years*, 1-28.

20. Edit. L. Duchesne, I, 390-91.

21. The letters of Gregory II have been published by E. Caspar in his study, "Papst Gregor II. und der Bilderstreit," in *Zeitschrift für Kirchengeschichte*, 52 (1933), 72-89. See also his *Gesch. des Papsttums* (Tübingen, 1933), II, 646ff.

22. The same title is claimed by the Emperor Leo III in the introduction to the *Ecloga*, a book of civil law that he had published. Cf. I. Zeppos, *Jus graeco-romanum* (Athens, 1931), I, 12. The emperor there declares that the Lord has commanded him, "as he commanded Peter, the supreme chief of the apostles, to feed his faithful flock."

23. St. Maximus the Confessor, in reply to a formal interrogation, emphasized the fact that the Emperor could not exercise priestly functions (PG 90, 1117).

24. See his letters to Pope Leo (PG 90, 1021-25), to Epiphanius (*Ibid.*, 1209), to the patriarch Thomas of Jerusalem (*Ibid.*, 1397), and to Naucratius (*Ibid.*, 1281).

25. See what I have said on this title and on the Greek monasteries in Rome in *Les légendes de Constantin et de Méthode*, 295-300, esp. 286-90.
26. Cf. E. Werner, "Die Krise im Verhältnis von Staat und Kirche in Byzanz: Theodor von Studion," in *Aus der byzant. Arbeit der deutschen demokratischen Republik*, I (1957), 127-33.
27. PG 99, 1417-1420.
28. See the life of St. John the Younger, PG 100, 1144.
29. PG 100, 597A, 621D. The patriarch offered a ringing eulogy of Peter, the leader. In the passage cited the leaders meant are Peter and Paul. It would seem that Nicephorus was also trying to pay honor to the old tradition that Rome had forgotten, which attributed the foundation of the see of Rome to both Peter and Paul.
30. *Ibid.*, 193-96.
31. Mansi, 12, 1056ff. Cf. G. Ostrogorsky, "Rom und Byzanz im Kampfe um die Bilderverehrung," in *Seminarium Kondakovianum*, 6 (1933), 76ff.
32. *Ibid.*, 1082. The Fathers could not help but subscribe to the affirmation of the Pope that the Church of Rome was the head of all the churches since that had been solidly confirmed by the councils. Doubtless, the veneration they all had for St. Peter was the reason why this passage was not altered. The Pope himself seems to attribute this supreme power to Peter, for he says: "For this reason, Peter himself, feeding the flock according to the command of the Lord, has always preserved and preserves the principate."
33. See p. 43, *supra*. K. Onasch, "Der apostel Paulus in der byzantinischen Slaven Mission,," in *Zeitschrift für Kirchengeschichte*, 69 (1958), 212-21, sees in this addition, a desire to replace the Primacy of St. Peter by a "consulate" of the two apostles, an interpretation which is surely exaggerated.
34. See pp. 46-47, *supra*.

PHOTIUS AND THE PRIMACY

THE EVOLUTION WHICH the idea of the Pentarchy underwent in the course of the eighth and ninth centuries deserves to be studied carefully. All the defenders of the cult of images shared this idea and Theodore of Stoudion expressed it very clearly in his letter to Leo the Sacellarius.[1]

We are not discussing worldly affairs. The right to judge them rests with the Emperor and the secular tribunal. But here it is question of divine and heavenly decisions and those are reserved only to him to whom the Word of God has said: "Whatsoever you shall bind upon earth, will be bound in Heaven and whatsoever you shall loose on earth, shall be loosed in Heaven" (Matt. 16.19). And who are the men to whom this order was given?—the Apostles and their successors. And who are their successors?—he who occupies the throne of Rome and is the first; the one who sits upon the throne of Constantinople and is the second; after them, those of Alexandria, Antioch and Jerusalem. That is the Pentarchic authority in the Church. It is to them that all decision belongs in divine dogmas. The Emperor and the secular authority have the duty to aid them and to confirm what they have decided.

It is interesting to notice that Theodore here attributes the apostolic character to all of the patriarchs, including Constantinople. They are the successors of the Apostles. It is possible that the Emperor Constantine IV or his Chancery shared in this idea. In fact when, at the end of the eighth session of the sixth ecumenical council, he ordered the decisions of the council to be sent to the five patriarchs, he attributed the apostolic character to the patriarchs of Rome, Constantinople and Alexandria.[2] In his letter to Pope Agatho,[3] in which he announced the convocation of the council, he spoke of "the Catholic and apostolic churches," no doubt having in view the five patriarchs.

Another outstanding partisan of the Pentarchic idea was the patriarch Nicephorus. In his defense of the cult of images,[4] after the passage in which he so clearly expressed the Primacy of Rome, the patriarch mentions that in addition to Rome, Constantinople and the three patriarchal and apostolic sees— apparently, Alexandria, Antioch and Jerusalem—had equally condemned Iconoclasm. He then continued:

It is the ancient law of the Church that whatever uncertainties or controversies arise in the Church of God, they are resolved and defined by the ecumenical synods, with the assent and approbation of the bishops who hold the apostolic sees.[5]

It is well known that it was at the Ignatian Council of 869-870 that this Pentarchic idea was particularly developed. It will suffice here to cite the words by which the patrician Baanes, the representative of Basil I, defined this idea:[6]

God founded His Church on the five patriarchs and in the Gospels He defined that it could never completely fail because they are the chiefs of the Church. In effect Christ had said: ". . . and the gates of Hell shall not prevail against her," which means: if two of them should happen to fail, they will turn to the three others; if three of them happen to fail, they shall address themselves to two others; and if by chance, four of them come to failure, the last, who dwells in Christ Our God, the Chief of all, will restore again the rest of the body of the Church.

* * *

The idea of the Pentarchy has often been considered as being very dangerous for the Roman Primacy and in direct opposition to it, but this opinion is surely exaggerated. We must understand the problem from the Byzantine point of view. The Pentarchic idea was an expression of the universality of the Church. This universality was no longer represented by the universality of the Empire, which at this period was considerably reduced by the loss of the eastern provinces. Besides, the idea that the teaching of Our Lord should be defined and explained by the five patriarchs, each of them representing the bishops of his patriarchate, was aimed at safeguarding the rights of the *Sacerdotium* which the *Imperium* should never infringe. From this point of view the pentarchic idea represented great progress in the contest which the *Sacerdotium* had carried on for so long against the *Imperium*, since the latter continued to misunderstand the true spirit of Christian Hellenism and sought to usurp the rights of the *Sacerdotium* in matters of doctrine. It was a long struggle that the Eastern Church had to wage, and she was to suffer many defeats which happened, in particular, when a large part of the hierarchy rallied to the side of emperors who were in heresy. However, they were always able to make a recovery with the aid of the Church of the West, represented by the papacy.

We should also recognize that the Pentarchic idea did not at all suppose absolute equality among the patriarchs. The see of the ancient city of Rome was considered the first. This is always made sufficiently clear by those who remained faithfully attached to the principle. We may cite, for example, the Patriarch Nicephorus who, speaking of the condemnation of the Iconoclasts by the seventh ecumenical council, added:[7]

that the Iconoclasts have been rejected by the Catholic Church we know from the wise testimony and from the confirmation in the letters which were, a short time ago, sent by the most holy and blessed archbishop of ancient Rome, that is to say the first Apostolic See.

Furthermore, it is important to remember that the Pentarchic principle also expressed, according to the Byzantine mentality, the idea of the infallibility of the Church in matters of doctrine, a doctrine which the Orthodox church still professes today with firmness. Also, the Pentarchic principle offered a certain foundation for a *modus vivendi* between Rome and Constantinople which sufficed for those times. This principle, no doubt, found its partisans even in Rome, as can be seen from what the famous Anastasius Bibliothecarius said in the preface to his translation of the Acts of the Council of 869-870. He defines the Roman conception of the Pentarchy in the following manner: [8]

Just as Christ has placed in His body, that is to say, in His Church, a number of patriarchs equal to the number of the senses in the human body, the well being of the Church will not suffer as long as these sees are of the same will, just as the body will function properly as long as the five senses remain intact and healthy. And because, among them, the See of Rome has precedence, it can well be compared to the sense of sight which is certainly the first of the senses of the body, since it is the most vigilant and since it remains, more than any of the other senses, in communion with the whole body. [9]

If the Pentarchic idea had put down such deep roots in Byzantium in the course of the eighth and ninth centuries, we must see in that fact a sign that the Roman principle concerning the organization of the Church—the apostolic character of a see—had also gained considerable ground in Byzantium in its encounter with the principle of accommodation to the political organization of the Empire. The defeat of Iconoclasm in Byzantium was also the defeat of the traditional conception of the *Imperium,* and an occasion for the Church to defend ever more vigorously its rights in matters of doctrine, rights for which She had so valiantly struggled. Further, this makes clear that the apostolic character of the see of Constantinople had been definitively accepted by the Orientals. Under such conditions it was quite natural that the legend which traced the apostolic origin of Byzantium to the Apostle Andrew and his alleged ordination of Stachys as his first bishop gained greater and greater acceptance in Constantinople.

*   *   *

It has been said that the legend as to the activity of Andrew in Byzantium had been created by Photius whom Western theologians have always considered as the bitter enemy of the Roman Primacy.[10] What we said above shows that Photius, surely, cannot be held to be the inventor of this tradition. But was he aware of it and did he make use of it in his conflict with Rome? This is an important matter for us to discuss. To be sure, the legend was known in his times. We have seen that the Patriarch Ignatius knew the two traditions: the one that attributed the apostolic character of the see of Byzantium to the fact that Constantinople had become the heir of Ephesus (founded by John the Evangelist) when the diocese of Asia was submitted to its jurisdiction, and the more recent tradition, which accepted the legend of Andrew as an historical fact. Photius, then, certainly had reason to know this legend. But did he make use of it?

Until very recently it was customary to attribute to him the authorship of a pamphlet entitled "Against Those Who Say That Rome is the First See." [11] The legend about Andrew is one of the principle arguments which this work employs to refuse to Rome its privilege. Since Andrew was the first one Our Lord invited to follow Him, the see which he founded in Byzantium is superior to that of Rome.[12] If Photius had made use of an argument of that kind against the Roman Primacy, it would be reasonable to expect that traces of it should be found in his other authentic writings, especially since the author of this pamphlet seems convinced of the validity of this argument and the tone he takes is combative and arrogant.

Photius could have made mention of it in his letter of enthronement of 856, or at least at the Synod of 867 which condemned the intervention of Pope Nicholas I in the internal affairs of the Byzantine Church, or finally in the account of the Council of 879-880 which reinstated him. If the followers of Photius had spread this legend in Bulgaria to make an impression on the Khagan Boris Michael, Pope Nicholas I would have learned of it from the missionaries who had followed them. In fact, we find no evidence at all of this. Neither Nicholas I nor his successor, Hadrian II,[13] had any knowledge of it. Photius did not use this argument in his letter to Boris Michael even though it would have served to enhance the prestige of his see.

On the contrary, if we look into another work of Photius, his *Bibliotheca*, we get from it the impression that he had no confidence in this legend. He seems to know nothing at all of the list of the bishops of Byzantium from Stachys to Metrophanes even though he cites two works, now no longer extant, where he could not help finding it mentioned: the history of the Church written by Gelasius, Bishop of Caesarea in Palestine and a work entitled *Politeia* which recounts the lives of Metrophanes, of Alexander, his successor, and of Constantine the Great.[14] Photius had also read the apocryphal Acts of Andrew and those of the other Apostles. There, he could have found mention of a visit to Byzantium by Andrew, the same story that must have inspired the inventor of the ordination of Stachys by Andrew. But, quite on the contrary, Photius shows himself completely distrustful of these stories since he says that these writings are full of false and heretical information and he warns his readers to beware of them.[15]

The most decisive reason why Photius could neither have invented nor made use of this legend is the *Typicon* of Santa Sophia, a liturgical book which contains the feasts to be celebrated in that great cathedral of Constantinople as well as detailed liturgical descriptions.[16] This *Typicon* is combined with a *Synaxarion* of Constantinople and it seems to have been revised and re-edited toward the end of the ninth century, almost certainly during the second patriarchate of Photius.[17] It is important to note that the feast of St. Andrew is indicated for the 30th of November in very brief fashion without any mention at all of Stachys nor of the visit of Andrew to Byzantium. The feast of Stachys is not found at all in this work. This must mean that during the second patriarchate of Photius (879-886) the legendary tradition of Andrew was not officially accepted in the Byzantine Church. If Photius ordered a revision of this *Typicon* and if he did not introduce the legend of Andrew into it, it is then quite clear that he did not himself believe in it, and that he could not have made use of it in his controversy with Rome.

All this seems to indicate that the legend was only accepted in Byzantium in the course of the tenth century. The re-edition of the life of Andrew by the famous hagiographer Symeon Metaphrastes[18] served to popularize this legend and thus it was introduced, at the same time that the feast of Stachys was instituted, into the liturgical books of the tenth century.[19] In general, these liturgical books found their material for the feast of Stachys (celebrated on the 30th of June), and for Andrew, in the account of Pseudo-Dorotheus.

This should dispose of for good, the attribution to Photius of the pamphlet mentioned above. In the ninth century the legend of Andrew could not yet have enjoyed a role such as that described in this pamphlet.

*　　*　　*

What then, really was the attitude of Photius as to the Roman Primacy? Must he really be regarded as its relentless enemy? Recent studies show that on this matter there must be a radical change of view. First of all, we must keep in mind that the bishops whom Ignatius judged on canonical reasons

—Gregory Asbestas of Syracuse, Zacharias, the Metropolitan of Chalcedon and Theophilus, the Bishop of Amorium—had appealed to Rome on the basis of the canon of Sardica (343) which authorized such an appeal. These bishops belonged to the group supporting Photius. This fact is significant since it shows that his supporters were not so hostile to Rome as has often been said.

Appeals from Byzantium to Rome were indeed rare enough. We recall, of course, the famous appeals of St. John Chrysostom and of St. Flavian but there, doctrinal questions were involved. Appeals to Rome on such matters had been quite numerous.[20] As for other types of cases, we know of the appeal of Stephen of Larissa in Illyricum whose election had been annulled by Epiphanius, Patriarch of Constantinople. The Pope received this appeal and convoked a Synod which decided in favor of Stephen.[21] Unfortunately the Acts of this Synod are not extant. It should be said, nevertheless, that in this case, Illyricum was really a part of the Roman Patriarchate. Hence, it was altogether natural that an appeal should be made to Rome against the intervention of the Patriarch of Constantinople. Much more interesting is the case of the priest, John of Chalcedon and of the monk, Athanasius, who appealed to Pope Gregory the Great with the authorization of their superior, the Patriarch John IV of Constantinople.[22]

It has been said that the Patriarch Ignatius appealed to Pope Nicholas I against the "usurpation" of Photius, but recent discoveries have shown that Ignatius did not make an appeal and this is proved by his own categorical declaration at the Synod of Constantinople in 861: "Ego non appellavi Romam, nec appello." [23] The appeal made to Rome by the monk Theognostus in 863, allegedly in the name of Ignatius, was therefore, false. Nevertheless the fact is of some importance because it shows that at Byzantium, in the ninth century, it was accepted that an appeal to Rome in disciplinary questions was a distinct possibility.

All of this explains the statements made by the Fathers of the

Synod of 861 which met to judge the case of Ignatius. At this Synod, the pontifical legates, Rodoald, Bishop of Porto, and Zachary, Bishop of Anagni, kept insisting that they were acting in accord with the canons of the Synod of Sardica which granted to the Pope the right to judge another bishop. Even if Ignatius had not appealed, one fact is significant, namely, that the Byzantine Church granted to the representatives of the Pope the right to judge its former Patriarch in a disciplinary matter. That the legates had not received from the Pope the authority to pronounce a definitive judgment in his name, is of little importance. What is of importance is that the Pope and the Byzantine Church gave the legates the right to examine the case.

In this connection the statement of the legates and the Byzantine bishops in the course of the second session of the Synod is very significant: "We believe, Brethren, that the fundamental reason why we wish to re-examine this case is that the Fathers of the Council of Sardica decided that the Bishop of Rome had the power to reopen the case of any bishop." Theodore, Bishop of Laodicea, replied to them in the name of the Church of Constantinople: "This is a source of pleasure to our Church; we have no objection to it and we find it in no way offensive." These words are important because they show that in 861 the Church of Constantinople had finally accepted the canons of Sardica which, up until that time, they had declined to observe.[24] Photius was the promoter of this Synod and Bishop Theodore was his spokesman. Unfortunately, this Synod was rejected in 863 by Pope Nicholas I and its Acts were destroyed by order of the council of 869-870. However, these Acts were in the archives of the Lateran and there they were discovered in the eleventh century by Cardinal Deusdedit. Recognizing the importance of these admissions of the Roman Primacy, the Cardinal inserted some extracts from them in his canonical collection. He was, unfortunately, the only one to recognize their importance. Other canonists of the times of Gregory VII, who had access to the pontifical archives, contented themselves with copying some extracts from the Council of 869-870 which had condemned Photius and which, ten years later, was declared invalid. They did not realize that this council developed the Pentarchic idea which they rejected. Therefore, without realizing it, they bore the primary responsibility for the origin and development of what we can call the "legend of Photius." We can imagine what would have happened if the canonists of the Middle Ages had known of the Acts of the Synod of 861. They would have certainly exploited them in their arguments in favor of the Primacy of the see of Rome over the entire Church.

*   *   *

On the other hand, Photius is criticized by Western theologians who accuse him of having altered the wording of the letters which Pope John VIII sent to him, to the Emperor and to the Fathers, before the Council of 879-880 which was to rehabilitate him. It is true that the Patriarchal Chancery suppressed in these letters everything that could throw a false light on the case of Photius. But these changes had been made with the consent of the legates who were convinced that the case of Photius, his "usurpation" (he had been canonically elected), his deposition (the great majority of the clergy considered this deposition as unjust and had remained faithful to him), and his other activities had been portrayed by his enemies in Rome in an altogether false light. At this period, communications[25] between Rome and Constantinople were extremely difficult and, to save the prestige of the Holy See, the legates decided to accept the facts as they were, and not to prolong the incident by a new consultation with Rome, hoping to be able to explain their action later to Pope John VIII. They could have been almost certain that the Pope would approve their step, for they became aware at Constantinople of certain things that John VIII did not know and which considerably changed the whole aspect of the Photian problem.

They had learned that Photius and Ignatius were reconciled before the latter became ill, that Photius himself had made use of his own competence in medical matters to ease the sufferings of his one-time adversary, and that the whole initiative for the convocation of the council, at which they were the representatives of the Holy See, had been stimulated not only by Photius and the Emperor but also by Ignatius himself. If Ignatius had still been alive at the time of their arrival in Constantinople everything would have been different and the Photian legend would probably never have been born. Further, the legates also learned that Photius himself had solemnly canonized Ignatius after his death.[26] All this contributed to convince them that the information which they had gotten in Rome on this whole matter was quite incomplete. Once they were on the spot, they realized that their information had come from the relatively few but intensely bitter enemies of Photius.

The legates could well have been satisfied on the matter of the rights of Rome and its Primacy when they saw the important passage which affirmed the Roman Primacy that was to be found and in fact was stressed in the Greek version of the letters of the Pope. Here is the passage in question. The letter is from the Pope to the Emperor:[27]

Since it has seemed desirable to us to bring peace to the Church of God, we have sent our legates so that they might execute our will, even though, in your charity, you have already anticipated us, in reinstating Photius. We accept this action, which was done not by our own authority, even though we have the power to do it, but in obedience to the apostolic teachings. Since in fact we have received the Keys of the Kingdom of Heaven from the High Priest, Jesus Christ, by the intermediary of the first of the Apostles to whom the Lord said: "I will give unto you the Keys of the Kingdom of Heaven; everything which you will bind upon earth will be found to be bound in Heaven and everything which you will loose upon earth, will be found to be loosed in Heaven"; therefore, this apostolic throne has the power to bind and to loose,[28] and according to the words of Jeremiah, to uproot and to plant. This is why, by the authority of Peter, the Prince of the Apostles, we announce to you in union with the whole Church and through you as intermediary, we announce to our dear confreres and concelebrants, the patriarchs of Alexandria, Antioch and Jerusalem and to the other bishops and priests and to all the Church of Constantinople, that we are in agreement with you, or rather in agreement with God, and that we consent to your request. . . . Accept this man without any hesitation.

These words are clear. The fact that this passage of the Latin text was retained in the Greek version and in fact underlined by the addition of the words of Jeremiah (Jer. I. 10) is very revealing of the attitude maintained by Photius and his Chancery with regard to the Roman Primacy. This famous passage of Jeremiah had been applied, in 866, by Nicholas I to the Emperor Michael:[29] "Behold, today I give thee authority over the nations and over the kingdoms, to root them up and pull them down, to overthrow and lay them in ruins, to build them up and plant them anew." It is more than merely probable that Photius and his Chancery knew this letter and the passage in question had not escaped their attention. This gives a particular interest to the addition of the passage in the Greek version of the letter of John VIII and to its application to the Pope.[30] It is extremely regrettable that this source has been, up to the present time, completely forgotten by historians and modern theologians.[31] But it was one of the great canonists of the Middle Ages, Ivo of Chartres,[32] who recognized its importance and inserted it in his canonical collection. He and the other medieval canonists made use of it as an important argument to prove that the Pope, by reason of the plenitude of power which he possessed, had the power to annul any sentence whatever.

The presence of this passage in the Greek version of the pontifical letters is by no means an isolated case. At the beginning of this very same letter, Photius placed another quotation from the Gospel, which is considered as a Scriptural argument in favor of the Primacy (John, 21.17). This portion of the

Greek version is longer than it is in the original. After having
emphasized the respect for Rome which the Emperor had
shown in sending an embassy to the Pope in the affair of
Photius, the Patriarch said to the Pope:[33]

We may well ask who is the Master who has taught you to act
in this fashion?—surely, above all, it is Peter, the leader of the
Apostles whom the Lord has placed at the head of all the churches,
when He said to him: "Feed my sheep" (John, 21.17). Nor is it
only Peter, but also the holy Synods and constitutions. And besides,
it was the holy and orthodox decrees established by the Fathers,
as is clear from your divine and holy letters.

Likewise, in a letter addressed by the Pope to the Oriental
patriarchs and to the Church of Constantinople,[34] the author of
the Greek version has retained the passage from Luke, 22.32,
which is frequently quoted among the Scriptural arguments in
favor of the Roman Primacy: "I have prayed for thee that thy
faith may not fail; and do thou, when once thou hast turned
again, strengthen thy brethren." Here we may add that Photius
always speaks of Peter with the greatest respect, calling him
the Chief and the Leader of the Apostles.[35] It is not at all surprising that the Greek version of this correspondence omitted
mention of the request which the Pope had made, namely, that
Photius should ask pardon before the Fathers of the Council.
When the Pope wrote his letter, he was still under the influence of the information supplied to Rome and the West by
the enemies of Photius. But Photius and his clergy considered
his deposition and the persecution he had suffered as a grave
injustice and they had good reason to think so. The legates
had no difficulty whatever in agreeing to this omission once
they were on the spot in Byzantium and had come to understand the true situation.

One other detail should be emphasized here. We have seen[36]
that every time that Peter was mentioned as the founder of the
see of Rome in a letter of the Pope to the Empress, the Chancery of Tarasius had always added the name of Paul. It is in-

teresting to note that Photius, on the contrary, did no such thing. This shows quite well that he and his contemporaries had accepted the tradition that was followed at Rome since the fourth century and which attributed the foundation of the Roman see to Peter alone. There we may well see a new rapprochement of the Byzantine mentality and Roman ideas.

* * *

It has often been said that it was in 867, on the occasion of the Oriental Synod which condemned Pope Nicholas I, that Photius denied the Primacy to Rome and transferred it to Byzantium. It is unfortunate that the Acts of this Synod have been destroyed, so much so that it is almost impossible to know the exact manner in which the events took place. It is difficult to say, for example, how and in what fashion Nicholas I was really condemned. Still it is interesting to note that the homily pronounced by Photius at the very end of the Synod, —probably the only official document that has been preserved,[37] contains no attack against Rome, against the papacy, against the person of Nicholas I, nor against the Church of the West. The fact is that the Synod condemned the "errors" spread by the Roman missionaries in Bulgaria, errors which Photius had enumerated in his encyclical letter to the Oriental patriarchs,[38] and in which the Pope was accused of having "invaded" the Bulgarian territory claimed by Byzantium, and of not respecting the autonomy of the Byzantine Church by condemning its patriarch who had been canonically elected.

Was there really a formal excommunication? It is not easy to see how this would have been at all in keeping with the traditional practice of the Church. A rupture of relations, joined to the condemnation mentioned above, would surely have been regarded as an exclusion from all communion with the other churches. In any case, even if a formal condemnation had taken place, it was not directed against Rome nor against the papacy as such, but simply against the person of a Pope. A similar case, much more serious since it was concerned with matters of doctrine, had already occurred in the case of Pope Honorius.[39] Obviously, this condemnation, although much more serious, had been directed against the person of Pope Honorius and not against the institution which he represented.

From another source[40] we learn the Emperor Michael III and his consort Basil had sent a copy of the Acts of the Synod of 867 to the Emperor of the West, Louis II. They offered to recognize his imperial title if he would depose Nicholas I by accepting the Acts of the Synod containing the reasons for the condemnation.

This account is very important for the conclusion that we may draw from it. For, if the Emperors had wished to gain the favor of Louis II, the Acts of the Synod could not possibly have contained a condemnation of the Western Church, nor any denial of the Roman Primacy as such. That is to say, it could not have contained a formal attack against the papacy nor any transfer of the Primacy from Rome to Constantinople. This would have been completely unacceptable to Louis II and the very Westerners whose support was sought.

*　　*　　*

There is another matter that is no less important. When we study the relations between Rome and Byzantium we must always keep in mind that the Byzantines regarded their Empire as a continuation of the Roman Empire and that they called themselves *Romaioi*, Romans. Therefore it would have been impossible for them to degrade Rome, in placing the Bishop of Rome in the second place after that of Constantinople. Rome remained the first Capital, the foundation of their Empire, and the Bishop of Rome must always remain the first. A transfer of the Primacy to any other place than Rome would have been unthinkable.

We are well aware how solicitous the Byzantines were to keep alive the idea of a universal Christian Empire which had at its head a Roman Emperor residing in the New Rome, Constantinople. Thus, the coronation of Charlemagne by Pope Leo III in 800 appeared in the eyes of the Byzantines as an expression of a revolt against the legitimate Emperor and Charlemagne was considered as a usurper. The war which followed this "usurpation" did not end until 812 when the Byzantine ambassadors acclaimed Charlemagne as Emperor at Aix-la-Chapelle. The Byzantines interpreted this gesture in the sense that Charlemagne was recognized as co-Emperor ruling over the Western part of the Roman Empire. Thus they saved the idea of the universal Empire having its supreme Emperor in the New Rome.[41]

It is most important here to keep in mind that the idea of the unity of the Roman Empire was still very much alive in Byzantium in 867. The offer made to Louis II to recognize officially his imperial title was a new step which was intended to make clear and to confirm this unity. We have good reason to think that Photius himself propagated this idea. If we read his *Bibliotheca* we see clearly the extent to which the learned patriarch was imbued with the ideas of the classical period which he knew and admired so much.[42] He was the guardian of the ancient traditions of Byzantium. This allows us to believe that the Acts, a copy of which had been sent to Louis II, could not have been in the slightest degree, offensive to a Westerner, nor could they have contained an attack on the Roman Primacy or a condemnation of the usages of the Latin Church. In fact, this would have been the worst possible method for gaining the sympathy of Louis II or trying to persuade him to depose Pope Nicholas I, with whom, incidentally —and Byzantium was quite well aware of this—he had not always been on the best of terms.

The affair of Photius has been considered down to very recent times as the most disastrous for any agreement as to the

Roman Primacy in Byzantium. But actually, it was concluded with the full agreement of Byzantium and Rome. The rehabilitation of Photius was accepted by Pope John VIII. Photius renounced all jurisdiction over Bulgaria, doubtless on the condition that the Greek clergy would not be expelled; the Emperor Basil I provided military support for the Pope in his struggle against the Arabs and even though he had been urged by Leo VI to abdicate and to cede his place to the brother of the Emperor Stephen, Photius, who had retired to a monastery, died in communion with Rome.

Without any doubt it is during the patriarchate of Photius that we can find important documents to support the Roman Primacy, as it was conceived and accepted in Byzantium. Now, by a tragic irony of history, these documents remained unknown, and they were destroyed at the very moment when the disagreement took place, and thus Photius was "promoted" to the role of bitter adversary of the Roman Primacy.[43]

There is one other point that should not be forgotten and which is equally linked to the history of Photius. We know that the Emperor Basil wished to replace the *Ecloga,* the manual of Byzantine law which the Iconoclast Emperor Leo III had introduced, by another collection destined for official use. The two commissions named by the Emperor presented to Basil two manuals, the *Procheiron* and the *Epanagogé.* The latter is particularly interesting because it is an illustration of the position which the *Sacerdotium* had acquired in Byzantium after the victory over Iconoclasm. The second and third paragraphs of the introduction to this manual define the respective rights and duties of the Emperor and the Patriarch in the religious domain.

According to this document, the Emperor "should in the first place defend and promote everything that is written in Sacred Scripture, as well as all the dogmas that are approved by the holy Synods; he should also follow the Roman laws." It is evident that the author of this text sought to limit the powers of the Emperor in the ecclesiastical domain and to prevent his intervention in doctrinal questions. Without doubt, he had in mind the last intervention, that of the Iconoclast Emperors.

Paragraph 3 also defines the rights of the patriarch: "The patriarch is the only one capable of interpreting the rules of the ancient patriarchs, the prescriptions of the Holy Fathers and the decisions of the Holy Synods." The exclusive rights of the *Sacerdotium* in doctrinal matters are expressed there more clearly and more strongly perhaps than they had ever been in the past.

There are reasons to believe that it was Photius who inspired the formulation of these two paragraphs. He wished to bring to an end the conflicts which opposed the *Imperium* and the *Sacerdotium* in the ecclesiastical domain and to define once and for all the rights of the church in doctrinal matters. The period of religious struggles should come to a definitive end with the triumph of the Church. All the defenders of the rights of the Church against imperial interventions were to be called upon, and we are reminded of their courage in the struggles against the Monothelites and the Iconoclasts.

However, the *Epanagogé* did not become the official manual of Byzantine law,[44] since the Emperor chose the *Procheiron*. Why did he do this? We can imagine that he was fearful of too radical a limitation of his rights. It is also possible that the Byzantine episcopate did not wish to see so great an extension of the privilege of the patriarch which restricted to him alone the right to interpret dogma. According to the Byzantine custom, such a right belonged to the bishops united in council. In spite of this, the *Epanagogé* still continued to be used in private, and many authors of juridical works inserted some titles from it in their manuals.[45]

Thus came to an end this long period in Byzantine history which was characterized by doctrinal controversies. A new era opened up in the relations between the *Imperium* and the *Sacerdotium*, and the personality of Photius largely contributed to bring this about.

NOTES

1. PG 99, 1417C, letter 129; cf. also 1420. St. Maximus the Confessor was quite favorable to the Pentarchy (*Epistula ad Joannem Cubicularium*, PG 90, 464; Disputatio cum Pyrrho, *ibid.*, 91, 352).
2. Mansi, 11, 681ff.
3. *Ibid.*, 200C.
4. PG 100, 597BC.
5. The patriarch also tried to reconcile the idea of apostolicity and the principle of accommodation to the civil structure of the Empire. After stressing the apostolic origin of the see of Rome, he has this to say of Constantinople: "She is the New Rome, the first and the most eminent of the cities of our country, a distinction which comes to her from the imperial majesty."
6. Mansi, 16, 140-41.
7. Published by A. Papadopoulos-Kerameus in his *Analecta de la glanure de Jerusalem* (in Greek) (St. Petersburg, 5 vols., 1891-98), 1, 454-60. This passage has also been utilized by Zonaras to prove that Rome was, indeed, the first see and that the Primacy had not been transferred from Rome to Constantinople by Canon XXVIII of Chalcedon; see p. 148, *infra*. V. Grumel, in his study, "Quelques temoignages byzantins sur la primauté romaine, "in *Échos d'Orient*, 30 (1931, 422-30) also cites a passage of a work of Nicephorus, *Apologeticus minor pro imaginibus* (PG 100, 841CD) as proof of the Primacy. However, this is not a very significant passage.
8. Mansi, 16, 7.
9. It was not until the twelfth and thirteenth centuries that the idea of the Pentarchy became an anti-papal weapon. On the history of this idea, cf. Hergenröther, *Photius* (Regensburg, 1869), 2, 132ff.; 3, 766; M. Jugie, *Theologia dogmatica* (Paris, 1931), 4, 451-63; R. Vancourt, "Patriarcats," DTC 11, 2269-77; D. H. Marot, "Note sur la pentarchie," in *Irenikon*, 32 (1959), 436-42.
10. Quite recently, F. Dölger did so in his study: "Rom in der Gedankenwelt der Byzantiner," in *Zeitschrift für Kirchenges-*

chichte, 56 (1937), 40-42, re-edited in his book *Byzanz und die europäischen Staatenwelt* (Speyer, 1953), 112ff.

11. Re-edited by M. Gordillo, "Photius et primatus romanus," in *Orientalia Christiana Periodica*, 6 (1940), 5ff. The work is translated into Latin in M. Jugie, *Theologia dogmatica christ. orient.* (Paris, 1926), I, 131ff.

12. "If Rome claims the Primacy because of the leader [Peter], Byzantium is really the first see because of Andrew, who was the first one called [to be an apostle], and because of this seniority, he occupied the episcopal chair of Byzantium some years before his brother came to Rome."

13. Not a trace of this legend is to be found in the letters of Pope Nicholas I, in those of his successor, Hadrian II, nor, indeed, in the controversies of Ratramnus of Corbie and Aeneas of Paris, which were written at the invitation of Pope Nicholas after he had received the report of the Latin missionaries. For more details, see *The Idea of Apostolicity*, 248-53.

14. *Bibliotheca*, codex 88, 256; PG 103, 289ff.; *ibid.*, 104, 105-20.

15. *Ibid.*, codex 114; PG 103, 389.

16. A. Dimitrijevskij, *Opisanie liturgič. rukopisej. Typica* (Kiev, 1895), I, 27. There is a new edition by Juan Mateos, "Le Typicon de la Grande Église," in *Orientalia Christiana Periodica*, 165-66 (Rome, 1962-63), 165, p. 116.

17. Cf. A. Baumstark, "Das Typicon der Patmos-Handschrift 266," in *Jahrbuch für Liturgiewissenschaft*, 6 (1926), 98-111. Juan Mateos, *op. cit.*, vol. 165, in his introduction to the edition (p. xff.), has shown that Baumstark's argument has some weak points. However, he is willing to admit that codex 266 of the Monastery of St. John the Theologian on the island of Patmos was written at the end of the ninth century, or the beginning of the tenth, at the latest. The script is the minuscule in use in Byzantium in the ninth and tenth centuries. The feast of St. Andrew is described in exactly the same fashion in all the known manuscripts. See p. 111, *infra.* what is there said about the canonization of Ignatius by Photius, himself.

18. Published in the *Menaia* (Venice, 1843), 235ff. re-edited in the *Menaion* of November (Athens, 1926), 318-25.

19. H. Delahaye, *Synaxarium Ecclesiae Constantinopolitanae*, AA. SS. Propylaea, Novembris (Bruxelles, 1902), 265ff.

20. On cases of recourse to Rome, see Batiffol, *Cathedra Petri*, 215ff., and P. Bernadakis, "Les appels au pape dans l'Église grecque jusqu'à Photius," in *Échos d'Orient*, 6 (1903), 30-42, 118-25, 249-57.

21. Cf. G. Bardy, "Boniface II," in DHGE (Paris, 1937), 9, 897. For more details, see L. Duchesne, *Autonomies ecclésiastiques, Églises separées* (Paris, 1896), 245-60.

22. See p. 80, *supra*.

23. See the edition of the Acts of the synod of 861 by W. v. Glanvell, *Die Kanonessammlung des Kardinals Deusdedit* (Paderborn, 1905), 607.

24. This is the way in which we must understand what Photius said in his letter to Nicholas I (PG 102. 600, 601, 604). What he had in mind was the canon which forbade the elevation of laymen to the episcopacy. Cf. the letters of Nicholas to Photius (MGH, *Epistolae*, VI, 450, 537, 538). In the first letter of 862, Nicholas mentioned only Canon XIII of the Synod of Sardica (Mansi, 3, 27), which forbade the elevation of laymen to high ecclesiastical posts. In his letter of 866 (MGH, VI, 537-38), he insists on that same canon, but he also has in mind Canon III (Mansi, 3, 23), since he makes mention of the appeal to the Pope, against the judgment of the patriarch, made by bishops Zachary and Gregory of Syracuse. The Pope was right when he said that the canons of Sardica were to be found in the Greek canonical collection of John the Scholastic, in the sixth century (*Synagoga 50 titulorum*, published by V. Beneševič [Munich, 1937] 63, canon III), but that Canon XIII was not there. The fact that Canon III was included in the Greek canonical collection explains why the Patriarch, Ignatius, could not ignore the appeal made by the bishops he had condemned. This also explains the attitude of the Byzantine bishops at Sardica. To be sure, they were not inclined to go quite as far as the legates in the interpretation of Canon III but, nevertheless, they realized they were obliged to accept it.

25. Cf. what I have said on this topic in *The Photian Schism* (Paris, 1950), p. 139.

26. Our information on the reconciliation of Photius with Ignatius and on the canonization of Ignatius by Photius come to us from an anti-Photianist, in a document which I found, quite by

chance, in a manuscript of Mt. Sinai (Sinait. gr. 482 1117, fol. 364^v, lines 32, 36-38). For more details, see F. Dvornik, *The Patriarch Photius in the Light of Recent Research* (Munich, 1958), 20, 35, 39, 56. This document, which is another version of the Synodicon Vetus, published by J. Pappe in J. A. Fabricius—G. C. Harles, *Bibliotheca Graeca* (Hamburg, 1809), vol. 12, will be published by Dumbarton Oaks. There exists another manuscript containing the same information.

The feast of Ignatius was placed in the *Typicon*, re-edited during the second patriarchate of Photius, on October 22. It is quite possible that the mosaic showing a portrait of Ignatius, which was recently discovered in Santa Sophia, was done under the aegis of Photius. It was reproduced for the first time by C. Mango, his book "Material for the Study of the Mosaics in St. Sophia in Istanbul," in *Dumbarton Oaks Studies*, 8 (1962), 61ff. table 62.

27. Mansi, 17, 400. There is no mention of Jeremiah in the original Latin version.

28. The Greek version cites Matt., 16, 19. The passage should be interpreted as being addressed directly to Peter, who is thus invested with universal jurisdiction. We are aware that Matt., 16, 18, was often interpreted in the East, as referring to the faith of Peter (on this rock), and not to his person. Cf. F. Dvornik, *The Photian Schism*, p. 187.

29. MGH, *Epistolae*, VI, 509. PL 109. 1042.

30. This passage is found in the Mass, *Pro Confessore Summo Pontifice*.

31. Even the editors of the letters of Photius in the MGH have omitted this phrase (cf. Epistolae, VII, 167ff.).

32. *Decretum*, PL 161, 56ff.

33. Mansi, 17, 396D; MGH, *Epp.* VII, 167

34. Mansi, 17, 452; MGH *Epp.* VII, 177.

35. See also what he says of St. Peter in his homilies. Cf. C. Mango, *The Homilies of Photius* (Cambridge, Mass., 1958), 50: "Foundation of the Church, bearer of the keys of heaven"; p. 59; "Bearer of the keys of heaven"; p. 312: "Bearer of the keys of heaven, foundation and rock of the faith." Cf. also, Th. Spačil, *op. cit.*, 38-41.

36. See p. 97, *supra.*

37. This has been shown by C. Mango, *The Homilies of Photius*, 296ff.

38. PG 102, 732ff.

39. See p. 92, *supra*.

40. Nicetas, *Vita Ignatii*, PG 105, 537; Mansi, 16, 417. Cf. F. Dölger, *Byzanz und der europäische Staatenwelt* (Ettal, 1953), 313ff.

41. Cf. Dölger, *op. cit.*, 282ff. On Charlemagne, his ideas and his relations with Byzantium, see my book, *The Making of Central and Eastern Europe* (London, 1949), 1-7, 41-47. The problem of the coronation of Charlemagne and the role played by Leo III on that occasion, as well as the reaction of the Byzantines to this "revolutionary" action, have been studied recently by W. Ohnesorge in "Das Kaisertum der Eirene und die Kaiserkrönung Karls des Grossen," *Saeculum*, 14 (1963) 221-47.

42. See my paper, "Patriarch Photius, Scholar and Statesman," in *Classical Folia*, 13 (1959), 3-18; 14 (1960), 3-22.

43. It is equally regrettable that the Ignatian Synod of 869-870 which condemned Photius, is still counted as the eighth among the ecumenical councils by Western canonists. The Orientals considered that this council had been suppressed by the Synod of Union of 879-880, and they recognize no more than seven ecumenical councils. They hold it against the Westerners for refusing them this small concession, in view of the fact that it had been shown that the council had only been added to the first seven councils by the reforming canonists of the eleventh and twelfth centuries. See Dvornik, *The Schism of Photius*, 433.

44. Contrary to what Congar thinks in *Conscience ecclésiologique*, 210.

45. For more details, See The *Idea of Apostolicity*, 271-75.

THE CRISIS OF THE

ELEVENTH CENTURY

GREAT HOPES WERE entertained in Byzantium that the Council of Union of 879-880 was going to open a period of good relations between Byzantium and Rome. The understanding that had been arrived at between the two Churches seemed to have been sealed for all time—at least that was what was thought at the time—by the first canon of this Synod [1] and by the proclamation made in the course of the fourth session which declared that each Church should preserve its own customs and maintain its own rights.[2] This appeared to be a solid base for good relations between the two Churches.

The matter was of great importance, for the two Churches —as we pointed out in our introduction[3]—had not been accustomed to follow the same usage in matter of canonical legislation. The Byzantines were content with the so-called "apostolic canons" and the decisions of the ecumenical councils and certain local Synods which they complemented by the imperial ordinances in religious matters. In the West, in the beginning of the sixth century they began to add to the conciliar canons the decretals of the Pope, without any concern

124

for imperial legislation.[4] In any discussion of the validity of the canons of Sardica in the affair of Ignatius and of Photius, we must keep in mind the complications which arose from the differences of acceptance and interpretation of certain canons.

The canon of the Council of Union and the declarations made during the fourth session kept these differences clearly in view. Tolerance of divergent practices and usages was required if new conflicts between the two Churches were to be avoided in the future. Unfortunately, this tolerance was not practiced by either side.

The story of the fourth marriage of the Emperor Leo VI, which the Church of the East considered as illicit, shows that the right of appeal to the Pope continued to be admitted and practiced in Byzantium. The Emperor Leo VI to whom the Patriarch Nicholas the Mystic had refused permission for this fourth marriage had turned toward Rome and toward the other patriarchs asking them if such a marriage would be permissible. Pope Sergius III (904-911) sanctioned the marriage even though it was to result in an internal schism in the Byzantine Church. This appeal of Leo VI can, quite properly, be regarded as an appeal to Rome in a disciplinary matter.[5]

It is true that in 920 when Nicholas the Mystic, after having been reinstated in his office by the Regent and co-Emperor Romanus I (920-944), convoked a local Synod, the fourth marriage was condemned by him in the presence of the legates of Pope John X. But this incident itself at least shows that the two Churches were always on good terms. This also appears in 933, when John XI, at the request of Romanus II (959-963), sent legates to Constantinople to sanction the elevation of Theophylactus, the son of the Emperor, to the patriarchal throne even though he was then only sixteen years of age. These two incidents show that the papacy had become dependent on the Byzantine emperors because of the disastrous conditions which obtained in Italy as a result of the deterioration of the Carolingian empire, the protector of Rome, and because of the intrigues of the Roman nobility who made and unmade Popes at will.

This situation changed in 962 when Otto I became Emperor and restored the idea of a Roman Empire of the West; from then on he acquired a direct influence over the election of the Popes. This was a sign that the new nations of the West, who had never lived under the direct government of ancient Rome and to whom the idea of a universal empire governed by a Roman Emperor resident in New Rome was completely strange, began to assert their part in the government of the Christian world.[6]

An incident that took place in 968 shows how little these newcomers understood the idea of a universal empire in which Byzantium believed so strongly. That year, Otto I sent a Lombard who knew Greek, Liutprand of Cremona, to the Emperor Nicephorus Phocas, to ask of him the hand of the Byzantine Princess for his son, the future Emperor. Pope John XII, recommending the ambassador to the Emperor, called Nicephorus "Emperor of the Greeks." He could have hardly offered a more striking insult to the Byzantines who thought of themselves as Romans. The report that Liutprand[7] made on his mission also shows how little the new nations understood the Byzantine mentality.

However, this incident was closed in 972 when the Emperor John Tzimisces (969-976) consented to the marriage of his niece, Theophano, to Otto II. His son, Otto III, who had been raised by his Greek mother, seemed as if he would bring about a new stage in the relations between East and West. A Byzantine Princess, who was to marry Otto III, was already on her way to Rome when suddenly the news arrived of the death of the young emperor (1002).[8]

*   *   *

During the pontificate of the Germanic Popes who had been installed by the Ottos and by Henry II, some innovations that were strange to the Byzantines were introduced in Rome. The most important was the introduction of the *Filioque* which was officially inserted into the Nicene Creed.[9] It appears that Pope Sergius IV (1009-1012) had sent to Byzantium, with the customary synodical letter on taking possession of the Papal throne, his profession of faith containing the *Filioque*. Naturally, this resulted in a refusal on the part of the Patriarch Sergius II and the name of the Pope was not inscribed in the Byzantine diptychs, the list of the names of those to be commemorated during divine service. It is possible that it was from this moment that the Byzantines discontinued their ancient practice of inscribing the names of the Roman patriarchs in their diptychs. This incident was later regarded by some as the beginning of the schism. Nicetas of Nicaea who in the eleventh century wrote a treatise on the Greek schism, speaks of a rupture which took place under Pope Sergius, but he admits that he was not aware of the reason for it.[10]

Nevertheless this incident was neither the denial of the Roman Primacy on the part of Byzantium nor, to tell the truth, the beginning of a schism. To be sure, since the end of the tenth century the two Churches had not had many points of contact but they were still not enemies. However, the estrangement of the two worlds continued to grow. Less and less did the Westerners understand the Byzantine concept of a universal Christian Empire and in the West, the idea that only the Emperor crowned by the Pope in Rome was the true successor of the Caesars began to receive general acceptance. The existence of a Roman Emperor in Constantinople had all but faded from memory.

In spite of all this, Byzantium remained close to Rome, as long as she still had possessions in the south of Italy, in spite of her refusal or her incapacity to defend them. As long as there existed in South Italy this bridge between Byzantium and the West, it was still possible that contacts between Constantinople and Rome could become more frequent and more cordial. Unfortunately, this bridge was suddenly broken down by the conquest of the Byzantine territory in Italy by the Normans.[11] This event was to have consequences more disastrous for the relations between the East and the West than the destruction of the bridge of Illyricum by the Avars and the Slavs in the sixth century.

*　　*　　*

One other circumstance was destined to bear an even greater responsibility for the separation which grew between the two Churches. This was the profound transformation which took place in Western Christendom as a result of the introduction of certain Germanic customs into ecclesiastical organization. The Germanic conception of real property was fundamentally different from that of the Romans and the Greeks. Being incapable of conceiving the possibility that an institution could become the owner of land or of real estate, the Germanic nations continued to regard the man who had built it, as the only owner of real property or of a building. The application of this idea to ecclesiastical institutions was the cause of a revolutionary development in the Western Church. Thus it was that the bishops lost the administrative control of churches which they had not themselves constructed. The founders considered the churches built at their expense as their own property and they arrogated to themselves the right of naming the priests who were to be charged with their administration.

This system of privately owned churches (Eigenkirchen) was also applied in France to abbeys and bishoprics. When it was joined to the feudal system, it permitted the kings of the Ottonian dynasty to transform the church of Germany into a "Church of the Empire" (Reichskirche), totally under the control of the King and the Emperor.

As a consequence of this state of affairs, Western Christendom became, in the eleventh century, a collection of autonomous and national churches, over which the princes, as "kings and priests," not only claimed administration but also ownership. As a result, the central power, the papacy, the very back-bone of the Church, found itself deprived of its prerogatives.[12] The abuses which resulted therefrom—simony, lay investiture, a married clergy—were responsible for the deterioration of the Church of the West in the tenth and eleventh centuries.

This provoked a reaction. Unfortunately this reaction—a reform movement—did not begin at Rome, the center of Christendom, but in the confines of France and the Empire, in Lorraine and in Burgundy, where the intervention of the Emperor or the King was not normally to be expected.[13] The reformers saw no other remedy than the restoration of the power and influence of the papacy as a means of freeing the Church from the stifling influence of the lay power. The principle was fundamentally good. As an antidote to the lay ownership of churches, the reformers invoked the ancient principle of Roman law according to which a moral person had the capacity to possess land and real property.

Unfortunately, these reformers were totally unaware of the peculiar situation of the Eastern churches and they naturally wished to extend everywhere the direct right of intervention of the papacy—even in the East where the churches had enjoyed a good deal of autonomy in running their internal affairs according to their own custom. In wishing to extend celibacy of the clergy which they were enforcing in the West, they forgot the practice of the East that priests were married. They also forgot that there were no churches under lay ownership in the East and that no reform was necessary in this matter. In preaching obedience to Rome and in enforcing observance of Roman customs they took no account whatever of the fact that the East had different customs and different rites.

An incident that took place in 1024 shows us well the danger for relations between the two Churches which could arise from the ignorance of the Byzantine mentality in reforming circles. Raoul Glaber, a Benedictine monk who spent some time in various monasteries, especially at Dijon under Abbot William and at Cluny under Abbot St. Odilo, reports in his chronicle that the reformers were very much disturbed when they learned "that the Byzantines wished, without any justification, to obtain Roman recognition of their supremacy." That is the way he entitled the chapter in which he told the story.[14] It is altogether probable that this is the way in which the reformers interpreted the intention of the Byzantines. However, even according to Glaber, the matter was not quite as scandalous as people wished to believe it was. According to him:

Around the year of Our Lord 1024, the Patriarch of Constantinople as well as the Emperor Basil and some other Greeks, decided to obtain from the Roman Pontiff authorization for the Church of Constantinople to be called "universal" in all parts of the territory which came under it, the same as the Church of Rome was considered in the entire world.

What are we to make of this piece of information? It is altogether likely that the Emperor Basil II (976-1025) had approached Pope John XIX (1024-1032), with a view to putting an end to the long controversy on the relative position of the two sees in the hierarchy of the Church. At this time, he was at the very summit of his power. After having stopped the advance of the Turks in Asia Minor and subdued Bulgaria, he dreamed of reconquering Sicily which was in the hands of the Arabs and of extending his influence over central Italy. In the accomplishment of this plan, an alliance with the Pope could not but have been advantageous. Basically, it was only a question of reissuing the ordinances of Justinian II, of Phocas and of Justinian I. If we may believe Raoul Glaber himself, the Greeks were ready to recognize the supreme power of the Roman see over the whole Church and even over Constantinople. But the intervention of the reformers—the Abbot William had addressed to the Pope a rather stiff letter—seems to have intimidated the Pope, for whom, incidentally, Glaber did not have a very high opinion. As a result, this last attempt at agreement was to be a failure.

*   *   *

After the election of Pope Leo IX (1049-1054), the nephew of Emperor Henry III, and quite favorable to reform, the Reform Movement took root also in Rome. The Pope had brought along with him to Rome some of the most zealous reformers, notably Humbert whom he named a Cardinal and Frederick of Lorraine who became Chancellor of the Roman Church. The Romans extended their activities over South Italy into the Byzantine territory where were found both Greek and Latin communities. Taking their stand on the privileges granted by the Donation of Constantine[15]—this forged document had become one of the most "decisive arguments for the extension of papal power—the Pope tried to extend his direct influence over the whole of Italy. He also laid claim to Sicily, a territory considered to be Byzantine although occupied by the Arabs and he appointed an archbishop there. He convoked a Synod at Siponto in 1050 where a great number of decrees were voted with a view to furthering the reform. Some of these decrees were directed against Greek liturgical usages which had been established in Italy. The reforming clergy, thereupon, launched into an active campaign in all of the provinces, including Apulia, which was a Byzantine area.

The Greeks began to be disturbed. The Patriarch Michael Cerularius (1043-1058),[16] an ambitious and haughty man, who had little love for Latins, reacted with counter measures. Since it seemed that the Latins intended to replace the Greek liturgy by the Latin rite in Italy, he gave orders that all the Latin establishments in Constantinople must adopt the Greek rite under penalty of being closed. Aiming at the Greeks in Apulia, he ordered Leo, the Archbishop of Ochrida, to compose a treatise defending the Greek rite and putting the blame on Latin usage.

Leo sent his famous letter[17] to the Latin bishop of Trani, in Byzantine territory, in which he criticized Latin practices and in particular the use of unleavened bread in the Sacrifice of the Mass. It is interesting to note that he made no mention of the *Filioque*. This letter was circulated at the worst possible moment. It served to increase the anti-Latin grievances in Apulia at a time when, because of the advance of the Normans who threatened both papal and Byzantine territory, a military and political alliance between the Pope and Byzantium was absolutely necessary. In order to win over the Latin population, the Emperor Constantine IX Monomachus (1042-1059), appointed as governor of the Byzantine territory a Latin named Argyrus who engineered a pact with the Pope directed against the Normans.[18] This caused the animosity of the Patriarch to grow still stronger because Argyrus was his personal enemy. Unfortunately, the papal and Byzantine armies were defeated by the Normans in June, 1053 and the Pope was taken prisoner.

Meantime, Humbert, at the request of the Pope, had composed a letter of reply to Leo of Ochrida, a long treatise full of abusive criticism against Greek usages. This treatise was not directed to Constantinople because, in the interval, the Emperor had sent a new embassy to conclude an anti-Norman alliance and he persuaded the Patriarch to address a friendly letter to the Pope. The Pope then decided to send Humbert, Frederick of Lorraine and Peter of Amalfi as legates to Constantinople. Humbert prepared a second reply to the attacks of Leo. This one was shorter but in the circumstances, it was still extremely undiplomatic. He tried to include in it everything that he had said in his former treatise and the Patriarch could not help but be offended because the Cardinal expressed doubts as to the legitimacy of his election, doubts which had no justification whatever. Humbert was annoyed also at the use of the title "ecumenical" which, he said, violated the rights of Alexandria and of Antioch who had precedence over Constantinople because of their direct connection with the Apostle Peter. He further said that this title was a usurpation of the right which belonged to Rome, the Mother of all the sees.

Once again, then, the Petrine argument was launched against the see of Constantinople.

The patriarch, who had been expecting a friendly letter in reply to his own, which had been short and polite, was surprised and suspected machinations on the part of his enemy Argyrus. He was offended by the attitude of Humbert whom he considered to be arrogant and he refused to continue the negotiations with the legates, declaring that they were not sent by the Pope at all but by Argyrus.

In reply, Humbert took the offensive, trusting, no doubt, in the assistance of the Emperor and probably encouraged by Argyrus in an attempt to depose the Patriarch. He published the first, very long letter which was translated into Greek as a sort of pamphlet against the Patriarch. In another dispute with the Monk Nicetas Stethatos, who had written a treatise in defense of the Greek usages attacked by the Cardinal, Humbert was the one to bring up the question of *Filioque*. His reply to the criticism of Latin usage which the Greek monk had discussed was impassioned and offensive.[19] The Emperor, however, who was most anxious to bring about an agreement with the Pope, forced Nicetas to repudiate his writings and to humble himself before Humbert.

The principles of the reformers became clear to the Byzantines for the first time in the pamphlets and letters of Humbert. Up to that time they had not realized the changes that had taken place in the mentality of the Roman Church. In all frankness, they simply did not understand them. If we consider the development that had taken place in Byzantine thinking with regard to the papacy and its position in the Church, we see that the extension of the absolute and direct authority of the Pope over all the bishops and the faithful such as it was preached by the reformers was, to the Byzantine mind, nothing less than a complete denial of the tradition with which they had been familiar. This extension would lead to the abolition of the autonomy of their churches. The liturgical uses of Byzantium were considered at least suspect, if not condemned outright. This is why the argument, which Humbert drew from the Donation of Constantine to support his view, was unacceptable to the Byzantines.

What they did find particularly offensive was the mode of behavior of the legates, so much so that far from turning them against the patriarchs as Humbert had hoped, the whole of the Byzantine clergy closed ranks around their leader. What Humbert had to say to them was much too new for them and his criticism of Greek usages offended their patriotic sentiments. Humbert lost all patience and even though he knew that the Pope had died, he composed his famous letter of excommunication against the Patriarch, laid it on the altar of Santa Sophia and departed from Constantinople.

The bull of excommunication composed by Humbert shows very clearly how far the mentality of the Roman Church had changed under the influence of the reformers and how little understanding they had of the Eastern Church and its customs. Humbert thought that he discovered in the East the roots of all the great heresies and he accused them of simony while, as a matter of fact, it was only in the West that simony was rampant. He condemned their married clergy, their beards and their long hair, and he accused the Byzantines of having suppressed the *Filioque* from the Nicene Creed, thereby showing his ignorance of the history of the Church.[20] The contents of the bull were found to be profoundly shocking not only by the Patriarch but also by the Emperor. The tumult that ensued among the people obliged the Emperor to abandon his efforts at peacemaking and to convoke the permanent Synod. This Synod condemned the bull, a copy of it was burned in public, and the Synod excommunicated the legates whom they said had been sent by Argyrus.

Thus it was that the embassy which was to have concluded an alliance between Byzantium and the papacy ended in this tragic rupture. The legates, especially Humbert, were gravely responsible. However, the correspondence between Michael

Cerularius and Peter, Patriarch of Antioch, also show us that Cerularius should bear some of the blame. At the same time this correspondence makes clear how far the separation between Byzantium and Rome had progressed, and we can also see that Cerularius had some inaccurate and preconceived ideas on the Roman Church and its practices.[21]

* * *

However, just as Cerularius had not been turned against the Pope and against the Latin Church as such and since the legates had excommunicated only the Patriarch and his supporters, it is not proper to say that the Roman Primacy had been rejected by Byzantium and that the schism was already in existence between the two Churches. New negotiations were broached during the pontificates of Victor II, Stephen IX and, in 1072, Alexander II, but the Norman question made these negotiations and any possible agreement extremely difficult.

At the invitation of Alexander II, St. Peter Damian composed a treatise on the errors of the Greeks,[22] which he dedicated to a patriarch—it is difficult to know which patriarch he had in mind—who had asked the Latins to explain their doctrine according to which the Holy Spirit proceeded from the Father and the Son. In this treatise Damian expresses his pleasure that the patriarch had sought information not from just anybody, but directly from St. Peter. He identified the Pope with the apostle "to whom God himself has deigned to unveil these secrets." After quoting the famous passage of Matt. 16 he continued:

The Creator of the world has chosen him before all other mortals on earth and has granted to him, in virtue of a perpetual privilege, the Chair of the Supreme Magisterium, so that any man who desires to know something that is profoundly divine, should turn toward the oracle and the doctrine of this teacher.

Damian went on to explain in irenic fashion the Catholic doctrine on the *Filioque*.

This definition of the Primacy of the Pope could have been accepted by the Greeks. St. Peter was always venerated in the Byzantine Church and they accorded him very great respect,[23] and his successors at Rome were always considered as the first masters in doctrinal matters. Although the approach made by the patriarch and the reply of Damian do not seem to have had any tangible results, the incident shows at least that it was always possible, even after 1054, to discuss in calm and friendly fashion the differences which existed between the two churches.

Curiously, it seems that at the outset of the negotiations broached by the Emperor Michael VII with Pope Gregory VII (1073-1085) they were of a nature to bring about a rapprochement between the two churches. The Byzantine Empire was then in great danger after the disaster of Manzikert. The Turks occupied a great part of Asia Minor and they threatened the eastern part of the empire. These difficulties caused the Emperor to turn to the Pope for military aid, in return for a promise of a renewal of friendly contacts with Rome.

The Pope replied in a cordial letter in which he expressed his satisfaction at this gesture. He planned to raise an army to come to the aid of Constantinople and to accompany it in person. Unfortunately, the appeal that Gregory made to the princes— it was also addressed to the Emperor Henry IV—failed to win any support for granting assistance to Constantinople.[24] Soon after, the violent opposition which Henry IV raised against the new papal ideology of the superiority of the spiritual over the temporal power forced the Pope to seek aid and protection from the Normans, the bitter enemies of Byzantium. The only result of this alliance of the Pope with the Normans was to put a definitive end to the possibility of agreement with Byzantium, and the memory of Gregory VII was always particularly hated by the Byzantines, if we are to believe what Anna Comnena said of him.[25] In general, we may well doubt whether Gregory would have been any happier in his relations with Byzantium than had been Leo IX. We only have to read his *Dictatus Papae*[26] to see the enormous distance which, from then on, separated East and West, since by now, the ideas of the reformers had been completely developed and they were applied to the relations of the *Sacerdotium* and the *Imperium*. We also get the impression that Gregory, in composing this document, also had in mind certain pretensions of Byzantium. The declaration that the title "universal" belonged exclusively to the Pope seemed to indicate this fact. The same is clear from the fact that the name of the Pope was to be the only one mentioned everywhere in the liturgy and that the title "Papa" was uniquely reserved to the Bishop of Rome. Likewise it was the Pope alone who should confirm the decisions of all Synods. Naturally there were many objections to these demands among the Byzantines. It was impossible for the Byzantines to grant the Pope the power of deposing an Emperor, of freeing his subjects from the obedience which was due to him even if he were failing in his duty; it was equally impossible for them to grant the Pope the right to wear the insignia of the Emperor and to oblige kings to salute him by kissing his feet.

The document issued by Gregory which proclaimed the superiority of the spiritual over the temporal power destroyed the last vestiges of Christian Hellenism which had remained in the West. The Roman Church now professed a new political ideology, very different from that which had existed up to this time in the East, and there was little chance that a compromise would ever emerge between these two ideologies.

It seems that even then the Byzantines did not fully understand how profound a change had taken place. For example, the Metropolitan of Kiev, John II (1080-1089),[27] sent a letter to the Anti-Pope Clement III which seems to indicate that he still believed in the possibility of agreement between Rome and Byzantium. The Metropolitan manifested a very friendly attitude to Rome and the Primacy did not seem to bother him as much as certain other "abuses" which he observed in the Latin Church, notably the *Filioque*. He exhorted Clement III to enter into contact with the Patriarch of Constantinople and to work for the suppression of these "abuses."

* * *

The alliance between Gregory VII and the Normans obliged the Emperor Alexis Comnenus (1081-1118) to turn to Henry IV [28] and toward his anti-Pope. The latter had already entered into contact with Constantinople when the successor of Gregory VII, Urban II, sent legates to the Emperor. The Emperor, at this juncture probably considering that Henry IV could not be very much use to him, opened negotiations with Urban II. He hoped that the Pope would be able to hold back the Normans from Byzantium.

We learn of all this from the Acts of the Synod which was convoked by the Emperor in 1089. [29] The Emperor who presided declared that the Pope was ready to establish harmony between Rome and Byzantium but he was said to be annoyed that the names of the Pope had been suppressed in the diptychs of Constantinople. He also asked if there had been any canonical decision authorizing the rupture with Rome. The prelates declared that there had been no such document, but since important differences existed in the customs of the two Churches they felt it necessary that these should be removed before the name of the Pope could be inscribed in the diptychs.

It was then that the Patriarch Nicholas III (1084-1111) asked the Pope to send, as a beginning, his profession of faith to Constantinople, since that had happened each time a new Pope had addressed to Constantinople his letter of enthronement. If this profession of faith was satisfactory his name would then be inscribed in the diptychs. In that case, a Synod would meet at Constantinople eighteen months later where, in the presence of the Pope and his envoys, they would discuss the differences which existed between the two Churches.

It seems fairly clear that the Pope was quite ready to go to

Constantinople and that the Norman Prince Roger Guiscard encouraged him in this intention.[30] Unfortunately, we do not have sufficient information to be able to decide if the Pope really sent the letter which the Patriarch asked for and if his name was inscribed in the diptychs.

Two documents of the same period show us the difficulties which barred the road to a renewal of more cordial contact. One is a letter of Basil, the Metropolitan of Reggio in Calabria. He had had to leave his see, being expelled by the Normans when he refused, after the conquest, to submit himself to the jurisdiction of the Pope. Before the convocation of the Synod by the Patriarch, Basil had been sent to the Pope and he met Urban II at the Synod of Melfi where he had a rather painful interview with him. His letter, full of bitterness, was addressed to Nicholas III at the end of 1089 and it is full of accusations against the Pope, the Normans, and the Latins in general.[31] This letter reveals to us the sentiments of the Greeks whom the Normans had forced out of Calabria and who saw their sees occupied by Latin prelates. Once again the Pope laid claim to rights over that part of Italy that had been Byzantine, which had been taken from him by the Iconoclast Emperor Leo III in 732-733.[32] The Byzantines, quite naturally, found this as a source of irritation.

The other document is a letter sent by Nicholas III to Symeon II, Patriarch of Jerusalem.[33] This letter informs us that Pope Urban II had addressed the other patriarchs in making the same request as he had made to the Emperor. Symeon communicated this demand of the Pope to his colleague of Constantinople, Nicholas III. The reply of the latter shows us that he was very much preoccupied with the "errors" of the Latins, especially that of unleavened bread and the *Filioque*. He quotes the usual arguments against these "errors," and he also discusses the citations from Scripture by which the Pope endeavored to prove his right to Primacy in the Church. But, he did allow to the Pope a certain primacy.

There was a time when the Pope was the first among us, since he shared the same sentiments as we do. Now that he holds such different views, how can we call him the first? If he will show us the identity of his faith with ours, he will then receive the Primacy . . . but, if he will not do that, he will never receive what he asks of us.

This letter was sent before the Synod of 1089. Subsequently, the Patriarch softened his view but the tone and content of this letter shows how strong was the memory of 1054 in Byzantium. In spite of this, the negotiations seemed to have continued, and the agreement between Rome and Byzantium always appeared as still a possibility.

*   *   *

It was once again an Archbishop of Ochrida, Theophylactus, who was invited to give his views on the "errors" of the Latins. This he did in a short treatise[34] and his judgment surprises us by its moderation and its obviously charitable intentions. He declares that the differences of rite and religious customs are not so important and they should not be allowed to lead to a schism. They should be considered with the eyes of Christian charity. He could also find excuses for the *Filioque*. He said that this formula had arisen because the Latin language did not possess a sufficiently accurate theological terminology, and he would allow the use of unleavened bread among the Latins, since the Scripture did not say precisely which bread was used during the paschal supper. As a result, he concluded, each Church should preserve its own customs and not reproach the other with having different usages from its own.

What is of real importance here, is the basic agreement in the matter of the true faith. If errors are found among the Westerners:

in the addition to the Creed of what concerns the Holy Spirit—this . . . an error affecting the doctrines of the Fathers as is the case is the greatest source of danger—those who would refuse to reject and to correct this error would surely be unworthy of pardon even if they spoke from the height of the throne which they professed to be the highest of all and even if they should put forth the confession of Peter and the blessing which he received from Christ for it, even if they should shake before our eyes the Keys of the Kingdom. For in proportion that they pretend to honor Peter by these keys, they dishonor him if they destroy what he established, if they root up the foundations of the Church which he is supposed to support.

We have cited this passage because it contains all that Theophylactus said on the Roman Primacy in his treatise. The words bear an ironical overtone, to be sure, but they show that Theophylactus accepted the Petrine thesis by which the Pope defended their Primacy, and this is an important fact. The whole treatise surprises us by the desire we find in it of a completely friendly relationship between the two Churches. For Theophylactus, the Primacy was not nearly as serious an obstacle to union as the *Filioque*.

Theophylactus also speaks of St. Peter in his commentary on the gospels. In commenting on Matt.16.18,[35] he stresses the fact that it is on Peter that Christ founded His Church. The confession of Peter is the foundation on which all believers should depend. "Since that has been affirmed to us in the confession of Christ, how can the gates of Hell, that is, sin, ever hold us in subjugation?" The Keys of the Kingdom were granted to Peter alone, but all bishops have the same power of loosing and of binding sin.

He is even more eloquent when he comments on the passage of Luke,22.32-33.[36]

"When you yourself have been strengthened, confirm your brethren." This obviously means: Since I have made you the chief of the Apostles, when you have wept and repented of having denied me, confirm your brethren. This is the way you must act, you who are, after me, the rock and the foundation of the Church. We must believe that this command, that they be strengthened by Peter, holds not only for the Apostles at the time of Our Lord, but for all the faithful unto the consummation of the world. For it is you, Peter, . . . who were an Apostle and you denied Him, but you are the one who, by your repentance, obtained the Primacy in the whole world.

In his commentary on John,21.15,[37] Theophylactus wrote "For the Lord entrusted the supervision over the whole flock to Peter alone and not to anyone else." A bit later on, he says "He has granted to Peter the supervision over all the faithful. If James obtained the throne of Jerusalem, Peter has obtained that of the whole world." Theophylactus did not here attempt to establish a direct link between Peter and his successors, but what he says of Peter is significant. He understood very well the Petrine argument for the Roman Primacy.

* * *

It is in this atmosphere of calm that preparations were made for that great enterprise of Western Christendom, the First Crusade. The Emperor Alexis I had halted the advance of the Turks in Asia Minor but since the Empire had lost a large part of that province and since it was from there that he recruited the largest proportion of his army, he turned to the West to seek additional troops. It seems that he had been engaged in conversation with the Pope on this matter since Anna Comnena writes in the *Alexiade*[38] that the Emperor in 1091 was awaiting a detachment of soldiers coming from Rome. In 1095 the imperial envoys petitioned the Synod which the Pope had convoked at Plaisance that the Christians of the West should come to the aid of their Oriental brethren to combat the infidel who was occupying the holy places so dear to all of Christendom.

It seems that it was this address and the conversations with the Emperor which suggested to the Pope the idea of inviting the faithful who were gathered at Clermont, some months later, to liberate the holy places from the hands of the infidel. The result was surprising, and the French nobility responded with enthusiasm to the exhortation of the Pope. But in the mind of the Pope, this First Crusade was launched not merely with the idea of assisting the Greeks in their struggle against the Turks and of liberating Jerusalem, but it was intimately linked, for him, with the idea of union of the two Churches. It is probable that he had come to an agreement with the Emperor and that they both hoped that the collaboration of Christendom, East and West, and the blood that would be spilled in common on the field of battle would seal for all time the union of the two Churches.[39] At the beginning, it looked as if these hopes would be realized. After the conquest of Antioch, the Crusaders reinstalled the Greek patriarch in that city. The relations between the legate of the Pope, Ademar of Puy, and the Patriarch Symeon II of Jerusalem before the conquest of the Holy City were most cordial. The Pope himself, at the Synod of Bari in 1098,[40] discussed with the Greeks of Italy and of Byzantium the question of union and he decided to convoke another Synod in Rome in the following year to continue these conversations.

Unfortunately the Pope died in the same year before he had the chance to name another legate to replace Ademar who died in 1098, and the selfish policy pursued by Bohemond, one of the chief Crusaders, spoiled everything. Although the Emperor had been promised that all the cities which belonged to the Empire would be returned to it, Bohemond decided to keep Antioch for himself and for his family.

The Emperor thought so highly of the possession of this important strategic center that he was prepared to go to every length to recover the city, if need be, by force. Thus it is at Antioch that we can see the first signs of schism, when in 1100 a Latin patriarch was installed there. Beginning with that year, the Greek patriarchs of Antioch continued, in exile, to reside in Constantinople and other cities.

Besides, the contact between the undisciplined army of the Crusaders and the local population had disastrous results for any agreement between the two Churches. The differences which had grown up between the two civilizations were now made clear to the general public. The depredations suffered by the population as the Crusaders passed through their towns made suspicion with regard to Latins universal throughout the Empire. The Greeks considered the Latins to be barbarians and savages; on their side, the Latins held the Greeks responsible for the disasters suffered by their army, even though most of these were due to their own fault, since they paid no attention to the advice which the Greeks had given them.[41] However, in spite of all it was still possible to discuss in a peaceful manner the differences that existed between the two Churches and the question of the Roman Primacy even at Constantinople. The debate which Bishop Anselm of Havelberg[42] was able to have in the capital in 1136 is most interesting from this point of view.[43] Naturally, Anselm was totally imbued with the ideas of the reformers as to the Roman Primacy. He based this primacy on the words addressed to St. Peter (Matt.16.18-19) and on the fact that Peter had preached and died in Rome with St. Paul. Making use of the Petrine argument of St. Leo the Great, he admitted only three principal sees in the primitive Church, those of Rome, Alexandria, and Antioch, because each of them had been founded by Peter and by his disciple, Mark. The Church of Peter had always remained true to the Faith and according to the words of Our Lord (Luke,22.32), that Church had the mission of confirming the faith of all the other churches. The Church of Constantinople, on the contrary, was nothing but the seed bed for all the heresies which had defiled the Eastern churches. It was for this reason that all the churches should venerate the Roman Church and follow whatever she proposed.

The reply of his opponent Nicetas, Bishop of Nicomedia, was very dignified. Here is what he says with regard to the Roman primacy:[44]

I neither deny nor do I reject the Primacy of the Roman Church whose dignity you have extolled. As a matter of fact, we read in our ancient histories that there were three patriarchal sees closely linked in brotherhood, Rome, Alexandria, and Antioch, among which Rome, the highest see in the empire, received the primacy. For this reason Rome has been called the first see and it is to her that appeal must be made in doubtful ecclesiastical cases, and it is to her judgment that all matters that cannot be settled according to the normal rules must be submitted.

But the Bishop of Rome himself ought not to be called the Prince of the Priesthood, nor the Supreme Priest, nor anything of that kind, but only the Bishop of the first see. Thus it was that Boniface III, who was Roman by nationality, and the son of John, the Bishop of Rome, obtained from the Emperor Phocas confirmation of the fact that the apostolic see of Blessed Peter was the head of all the other Churches, since at that time, the Church of Constantinople was saying that it was the first see because of the transfer of the Empire.

In order to make sure that all the sees profess the same faith, Rome sent delegates to each of them [Perhaps Nicetas was thinking of the delegations who carried letters of enthronement and the profession of faith joined to them], telling them that they should be diligent in the preservation of the true Faith. When Constantinople was granted the second place in the hierarchy because of the transfer of the capital, this custom of the delegations was likewise extended to that see.

We find that, my dear brother, written in the ancient historical documents. But the Roman Church to which we do not deny the Primacy among her sisters, and whom we recognize as holding the highest place in any general council, the first place of honor, that Church has separated herself from the rest by her pretensions. She has appropriated to herself the monarchy which is not contained in her office and which has divided the bishops and the churches of the East and the West since the partition of the Empire. When, as a result of these circumstances, she gathers a council of the Western bishops without making us (in the East) a part of it, it is fitting that her bishops should accept its decrees and observe them with the veneration that is due to them . . . but although we are not in disagreement with the Roman Church in the matter of the Catholic faith, how can we be expected to accept these decisions which were taken without our advice and of which we know nothing, since we were not at that same time gathered in council? If the Roman Pontiff, seated upon his sublime throne of glory, wishes to fulminate against us and to launch his orders from the height of his sublime dignity, if he wishes to sit in judgment on our Churches with a total disregard of our advice and solely according to his own will, as he seems to wish, what brotherhood and what fatherhood can we see in such a course of action? Who could ever accept such a situation? In such circumstances we could not be called nor would we really be any longer sons of the Church but truly its slaves.

If the authority of the Pope was such as described by Anselm what good could be served by Scripture, by studies and by Greek wisdom? If that is the way things are, the Pope is the only bishop and the only master.

But if he wishes to have collaborators in the vineyard of the Lord, let him dwell in humility in his own primatial see and let him not despise his brothers! The truth of Christ has caused us to be born in the bosom of the Church, not for slavery but for freedom.

In confirmation of these words, Nicetas quoted John,20.23 and Matt.,16.19, the words by which Our Lord had granted the power to forgive sins, of binding and of loosing, to all the Apostles without exception. Anselm, while admitting this fact, quite rightly made the point that the Lord had also spoken to Peter alone and he stressed the predominant role which Peter had played among the Apostles and in the primitive Church.

Nicetas brought his declaration to an end by speaking of the part played by the Oriental bishops and by the Popes in the suppression of heresy:[45]

In the archives of Santa Sophia we possess the account of the great deeds of the Roman Pontiffs and we possess the Acts of the councils wherein are described all that you have said about the authority

146

of the Roman Church. For this reason it would be a source of great shame to us if we were to wish to deny what we have seen with our own eyes and what was written by our Fathers. However, in all truth, we must recognize the fact that neither the Roman Pontiff nor his legates would have had any part in the condemnation of heresies in the East, if the Orthodox bishops established in the East had not welcomed, aided, and encouraged them. For it was they who, full of zeal for the faith, condemned these heresies and provided confirmation of the true Catholic faith, sometimes with the Roman Church and sometimes without her.

These words of Nicetas illustrate very well the position taken by the Byzantine Church. From them we see that the Orientals continued to prefer the principle of accommodation to the principle of apostolicity. They rather looked for reasons for the Roman Primacy in the decisions of the councils and of the Emperors. Nicetas, however, did not deny the Scriptural argument (Matt., 16.18-19), used by Anselm. In recalling the words by which Our Lord had granted to the Apostles a similiar power to that which He had given to Peter, he raised a problem which even today has not been resolved in definitive fashion by the Roman Church, that of the relation between the full power accorded to the successors of Peter and the powers granted to the bishops.

Drawing his inspiration from the ideology of the reformers, Anselm went even further in demanding not only the recognition of the Primacy of the Roman Church—in principle this had not been denied, as we have seen—but also the acceptance of all the liturgical practices that were proper to the West, especially the abandonment of the use of leavened bread in the celebration of the Mass. We can easily understand how strenuously the Orientals would defend their own usages and their autonomy in this matter. It is regrettable that, on both sides, they forgot the recommendations made by the Council of 879-880, that each Church should preserve its own proper customs and that there was no place for any quarrel with regard to such minor differences. Even so, it is quite surprising to observe that given these circumstances, during the first half of the twelfth century, the Byzantines still recognized the principle of the Roman Primacy in the Church in spite of all that had happened in 1054 and after.

We can also quote the declaration of the most famous of the Byzantine canonists, Zonaras,[46] who composed his canonical work in the first half of the twelfth century. In his explanation of Canon XXVIII of Chalcedon, he shows with considerable emphasis the words attributing to Constantinople the same advantages as to ancient Rome should not be extended so far as to imply the transfer of the Primacy from Rome to Constantinople. The preposition *after* means a relationship of dignity and does not imply succession in time. To prove that his interpretation is correct he quotes a passage from the profession of faith of the Patriarch Nicephorus[47] where he spoke of the condemnation of the Iconoclasts:

That the Iconoclasts have been rejected by the Catholic Church, we know from the wise testimony and from the confirmation in the letters which were, a short time ago, sent by the most holy and blessed archbishop of ancient Rome, that is to say, the first Apostolic See.

NOTES

1. Mansi, 17, 497. It was stated in this canon that sentences passed by the Pope against anyone in the East should be approved by the patriarch, and vice versa. "However," the canon continued, "the privileges that belong to the most holy see of Rome or to its bishop should not suffer any change, neither now nor later on."

2. *Ibid.*, 489: "The holy synod has said: Each see has a number of ancient traditional practices. There is to be no discussion or quarrel on this matter. It is proper that the Roman Church

should hold to its practices, but the Church of Constantinople should also preserve the customs that it has inherited from the past. And, the same is to be said for the rest of the Oriental sees."

3. See p. 19, *supra*.

4. See p. 63, *supra*.

5. It is true that the Emperor addressed himself to the other patriarchs, as Nicholas the Mystic mentions in his Letter 32, but, from all the evidence, it emerges from this letter that Nicholas himself, as well as the Emperor, considered the appeal to Rome and the intervention of the legates as of primary importance.

6. The reaction of the Byzantines to this "intrusion" by the Germanic emperors into Roman affairs and the election of popes was quite violent. During the period of decadence of the Carolingian Empire the Byzantines regained a certain measure of control over papal elections. The struggle between the two parties of the Roman aristocracy, the one favoring the Franks and the other preferring Byzantine influence, poisoned the relations between East and West during the second half of the tenth century. When, for example, Pope Boniface VII, who upheld the Byzantine side, was expelled from Rome and had to take refuge in Byzantium (974), the Byzantines manifested their displeasure by "degrading" the patriarchate of Rome, which had at its head a pope they did not recognize, by putting it in the last place in one of their lists of patriarchates and bishoprics. Cf. H. Gelzer, *Texte der Notitiae episcopatuum*, Abhandl. d. Bay. Akad. (Munich, 1901), 569. The *Notitia* should be dated 974-76.

7. Cf. *De legatione Constantinopolotana*, MGH, *Scriptores* III, 347-63. See also his *Antapodosis, ibid.,* 273-339.

8. Cf. F. Dvornik, *The Making of Central and Eastern Europe*, 95-185.

9. Cf. J. A. Jungmann, *Missarum solemnia*, (Vienna, 1948), on the singing of the *Credo* during Mass in Rome. The evolution seems to have been quite slow, and the practice of adding the *Filioque* did not become general until after 1014.

10. PG 120, 717ff. Cf. Dvornik, *The Photian Schism*, 410.

11. The best work on the Norman Conquest in Italy is that of

F. Chalandon, *Histoire de la domination normande en Italie et en Sicilie*, 2 vols. (Paris, 1907).

12. A. Fliche, *La réforme grégorienne* (Paris, 1924), I, 17ff.
13. This reform movement should not be confused with the monastic reform stemming from Cluny. See my study, *National Churches and Church Universal* (London, 1943), 33ff.
14. *Historiarum libri quinque*, II, ch. 1, PL 142, 671; Hugh of Flavigny, *Chronicon*, PL 154, 240-41. Cf. F. Grumel, "Les préliminaires du schisme de Michel Cérulaire ou la question romaine avant 1054," in *Revue des Études Byzantines*, 10 (1952), 18-20.
15. On the *Donatio* and its utilization by the Greeks in the twelfth century, see the bibliography given by F. Dölger, *Byzanz und die Europäische Staatenwelt*, 107ff. The *Donatio* was already known in Byzantium in the tenth century.
16. See E. Amann, "Michel Cérulaire," DTC, 10, 1683-84. Also, A. Michel, *Humbert und Kerullarios*, 2 vols. (Paderborn, 1924-30); V. Grumel, "Les préliminaires . . ." 5-24, and P. L'Huillier, "Le schisme de 1054," in *Messager de l'exarchate du patriarche russe en Europe occidentale*, 5 (1954), 144-64.
17. In PG 120, 836ff.
18. On this question, see J. Gay, *L'Italie méridionale et byzantin de 867 à 1071* (Paris, 1904), 450-72. See also, D. M. Nicol, "Byzantium and the Papacy in the Eleventh Century," in *The Journal of Ecclesiastical History*, 13 (1962), 1-20.
19. Cf. the writings of Humbert against the Greeks, in PL 143, 744-69 (among the letters of Leo), 929-1004. A new edition of the writings of Nicetas has been made by A. Michel in *Humbert und Kerullarios*, 2, 322-42.
20. Here is what M. Jugie has to say of this Bull in his *Le Schisme byzantin* (Paris, 1941), 205-06; "This theatrical gesture was regrettable from every point of view; regrettable, because one might well ask himself if the legates, since the Holy See was vacant at the time, were sufficiently authorized to take so grave a step; regrettable also, because it was useless and ineffectual . . . ; regrettable especially, by the content of this sentence and the tone in which it was drawn up. It reproached Cerularius and his partisans, and indirectly even all the Byzantines, side by

side with some legitimate complaints, of a whole series of heresies and imaginary crimes."

21. See this correspondence in PG 120, 751-819.

22. PL 145, 633-42.

23. See what J. Meyendorff says in his study, "S. Pierre, sa primauté et sa succession, dans la théologie byzantine," in *La primauté de Pierre dans l'Église orthodoxe* (Neuchatel, 1960), 96ff. See also his article, "St. Peter in Byzantine Theology," in *St. Vladimir Seminary Quarterly*, 4 (New York, 1960) 26-48.

24. See the edition of E. Caspar, *Das Register Gregors VII*, MGH, *Epistolae Selectae* (Berlin, 1920), 29 (Letter to Michael); 70, 75 (appeal to the princes); 167 (Letter to Henry IV), 173.

25. Anna Comnenus, *Alexiade*, edited and translated by B. Leib (Paris, 1937), I, 47, 48, 50, 52.

26. Published by E. Caspar, *op. cit.*, 202-08. Cf. H. X. Arquillière, *Saint Grégoire VII* (Paris, 1934), 130ff. See the study of J. T. Gilchrist, "Canon Law Aspects of the Eleventh Century Gregorian Reform Programme," *Journal of Ecclesiastical History*, 13 (1962), 21-38.

27. Ed. by A. Pavlov, *Kritičeskie opyty po istorii drevnejšej greko-russkoj polemiky protiv Latinjan* (St. Petersburg, 1878), 169, 186.

28. This probably earned him an excommunication by Gregory VII. The latter, who was faithful to Michael VII with whom he was in contact, in 1078 had excommunicated Nicephorus III Botaniates who had deposed Michael VII. These were the first applications of the *Dictatus papae*. Cf. E. Caspar, *op. cit.*, 400. 401, 524.

29. Published by W. Holtzmann, in his study, "Unionsverhandlungen zwischen Kaiser Alexios I und Papst Urban II, im Jahre 1089," in *Byzantin. Zeitschr.*, 28 (1928) 38-67, 60-62. See also V. Grumel, *Les Regestes des Actes du patriarcat de Constantinople* (Paris, 1947), I, fasc. 3, 48.

30. This is confirmed by Godfrey Malaterra in his *Historia Sicula*, PL 149, 1192.

31. See Holtzmann, *op. cit.*, 64-66.

32. On this problem, see M. V. Anastos, "The Transfer of Illyricum, Calabria and Sicily to the Jurisdiction of the Patriarchate

of Constantinople in 732-733," in *Silloge Bizantina in onore di S. G. Mercati,* Studi bizantini e neoellenici, 9 (Rome, 1957), 14-31.

33. Published by A. Pavlov, *Kritičeskie opyty* . . . , 158-69. See V. Grumel, "Jerusalem entre Rome et Byzance. Une lettre inconnue du patriarche de Constantinople Nicolas III à son collègue de Jerusalem," in *Echos d'Orient,* 38 (1939), 104-117.

34. *Liber de iis quorum Latini accusantur,* PG 126, 221-49.

35. PG 123, 320.

36. Ibid., 1073D.

37. PG 124, 309A-313A.

38. *Alexiade,* 8, edit. of B. Leib, II, 139. Cf. Holtzmann, "Die Unionsverhandlungen," *op. cit.,* 38-67. On Alexis I, see also F, Chalandon, *Les Comnenes,* I, "Essai sur le régne d'Alexis I, Comnène" (Paris, 1900).

39. On the history of the Crusades, see R. Grousset, *Histoire des croisades,* 3. vols. (Paris, 1934-36), and S. Runciman, *A History of the Crusades,* 3 vols. (Cambridge, 1951-53).

40. Cf. B. Leib, *Rome, Kiev et Byzance à la fin du XIᵉ siècle* (Paris, 1924), 287-97.

41. The disastrous results which the clash of the crusaders and the native population had for the possibility of union have been illustrated by Runciman in his book *The Eastern Schism* (Oxford, 1935), 124ff. See also B. Leib, *op. cit.,* 236-75, 302-07 (Guibert de Nogent).

42. See the two new studies on Anselm: Kurt Fina, "Anselm von Havelberg. Untersuchungen zur Kirchen- und Geistesgeschichte des 12. Jhts.," in *Analecta Praemonstratensia,* 32 (1956), 33 (1957), 34 (1958), and G. Schreiber, "Anselm von Havelberg und die Ostkirche," in *Zeitschrift für Kirchengeschichte,* 60 (1941), 354-411. On the discussions which the Greeks and the Latins had, in the twelfth century, on religious problems, especially on the *Filioque,* see P. Classen, "Das Conzil von Konstantinopel 1166 und die Lateiner," in *Byz. Zeitschr.* 48 (1955), 339-68; M. Anastos, "Some Aspects of Byzantine Influence on Latin Thought," in *Twelfth Century Europe,*" edited by M. Clagett, G. Post, R. Reynolds (Madison, Wisconsin, 1961), 131-87.(On Hugo Eterianus and Nicetas of Nicomedia, 140-49.) According to Grumel, "Notes d'histoire et de littéra-

ture byzantines," in *Échos d'Orient*, 29 (1930), 336, the discussion took place on Oct. 2-3, 1154.

43. *Dialogi*, lib. 3, PL 188, 1213ff.
44. *Ibid.*, 1217ff.
45. *Ibid.*, 1228.
46. PG 137, 488-89.
47. See p. 103, *supra*.

THE CATASTROPHE OF 1204

THE EMPERORS made substantial efforts to maintain good relations with the papacy, and the popes, urged on by Henry V and Frederick Barbarossa, were not unfavorable to overtures coming from Byzantium. The Emperors Alexis, John II and Manuel [1] even proposed the idea of a Roman Empire and showed themselves ready to accept union, on condition that the Popes would recognize the Byzantine emperor as the only true Emperor. Manuel Comnenus (1143-1181) was particularly inclined to make an alliance with the papacy since he himself was quite favorable to Latins.[2]

All of these projects met shipwreck on the rock of the new politico-religious conception of the papacy. Full of the Gregorian idea of the superiority of the spiritual over the temporal power, the Popes were particularly solicitous to maintain their domination over the Empire, both East and West, and over the Latin principalities in the East. They could not accept the supremacy of an Eastern Emperor, for the Christian Hellenism which the Byzantines professed had long since been dead in the West. Besides, the attempts made by the Byzantine Emperors encountered an increasingly strong opposition from their own clergy and from the population who, out of the experience acquired by their contact with the Crusaders, had learned to hate all Latins. They had no understanding of the new conceptions of the papacy and they rejected the papal idea of universal domination.

The result of this development was, in 1182, the massacre by the Greek populace of all Latins residing in Constantinople.[3] This terrible tragedy provoked an anti-Greek reaction in the West. The idea that had already been suggested by Bohemond became general, that the only way the Crusades could be successful would be the conquest of Constantinople and the replacement of the Greek Emperor by a Latin Emperor, and this came to pass in 1204 during the Fourth Crusade. The scenes of horror that unfolded in the city after the victorious entry of the Latins have never been forgotten by the Byzantines. This tragic evolution was crowned by the installation of the Latin Patriarch in Constantinople and the schism reached its summit.

* * *

It was only after the conquest of Constantinople by the Latins that the Byzantines fully understood the development that had taken place in the idea of the Roman Primacy. The simple nomination of a patriarch by the Pope, the designation of bishops without any consultation of Synods and without confirmation by the Emperor were for them experiences they never dreamed of. If they were aware that that was the way things were done in the West, they surely never thought that such a thing could happen in their Church.

There is a short anonymous treatise that reveals best the despair that the Greeks felt after the conquest.[4] This treatise is entitled "Why the Latins have Triumphed over us." The author deplores the spoliation of churches by the Crusaders, and the replacement of Greek priests by Latin priests; he protests in especially vehement fashion against the designation of the Venetian, Thomas Morosini, as Patriarch of Constantinople. In his lamentations we perceive an overtone of hatred against the Latins. The author of this treatise also went much further than all the other Greek controversialists in what concerns the Primacy of the Pope. He not only purely and simply denied it, but he also denied the Primacy which Peter was thought to have enjoyed in the circle of the Apostles.

The catastrophe of the taking of Constantinople by the Latins not only had serious consequences for the religious and political life of the Byzantines, but it also profoundly influenced all Greek theological speculation concerning the Primacy. Obviously, the general atmosphere would be negative on this point. In their discussions with the Latins and in their controversial writings, the Greek theologians rejected the Latin conception of the Primacy such as it had been suddenly revealed before their eyes. However, in spite of the hostility which they cherished against anything of Latin origin, they did not dare to go as far as the author of the anonymous treatise mentioned above. There were certain facts which they felt obliged to respect. First of all, they preserved a veneration for St. Peter,[5] whom they continued, in general fashion, to call the leader of the Apostles and whose Primacy they admitted. Next, they recognized the decisions of the councils concerning the situation of the patriarchs, the decisions of the Council of Nicaea, those of the First Council of Constantinople and, naturally, those of the Council of Chalcedon. Finally, they accepted the decisions of the Emperors, especially those of Justinian who, on many occasions had confirmed the first place occupied by the Bishop of Rome in the hierarchy. Also, the quotations from the Gospels which the Latins produced to prove the Primacy of the successor of Peter, and which had so strongly impressed certain Greek theologians of the past, were not without their power to create an embarrassment which the Greeks would have loved to have been able to surmount.

* * *

With the exception of the anonymous author, practically all of the Greek controversialists of the twelfth and thirteenth centuries continued to grant Peter the honorific title of leader. However, the Patriarch John Camateros (1198-1206) in his letter to Pope Innocent III recalled that Paul was also called "a vessel of election" (Acts, 9.15), and that James presided over the council of Jerusalem.[6] The real foundation of the Church is the Apostles and the Prophets (Eph. 2.20), and it should be remembered that the real cornerstone of the Church is Christ Himself. This priority of Christ over Peter is emphasized even more strongly by an unknown patriarch of Constantinople in his letter to the patriarch of Jerusalem. He declares simply that the Head of the Church is Christ and he refused to say that that title belonged to the Pope, as the Latins insisted.[7]

To weaken the conclusions which the Latins drew from the fact that the Pope was the successor of Peter, the Greek theologians renewed the thesis according to which the Apostles were the teachers of the whole Church and could not be considered as the bishops of an individual city.[8] Thus, the first Bishop of Rome was not Peter, but Linus who had been ordained by Peter.

Nicholas Mesarites made use of this argument even more explicitly in the dispute which took place in August, 1206 in the presence of the Patriarch Thomas Morosini.[9] In his view, the connection of Peter with Rome was nothing more than a Jewish practice. The words of Matt., 16.18 must be interpreted as referring not only to the Roman Church, but to the universal Church.

A similar argument was made use of by his brother John, in the course of a debate held on September 29 in the same year, in the presence of Cardinal Benedict.[10] John asserted that the Apostles had fulfilled their ecumenical mission and that they had ordained sixty-six disciples as bishops of different cities.

The Patriarch Germanus II (1222-1240), in one of his letters to the Cypriotes,[11] declared that the only Primacy was that of Christ and he said that the Roman attitude destroyed the ecclesiastical Pentarchy. Mesarites' argument was taken up by the anonymous author of a treatise entitled "Against Those who Say that Rome is the First See," which was falsely attributed to Photius.[12]

In making capital of the idea that the Apostles were the universal teachers and could not be considered as the bishops of the different cities, the Greek controversialists lost the habit of making use, to the profit of Constantinople, of the tradition by which that see had been founded by Andrew, the first to have been called by Christ and the one who introduced Peter to the Lord. In fact the only writers who tried to make use of this argument were Mesarites and the anonymous pamphleteer against the Primacy who followed his lead.

This argument, of course, only had validity when it was used in conjunction with the Petrine argument. It provided an answer for the Greeks against the Latins who, at one time, had made use of the Petrine argument as their most powerful weapon against the pretensions of Constantinople. If the Latins based the Primacy of Rome on the fact that Peter had lived there, Antioch had still greater right to claim Primacy since Peter had preached there before he ever came to Rome. In fact, Jerusalem could claim the Primacy and that with even greater right because Our Lord himself had preached and died there. In the light of such argumentation it is easy to see that the Greeks did not attach any great importance to the fact that a bishopric had been founded by an Apostle.[13]

*   *   *

However, despite the bitterness against Rome which the Greeks harbored after 1204, they were not able to ignore the tradition of the accommodation of the ecclesiastical organization to the political division of the Empire. This had been sanctioned by three councils and by the decrees of Justinian and it had always granted to Rome the first place in the ecclesiastical hierarchy. The Greeks continued to make use of this tradition to deny the divine character of the Roman

Primacy. Not that the Primacy was a bad thing, but it had only been accorded to Rome because of the importance it held in the Empire as the capital. The Patriarch Michael of Anchialos (1170-1177), in reply to the Emperor Manuel at the Synod where the possibility of union was being discussed,[14] even admitted the validity of the Donation of Constantine as the first imperial document granting the Primacy to Rome. This Primacy, he said, remained valid and was recognized as long as the Pope professed the true faith. He lost his Primacy when he adopted the heresy of the *Filioque*.

In this view Michael was followed by his contemporary, Andronicus Camateros.[15] The unknown patriarch who wrote a letter to the Patriarch of Jerusalem was also expressing the same view when he said that the Pope was at one time the first because then he professed the same faith. "Once this identity of faith is established, then he will regain his primacy."[16] It seems that Michael of Anchialos wished to transfer the Primacy to the see of Constantinople, the second in rank of the patriarchal sees, since the first see, Rome, had become heretical. This is also the view of the rhetorician Manuel, in his reply to a Dominican Friar.[17]

John Mesarites went even further still.[18] He admitted that the Pope could act as supreme judge if someone who had been condemned by a patriarch or by a Synod made appeal to him. Obviously the Pope could not use this privilege if he did not profess the true faith. Therefore the privilege is not of divine institution but has its foundation only in Canon Law. The brother of John Mesarites, Nicholas, defended a similar opinion in a dispute which took place in 1214.[19] All of these statements are important, for in them we find an echo of the declarations of the Synod of 861.

*   *   *

The interpretation of the words of Our Lord (Matt., 16.18), given by certain theologians of this era, had very important consequences for the development of ecclesiology among the Orthodox after 1204. Here is how the unknown patriarch in his letter to Jerusalem explained them:[20]

Christ is the [Sole] Shepherd and the Master but He confided the pastoral ministry to Peter . . . however, we see today that all the bishops possess this same function. As a consequence, if Christ has granted to Peter the Primacy in giving him the pastoral charge, this Primacy should, in the same fashion, be accorded to others, since they are also shepherds; and so, they are *all* first.

Mesarites declared that the promise given to Peter (Matt., 16.18) must be explained in a Catholic sense, "in relating it to all those who have believed and who believe . . . The whole Church has its foundation on the rock, that is to say on the doctrine of Peter, in conformity with this promise." [21] The anti-Latin controversialists of the thirteenth century did not develop any doctrinal theory with regard to the Roman Primacy and the Church. Still, their deductions, often improvised under the pressure of events, have remained a solid base for Greek theological speculation in the fourteenth and fifteenth centuries. This period produced very many sound theologians and their doctrine on the Primacy is presented in more systematic fashion.

They all make a very sharp distinction between the function of an Apostle and that of a bishop, repeating as their predecessors had done, that the Apostles were the universal teachers. It is for this reason that Barlaam, before his return to the Roman Church, declared that Peter could not have passed on to Clement his character as leader of the Apostles but only the episcopate. And so, from that time on, the Bishop of Rome could not be considered as the leader of the other bishops.[22] Barlaam granted the Pope a certain primacy, but only that which was granted by the Emperors, by Constantine—and here we must see an allusion to the Donation of Constantine—and by Justinian and the councils. Every bishop who professed the faith of Peter is a successor of the Apostles.[23] Nilus Caba-

silas reiterates the statements of Barlaam as to the character
of the Bishop of Rome,[24] but he departs from him in adopting
the interpretation of Matt., 16.18, which was given by the controversialists. "Christ has founded His Church on the profession of Peter and on all those who have been the guardians of
this profession." These guardians are the bishops who thus
all become successors of St. Peter.[25] The result of this interpretation is clear: The universal Church is represented by the
bishops who, because they are all the successors of Peter and
profess his faith, are equal.

*　　*　　*

Although Symeon of Thessalonica interpreted the succession
of Peter as a succession in the true faith, he is the most explicit
of all the theologians of the fifteenth century. This is what he
says on the Primacy:[26]

When the Latins say that the Bishop of Rome is first, there is no
need to contradict them, since this can do no harm to the Church.
If they will only show us that he has continued in the faith of
Peter and his successors and that he possesses all that came from
Peter, then he will be the first, the chief and head of all, the
Supreme Pontiff. All these qualities have been attributed to the
patriarchs of Rome in the past. His throne is apostolic and the
Pontiff who sits there is called the successor of Peter as long as he
professes the true faith. There is no right-thinking person who
would dare to deny this.

After recalling what the council said on the place of the Bishop
of Rome, he goes on to quote what he had declared to the
Latins in a discussion on the Primacy:

We are in communion in Christ and we have no reason to separate
ourselves from the Popes and Patriarchs such as Peter, Linus,
Clement, Stephen, Hippolytus, Sylvester, Innocent, Leo, Agapitus,
Martin, and Agatho. This is clear since we celebrate their memory

by calling them Doctors and Fathers. . . . If another should arise who would be like to them by the faith that he possesses, by his life, and by the traditions of orthodoxy, he will be our common father. We will accept him as Peter and the bonds of union will continue for a long time and to the end of the world.

Unfortunately, he adds, the present Pope does not profess the faith of Peter since he has added the *Filioque* to the Creed and for that reason he has lost the Primacy.[27] In these words of Symeon we hear an undertone that is almost nostalgic, a longing for the times when the Popes were the defenders of the faith, recognized as primates and venerated as the successors of Peter. The same sentiments seem to animate an unknown author whose treatise I found in the Vatican library.[28] It is listed as a treatise on the councils but it really is a letter written to the Pope by a Byzantine. The author stresses the fact that the bishops of ancient Rome have participated in the seven general councils which defined the faith of all Christians:

These seven holy and ecumenical councils were accepted by the bishops who were the successors of Peter, he who is the leader of the saints and of the famous apostles and they agreed to them in unanimous fashion, some of them even being present at them in person [sic!]. They associated themselves with what was done at those councils and they gave their assent to what was said there, and some of them sent men who were very close to them and who shared their opinions, to work with the Fathers of the council and they confirmed all that had been decided in a definite and clear fashion from the height of your divine and apostolic chair.

The author then enumerates all the Popes under whose reign the councils had taken place and then he regrets that someone has sown so many evil seeds in Rome. After which, he enumerates the "abuses." It is regrettable that the manuscript is incomplete; the letter probably dates in the fourteenth century.

From these controversial writings it is possible to see that the Primacy was one of the first preoccupations of the Byzan-

tines even after the schism had been consummated as a result
of unhappy military and political events.[29] The Greek controversialists found it necessary to take a strongly defensive
and negative attitude with regard to the Latins and their pretensions, and this prevented them from developing their own
ecclesiological system or of sharpening their theory so as
to oppose it to the Latin system. Nevertheless, it is possible to
recover from their speculations a certain number of common
traits. For example, save for one or two exceptions, they did
not dare to deny the Primacy of Peter but they considered all
the bishops to be successors of Peter. The Church was founded
on the rock of his profession and only those who had preserved his faith could be regarded as his successors. God had
given His Grace to the whole Church, to every Church which
had a bishop who taught the faith of Peter and hence, possessed the plenitude of the sacraments. The Primacy, which
Rome enjoyed as long as the Popes held to the faith of Peter,
had been granted to its bishop by the councils and the Emperors.

In many of these statements one could very probably find
similarities to what Cyprian, Irenaeus and even Origen and
Pseudo-Dionysius[30] had thought of the life of the Church, but
the Greek controversialists were not aware of them because
they did not look for arguments in those early works. Their
hostility to the pretensions of the Latin clergy and the bitterness which they felt against the destroyers of their Empire was
what urged them to seek for another solution to the problem
that obsessed them: how can we reconcile the idea of the
Primacy with the idea of the Church of Christ?

* * *

The picture that we have here attempted to trace of the
problem of the Roman Primacy in Byzantium is far from complete. We have done no more than examine the most important
and most characteristic witnesses. However, it seems clear that

this idea of the Primacy underwent a profound change in Byzantium beginning with the eleventh century. Without doubt, the period between the fourth and the tenth century is of the greatest interest to us since the Primacy of Rome was then accepted as a natural thing because Rome was the capital of the Empire and its ideological base. Further, Rome was the "home of the apostles," of Peter and of Paul who had lived there. The Council of Nicaea had no need to define or to confirm this Primacy since it had been recognized well before Constantine as a fact which it was neither necessary to discuss nor to prove.

However, since the principal of accommodation to the political division of the Empire had been accepted as the basis for the organization of the Church, the Byzantines were encouraged to try to derive this primacy from the decisions of the councils of Nicaea, Constantinople and Chalcedon, and from the decrees of Justinian I, Phocas and Justinian II.

Since there were a great number of sees in the East that had been founded by an Apostle, the apostolic origin of the see was not appreciated at its full value; for this reason it was not too easy for the papacy to bring the Byzantines to accept the divine origin of the Primacy by basing it on the words of Our Lord (Matt. 16.18-19).

The whole crisis that was provoked by the vote on Canon XXVIII of the Council of Chalcedon (which confirmed the position of second place after Rome for Constantinople and placed under its jurisdiction three civil dioceses of the empire), and by the attitude of St. Leo the Great, should both be attributed to the fact that the Fathers of the Council had failed to make mention in Canon XXVIII of the apostolic and Petrine character of the see of Rome, even though this character was admitted by them both during and after the council. The effort made by the Popes to substitute the principle of apostolicity for the principle of accommodation had a certain effect in the seventh century when Byzantium began to attribute an apostolic character to the see of Constantinople because it had succeeded

Ephesus—which had been founded by St. John—in the administration of the diocese of Asia. The legend claiming the apostle Andrew as the founder of the see of Byzantium which began to circulate in the eighth century also developed under the influence of the "apostolic" propaganda from Rome.

The Byzantines had been able to appreciate the firm and orthodox attitude of the Apostolic See of Rome and the aid which it always brought to the supporters of orthodoxy during the numerous doctrinal crises that arose as a result of the intervention of the Emperors in the domain reserved to the *Sacerdotium*. But their fear of compromising the autonomy of their churches prevented the Orientals from accepting the claims that were made by certain Popes, especially Gelasius, Symmachus and Nicholas I, the claim to direct and immediate jurisdiction over the whole Church, including the East.

A compromise had to be reached. In the ninth century this compromise was found by the Patriarch Photius who, by a sort of irony, has always been considered as a bitter enemy of the Primacy. The right of appeal to the Pope, a right which resulted from his Primacy, was put into practice by Byzantium and was fully recognized, for the first time, at the Synod of 861. The Roman tradition which claimed St. Peter alone, without any mention of Paul, as the founder of the see of Rome was finally accepted in Byzantium, and the words of Our Lord by which He had conferred on Peter the Primacy remained in the Greek edition of the papal letters which were sent to the Synod of 879-880. Photius defended the autonomy of his Church but, with his flock, he accepted the Primacy of the Apostolic See of Rome.

That provided a solid base for a further development of the principle of the Roman Primacy in Byzantium. But the prestige that Rome had gained in the ninth century was destined to decline in the course of the following century which was marked by the decadence of the papacy.[31] The influence which the German kings, after the restoration of the Roman Empire in the West, exercised over the election of Popes also contributed to lower the prestige of the papacy in the eyes of the Byzantines.

All these events speeded up the separation which grew between the Roman and the Byzantine Church. When communication between Rome and Byzantium was substantially interrupted, the Orientals were not aware of the profound changes that were taking place in the West under the influence of the reform movement which had begun in Lorraine and in Burgundy. The conception of the Roman Primacy which had been accepted in Byzantium, although never defined in clear and sharp fashion, was not enough for the reformers. In their zeal to raise the prestige of the papacy they went much further than Gelasius and Symmachus or Nicholas. They claimed for the Pope not only direct and immediate jurisdiction over all the bishops and over the faithful, but also, in their ignorance of the liturgical and ecclesiastical differences which existed in the churches in the East, complete conformity to Roman usages in the East and in the West.

The regrettable conflict which arose in 1054 was the result of this divergent evolution of the ecclesiastical ideology in the two worlds. However, even though this unhappy incident increased the suspicion between the two Churches, we cannot say that it was at this moment that the schism really took place. The Byzantines did not always realize that when the West affirmed the superiority of the spiritual over the temporal power they were thereby definitively abandoning the political system of Christian Hellenism which the Orientals professed. Hope was still cherished that the Crusades would cement the union for all time and they were content to discuss the differences between the two Churches in an academic fashion and without any positive results. The declarations of Theophylactus of Ochrida and of Nicetas of Nicomedia show us very clearly that, basically, Byzantium accepted the idea of the Roman Primacy in the framework of compromise which had been arrived at in the ninth century. It is unfortunate that the Crusades had a result that was far from what was anticipated.

The Crusaders made all Latins very unpopular among the masses of the Greek population by their way of behavior. The taking of Constantinople by the Latins and the destruction of the Byzantine Empire put an end to all possibility of agreement. It was at this moment, in 1204, that the schism reached its completion. The Roman Primacy was thereafter denied and rejected by the Byzantines. However, despite the hostile attitude of the Greek theologians we can see that the memory of the past was still vivid in Byzantium. The Primacy of the Pope was rejected under the pretext that he had become a heretic in accepting the *Filioque* but Symeon of Thessalonica was quite ready to grant him the Primacy if he would only abandon his "heresy."

There is no doubt that the arguments of Greek theologians after 1204 were heavily charged with prejudice brought about by political developments. It would be altogether regrettable if the writings of these theologians and controversialists were utilized as a base on which modern Orthodox theologians should build an "Orthodox ecclesiology." [32] It is equally regrettable that Western theologians restricted themselves to these writings in judging the theological thought of the Byzantines. Neither of these attitudes is correct. No agreement can ever be reached on material that is out of date and stained with the prejudices which have resulted from errors and from unjust treatment in the past. If there is, on one side and on the other, a sincere desire to work for a rapprochement and perhaps even for union, both, both must turn to the period of the fourth to the eleventh centuries. It is there that we can find a foundation for an agreement.

NOTES

1. For more details, see F. Chalandon, *Les Comnènes*, vol. 2; Jean II Comnène et Manuel I Comnène (Paris, 1912). Cf. also, W. Norden, *Das Papsttum und Byzanz* (Berlin, 1903) 88ff.

2. Cf. V. Grumel, "Au seuil de la IIe croisade. Deux lettres de Manuel Comnène au pape," *Revue des études byzantines*, 3 (1945) 143-67.

3. In retaliation, the sailors of the Latin ships attacked the population of the city. And further, in 1185, William II, King of Sicily, who had occupied Thessalonica, massacred a large part of the people of that city.

4. Published by Arsenij, *Ti staty neizuvestnago grečeskago pisatelja načala XIII veka* (Three articles of an unknown Greek writer at the beginning of the thirteenth century) (Moscow, 1892) 84-115.

5. For more details, see M. Jugie, *Theologia dogmatica*, IV, 320-48. See also *La primauté de Pierre*, studies by A. Afanassieff, N. Koulomzine, J. Meyendorff, A. Schmemann (Neuchâtel, 1960). The paper by Meyendorff is the best. Cf. also, E. Stephanou, "La primauté romaine dans l'apologie orthodoxe," in *Échos d'Orient*, 30 (1931), 212-32 and especially D. T. Strotmann, "Les coryphées Pierre et Paul et les autres Apôtres," in *Irenikon* (1963) 164-76. The author examines the titles which the texts of the Byzantine offices give to Peter and Paul.

6. This letter has not yet been published, from the Manuscript *Parisinus graecus* 1302 (XIII cent.) fol. 272^v-273^v. Though it is very difficult to read, some extracts from it concerning the primacy have been quoted in M. Jugie, *Theologia dogmatica christianorum orientalium* (Paris, 1931) IV, 341-42.

7. Edited by A. Pavlov, *Kritičeskie opyty*, 164-65.

8. John Camateros, *Parisinus graecus* 1302, fol. 272 *bis;* the Anonymous author, cf. Arsenij, 107, 111; the Patriarch of Jerusalem, cf. Pavlov, 165.

9. A. Heisenberg, "Neue Quellen zur Geschichte des lateinischen Kaisertums und der Kirchenunion," in *Sitzungsb. d. Bayr. Akad.* Phil.-hist. Kl., 2 (1923), 22-24. For more details see the study of R. Janin, "Au lendemain de la conquête de Constantinople. Les tentatives d'union des Églises (1204-1208; 1208-1214), in *Échos d'Orient*, 32 (1933), 5-20, 195-202. See also V. Grumel, "Le patriarcat byzantin de Michel Cérulaire à 1204," *Rev. d. études byz.* 4 (1946), 257-63.

10. Edited by A. Heisenberg, *op. cit.*, 1 (1922) 54ff.

11. PG 40, 616C-617A.
12. Edited by A. Gordillo, "Photius et primatus romanus," in *Orientalia christiana periodica*, 6 (1940), 5-39. Cf. F. Dvornik, *The Photian Schism*, 126ff., and *The Idea of Apostolicity*, 247-53.
13. As was to be expected, many polemicists and theologians used the idea of the Pentarchy as a weapon against the Roman Primacy. Cf. Jugie, *Theol. dogmat.*, IV, 456ff. The patriarch Nilus (1379-1388), in a letter to Urban VI, seems to attribute a primacy of honor to the pope. Cf. F. Miklosich-Müller, *Acta patriarchatus Constantinopolitani*, II, 87. He also speaks of the Pentarchy, p. 40.
14. See this dialogue in *Vizantijskij Vremennik*, 14 (1907), 344-57, published by C. Loparev.
15. Cf. Hergenröther, *Photius* (Ratisbon, 1867-69), III, 813.
16. Edited by Pavlov. *loc cit.*
17. Cf. Arsenij, *Manuila velikago ritora otvet dominikanu Francisku* (Moscow, 1889), 19.
18. A. Heisenberg, *op. cit.*, I, 57.
19. *Idem*, III (1923) 34ff.
20. Edited by Pavlov, 165. See the study of J. Meyendorff, "Saint Pierre, sa primauté et sa succession dans la théologie byzantine," in *La primauté de Pierre dans l'Église Byzantine* (Neuchâtel, 1960), 104.
21. Mesarites (edit. Heisenberg, I, 57-58), also rejects the canons of Sardica which, he says, are valid for the West but not for the East. The anonymous treatise edited by Gordillo, *loc. cit.*, 14ff. is also very hostile to this Synod.
22. *Contra Latinos*, PG, 151, 1260-63.
23. The treatise of Barlaam is still unedited, *Paris, graec.* 1218 (XV cent.) fols. 101, 127^v. 130^v. It is also cited by Meyendorff, *op. cit.*, 109.
24. *De primatu papae*, PG 149, 704-05.
25. *Ibid.*, 708B.
26. *Dialogus contra haereses*, ch. 29. PG 155, 120-21.
27. Gennadios Scholarios, the first patriarch under the Turkish regime, saves most of his efforts for the attack on the *Filioque*. The few allusions to the Primacy that appear in his writings

are found in his treatise on the Procession (edited by L. Petit-M. Jugie [Paris, 1929], II, 62-63) and in his letters (*ibid.*, IV (1935), 206-07. He shares the ideas of his contemporaries on Peter "Bishop and Pastor of the Universe," a distinction never enjoyed by the successors of St. Peter.

28. *Vaticanus graecus* 166. fol. 179ᵛ, 180. The script is that of the end of the fourteenth century or the beginning of the fifteenth.

29. See also J. Darrouzès, "Conférence sur la Primauté du pape à Constantinople en 1357," *Revue des études byzantines,* 19 (1961), pp. 76-109. The monk and deacon Athanasius refutes, in his discussion with the papal legate Peter Thomas, sent to Constantinople in 1357, not only all scriptural proof of the papal primacy put forward by the legate, but uses also the condemnation of Pope Honorius by the sixth ecumenical council. This is probably the only time when the case of Honorius was used in Greek polemical literature as proof against Roman Primacy. Cf. also J. Meyendorff, "Projet de concile oecuménique en 1367," *Dumbarton Oaks Papers,* 14 (1960), 149-177, and V. Laurent, "Les préliminaires du Concile de Florence. Les neuf articles du Pape Martin V et la réponse inédite du Patriarche de Constantinople Joseph II," *Revue des études byzantines,* 22 (1962), 11-60. The answers of the Patriarch show clearly the Byzantine mentality and their lack of enthusiasm for a union.

30. J. Meyendorff, *Saint Pierre, sa primauté, etc.,* 114.

31. This decline is also apparent in the realm of ideas. Cf. H. M. Klinkenberg, "Der römische primat im 10. Jahrhundert," in *Zeitschrift für Rechtsgeschichte,* Kan. Abt., 42 (1955), 1-57.

32. If we read the essays on Orthodox ecclesiology, which, incidentally, are not all of equal value, it becomes clear that modern Orthodox theologians are quite in agreement that the ecclesiological problems that face them and other theologians are far from solved. See especially what is said on this by G. Florovsky, in his study, "L'Église, sa nature et sa tâche," in *L'Église universelle dans le dessein de Dieu* (Vol. I of Documents of the Amsterdam Assembly) (Neuchâtel-Paris, 1949), 61; *idem,* "Le Corps du Christ vivant," in *La Sainte Église Universelle. Confrontation oecuménique* (Neuchâtel-Paris, 1948), 11; J. Meyendorff, *L'Église Orthodoxe hier et aujourdhui* (Paris, 1960), 179;

P. Evdokimov, *L'Orthodoxie*, (Neuchâtel-Paris, 1959), 123. See the detailed and irenic examination of recent ecclesiological treatises done by D. E. Lanne, "Le mystère de l'Église dans la perspective de la théologie Orthodoxe," in *Irenikon*, 35 (1962), 171-212.

INDEX

Index

Index